THE
DEVOURING
LAND

BOOK TWO OF THE ECOSYSTEM SERIES

JOSHUA DAVID BELLIN

For our planet

THE ECOSYSTEM

SENSOR
VILLAGE

GREAT FOREST

PAIN TRE

SOUTHERN FOREST

BOOK ONE

SWARM

Nature's silence is its one remark, and every flake of world is a chip off that old mute and immutable block.

—Annie Dillard, "Teaching a Stone to Talk" (1982)

I'M JUMPY.

Can't sit still. I keep springing from my chair, rushing to the window, spying outside. As though I expect to see something other than the stunningly gray day smearing its light over the gray village stone.

Something. Or someone.

Lanky body, shaggy hair hanging across his forehead. Walking with a staff and a limp, byproducts of his near-miss with death three weeks ago. Soft brown eyes that make my heart dance uncontrollably in my chest. And a smile I learned to love so much, I literally ache now that it's sequestered on the far side of the village.

Isaac.

I haven't seen him for over a week, not since Aaron's funeral. I studied his face across the swirling flames of my grandfather's pyre, but he wouldn't meet my eye, would do no more than bow stiffly when he passed me in the condolence line. Ever since, he's been avoiding me, or I him—no easy thing in a community of fewer than two hundred souls. By unspoken consent, we've stationed ourselves at opposite ends of the village, he among the houses of the healers, I in my lonely cottage in the Sensors' quarters. I can't help thinking that though he's where he belongs, I'm anything but.

Technically, I'm still a Sensor. But I'm a healer too, or

could be. My hands hold a power I don't understand, a power first manifested in Isaac's presence. When I touched his face, held his hand, kissed him, it brought that power alive in me: the power to reach inside others, find what ails them, and start the process of healing. It's a power my mother—though also a Sensor—possessed as well. The day before my grandpa's funeral, I made the decision to explore that power, to commit myself to the healer's path.

But my plan, like so many others, has vanished in the time since. I might train to become a healer, but it'll be with Chief Warden Daniel or with the midwife Judith, not with Isaac. He and I might work side by side one day, but it won't be anything other than work. We might plumb the secrets of the Ecosystem together, but we'll never be able to speak what's inside our own hearts.

Not after today.

I leap up once more, bypassing the window and heading out the door to the village commons. My body's still recovering from my own near-death experiences; my shoulder is stiff and sore from the arrow our former Chief Sensor shot through it, while my legs look terrible, crisscrossed by ragged scars where the urthwyrms wolfed chunks of my flesh. I move with a lurching, unsteady gait so unlike the fluid sprinter who exists in my mind. It's a mercy I'm not expected to do much of anything today.

The morning spreads before me, gray on gray, the somber green of the forest a backdrop to the sunless stone. Clouds swell, gravid with rain. No one is about. Far off, the chopping sound of the threshers breaks the quiet. The Sensors, the few who remain, must be in the woods by now. Chief Sensor Esther and Judah and the others. Levi, though not strictly ready, has been added to their numbers out of necessity. Jarrod will be next. Relations between Sensors and villagers have been strained since the death of Chief Sensor Nathan, but under Esther's command, the Sensors continue to do their job, continue to risk the Ecosystem's anger to gather the food, water, and fuel we need to survive.

And Sarah, they wonder—when will Sarah hunt again?

For a week after my return to the village, they accepted the physical excuse, my need to recuperate. Now, they look at me sidelong, with suspicion and resentment if not outright hostility. They know my part in the death of our former Chief Sensor, know that I've courted friendships with the healers. That they don't know, can't know, how I feel about one healer in particular doesn't change the fact that they see me as a threat to the Sensor order, harbinger of a new world. A new world, they also don't know, that even I'm uncertain I want to bring into being.

All would be forgiven if I would declare myself, return to the field. I've seen their eyes. *We need you, Sarah*, they say. *Your village needs you. You're the daughter of a Sensor, the granddaughter of a Sensor. All those years of training, Aaron would expect you to....*

Enough.

Only Esther, Chief Sensor this past week, knows the truth. Only she knows I'll never hunt again.

I stand still and silence my breath, close my eyes on the cloudy day and attempt to send tendrils of Sensation into the wide world. Truth be told, my Sense is no stronger than my legs: ever since my narrow escape from the urthwyrms' lair, my power's been twitchy, unable to lock onto the Ecosystem's mind. It pulses feebly from time to time, enough to make hope rise to my throat. But it's never more than that, a glimmer of light in a darkened cave. I was nearly eaten alive three weeks ago, and the damage I suffered seems to have forced into hibernation a gift I've possessed since birth.

That's not it, Isaac would say.

My troubles, he'd say, are because I'm discovering everything anew, not only the Ecosystem but my place in it. After years of viewing the Ecosystem as my enemy, a predator that killed my mother and nearly devoured my heart, I've spent the past few weeks balanced on the proposition that it might be my—our—last hope. But I don't trust that thin sliver of possibility, he'd say: I'm not willing to open myself to it. I'm afraid that if I take a step off my knife-slim perch, I'll find myself falling into space. Afraid, as I've always been afraid, of surrendering my heart to something I don't know I can trust.

You won't be a Sensor, he'd say. *But you won't be one of us, either. When will you choose, Sarah?*

"You ask too much of me," I say aloud. "You ask for my all, yet you offer nothing in return."

I reach into my shirt pocket and withdraw my healer's token, the one I inherited from my mother. A serpent twining around a staff, carved of pink stone that, in sunlight, sparkles with an iridescence that makes the coils seem to come alive. Today, it's as dull as everything else. I've rubbed its smooth, scaly surface a hundred times since it came to me a little more than a week ago. In the absence of its original owner, it provides some solace, if no wisdom.

"Why?" I ask the gray sky, the woods, the earth. Not

expecting an answer, only hoping to trick my ears into believing I'm less alone. "Why, why, why, why, why?"

I Sense a murmur of response, then the Ecosystem falls silent again.

But the village, of all things, spits back an answer. Not the one I'm looking for—in fact, the exact opposite of the one I'm looking for—but, you could say, the one I summoned. The one who holds the other token I received from my mother: my Sensor's token, passed from teacher to student. Even from a distance, there's no mistaking her: frowzy hair, spastic body not so much walking as squirting across the pavilion, limbs so thin they're little more than bone. The only feature that redeems her, physically, is too far away to discern: wide lavender eyes like night sky reflected in water. They're beautiful, and my breath catches when I think of all he sees in them. All he'll see in them every day for the rest of their lives.

Miriam.

She's at my side in less time than I need to compose my heart, though I hope I succeed with my face. My mother's Sensor token, a shard of tooth carved with a blue-branched tracery like veins, hangs on a string at her throat.

"Shouldn't you be getting ready?" I ask.

"We have till later today," she says. "I need to stretch my legs."

Taking a stroll with Miriam on this day of all days is the last thing I want to do, but I feel trapped. As my ex-student, she exerts a power over me that's a combination of guilt, responsibility, and anxiety lest anyone think I've failed in my duties. Not that she's aware of any of this—nothing could be more guileless than those trusting eyes—but I feel the sting of conscience nonetheless. Maybe it's because I was the one who dragged her into the Ecosystem before she was ready, which led to a rescue attempt, which led to me spending days on the road with Isaac, which led to....

"Where are the children?" I ask.

"They're headachy."

"Both of them?"

"Rebecca the more so," she says. "She would have come, but Esau convinced her to stay home."

This sounds familiar. The two youngest recruits to the Sensor order are mine to train, but nine-year-old Esau is adept at little but finding ways out of work. Rebecca, at seven, might be salvageable, if she can develop the courage to stand up to her older companion.

"Fine," I say. "But if you come back stinking of dead meat, it's on you."

"In a manner of speaking," she says, and we're off.

We race across the stone terrace, aiming for the open lawn that surrounds the village. Or Miriam races: I lag several steps in her rear. Up ahead, the only signs of brightness I've seen this day flit across the sward, ruby-throated huntingbirds seeking poisonrose blooms to pierce with their sharp beaks. My first step onto the lawn offers the premonitory quiver I keep hoping will blossom into full Sensation, but again, I'm disappointed. My legs, however, carry me more confidently on grass and earth than on the village stone, and by the time we reach the first of the trees, I've nearly recovered my stride.

The forest opens its arms to admit us. A warning wind rustles the leaves, but the low-lying clouds cradle the raindrops for now. This isn't the first time I've been within the forest's embrace since my encounter with the urthwyrms. Miriam and I have gone out every day since my grandpa's funeral. Esther's idea, not mine. The Chief Sensor took me aside after the pyre had died to cinder and ash, asked my plans for the future. When I told her I had none, she suggested I pair with Miriam to complete her training. To the objection forming on my lips, she raised a hand, and that was that. I doubt her obsidian eyes were keen enough to see the phantom blade she'd plunged into my chest.

"Which way's the wind?" I ask Miriam as the village vanishes behind us.

"East," she says.

"The bloodbirds?"

"None within leagues," she answers, and I wish I could confirm if she's right. My Sense catches the edge of a blood-red wing before it sputters and dies.

"And what is its mind?" I ask warily, knowing I'll not be able to certify her response.

She's silent for a long moment. The forest flashes by, and I can almost—almost—feel the webs of thought and will radiating from the earth and trees.

"It...flutters," she reports. "It withholds its true thought, and I—"

"Your purpose is to name its true thought," I say. "Or should we wait for it to name ours?"

"It hides from me," she says, concentration knotting her brow. "I Sense unrest. Division. It is...troubled today. Unwell."

"Then by all means, let's go easy on it," I say. "We wouldn't want to hurt its delicate feelings."

She broods, or pouts, which on that baby face are much the same. I know I'm being unfair, particularly since the mind of the Ecosystem is hidden from me as well. I suspect that's what's making me so edgy. I'm not crazy to hear Miriam describing the interruptions in the stream very much the way they're occurring to me.

She glances over. "Shall I try again?"

For no good reason, I soften.

"Pick up the pace," I say. "And take care."

We speed through the trees, and all I can think of is the companion I'd rather have at my side.

THE SENSORSHIP HAS existed for tens of thousands of years. The Ecosystem has lived for just a little while longer. A planet-wide entity that grew from innocence to conscious rage, it knitted all living things into one mind, one thought. Without the Sensorship to protect our kind, it would have destroyed us altogether. But it's never played host to a Sensor like Miriam.

She's a mess. And a marvel. The apprentices call her Weird Miri. I'm not sure if they mean it as an insult or a compliment.

She's as scrawny as she was the day she started the training, and as awkward. She trips over vines, stubs her toes on tree roots. I'd never seen her run before we went out in the field together—the only time she ran with me previously was in the underground lair of the urthwyrms, where it was too dark to see—and though she's fleet enough, she moves with a jerky, rolling motion of her hips that reminds me of a spavined killdeer. With my gammy legs, the two of us must make quite the pair. If the Ecosystem had half a mind to, it could devour us in record time.

But I've yet to detect a sign that it's interested. And though my Sense is hardly to be trusted, I suspect I know why it seems so docile and unalarmed.

Miriam doesn't kill anything. Instead, she scavenges.

Ordinarily, I'd call that a dreadful idea. Dead meat, however freshly dead, is perilous, both for the predators it attracts and the disease organisms it breeds. Sensors have always hauled their catch back to the village immediately, even if that means forsaking the hunt before the kill sack is full. It's better to return with a pittance of edible game than a stuffed sack crawling with germs and the four-footed scavengers we call jekylls.

But Miriam is so creepily Sensitive, she's on carrion before anything else knows it's down.

Watching her is amazing. And unnerving. She stands with her head lowered and hands balled, in total defiance of the posture I taught her: head up, fingers splayed to catch the threads of Sensation that float like gossamer currents on the air, invisible to any but a Sensor. The first sign that she's on to something is her black hair rising like antennae, each strand waving blindly before settling in a bushy halo around her head. I asked her about it the first time I saw it happen, and she said something I'd have considered completely insane coming from anyone but her.

"It Senses the death," she said.

"What does? Your hair?"

She nodded serenely, then led me to a copse of ache trees a good two hundred rods away and plucked a runt warhog's carcass from the forest floor. Abandoned by its mother. So newly dead its rubbery skin held its living warmth, and the grabgrass hadn't begun to pull it underground. Hardly a prime catch, but the point is, she'd Sensed its death and harvested it right away. Or technically, since Sensors can't detect what's no longer alive, she'd

Sensed it dying and steered us to the spot, just in time for its final heartbeat.

And the scariest part was, all the while she was tracking it, she didn't know. Couldn't have said what she was locking onto, why she was heading in that direction. And yet, when we got there, her prize was waiting to be retrieved.

"Your hair," I said then.

"My hair," she said with a smile. And we headed back to the village carrying her catch.

Miriam's style of hunting, I'm forced to conclude, escapes the Ecosystem's notice because the creatures she takes from it have already vanished from its mind. She deals in death only, and death is beyond the Ecosystem's ken.

I don't know where she learned this method. Certainly not from me. Maybe her experience with the urthwyrms changed her. But regardless, there's nothing left for me to teach. What am I supposed to do, train her hair? The evasive strategies I could impart to her are needless when the Ecosystem has no interest in her presence. Killing techniques would be wasted on her, since she doesn't kill anything. We could spend all day cataloguing species, but why bother? The only species she pays attention to are the ones that drop dead at her feet, ready to be dragged home. Miriam's newfound powers are beyond *my* ken, and her fate is none of my business.

When I informed Esther of this, the Chief Sensor pursed her thin lips, but said nothing.

"Maybe it's best if I focus on the children," I said.

"No," she responded. "They're years from the hunt. We need Miriam now."

"Let her hunt alone, then."

"You will accompany her," she said. "Until I instruct otherwise."

"But she doesn't need me."

"Perhaps," she said, which ended the conversation the way all conversations with Esther end. Unsatisfactorily.

So while Miriam hunts, I search.

For what, I don't know. Something I tell myself is out there, something that'll show me what I'm meant to do. I've learned to identify a handful of shrubs and blossoms the healers believe hold medicinal powers, but these grow so sparsely in the vicinity of the village, I'm never able to find enough to make it worth the time it would take to gather them. The deeper secrets, like the Ecosystem's true wishes for me or my place in its vast inhuman design, lie hidden in plain sight: in the warp and woof of the trees, the skein of the soil, the scents that twirl on the breeze. I don't know how to find the answers, don't know what to ask. Don't know which of the countless threads of life to start with.

That's an excuse, he'd say. *You could learn all of these things from Daniel, if you'd accept him as your teacher. It's not the Ecosystem, it's you. Pick up a thread and follow where it leads.*

"You ask too much," I whisper. Let Miriam's hair try to Sense *that*.

My companion pulls up short on the edge of an open glade. The aura of prey hangs so heavily in the air, even my stuttering Sense drinks it in: a family of pigdeer, two tiny fawns and their miniature mother. As we creep closer, I see them flickering through the shadows of the low-lying clouds: the doe standing guard, her babies nuzzling at the saplings that sprinkle the dell. A perfect catch for the traditional Sensor, who'd easily take down both of the young and maybe the dam too. But Miriam being the Sensor she is, it can't be because of this golden opportunity that she's paused.

She regards the animals placidly. She's masking herself, and I must be managing it well enough, because the mother hasn't realized we're here. The instant our presence registers in the Ecosystem's consciousness, it'll send a jolt through the sentinel's legs, and she'll bound for safety, her offspring following.

"We'd best move on," I say.

"In a moment." Her hand plays with the token at her throat. "Just let me watch them."

I do, for another moment.

"Miriam," I say.

Midnight eyes slant to mine. "So peaceful," she says.

"It's lovely," I say. "But unless you plan to snare them…."

"I was working on snares," she says. "Just this morning. I think I've got the basics. The slip-knot, the way the animal's momentum tightens the noose. I think I could set one."

"Do you intend to?"

She's silent, her gaze returning to the deer. The fawns have finished their nibbling and are busy sharpening the nubs of their antlers against an ache tree. Their budding desire to stab and rend should assault my Sense, but all I see are tawny hides, spots of white catching the gray morning light.

"It's funny," Miriam says.

"What is?"

She gestures at the deer. "Here we are, almost close enough to touch them, and they don't seem scared at all. But as soon as they see us, they'll scamper off."

"That's how it works," I say. "They conserve their energy until they need it."

"If we were in their place, we'd be scared."

"Because we know what's out there."

"We're out here."

I've begun to tire of the conversation as much as of the wildlife exhibit. "Is there some point to this?"

"Just," she says, "I've been thinking. I have no wish to hurt them, but if they were to die, I'd collect their bodies for the village. So their deaths would benefit me."

"That's the way of the Ecosystem," I say. "If we die, grabgrass will pull our bodies belowground, where we'll become fertilizer for the plants the deer are feeding on. Our deaths will benefit them."

"But when we were in the borers' lair," she says, "I had a thought. Maybe it was because I was convinced I was going to get eaten myself."

The reminder turns my stomach.

"What if it doesn't have to be that way?" she says. "What if we don't have to be…killers?"

"What are you suggesting we eat?" I ask. "Rocks?"

"No…." That's Miriam: feet or tongue, forever tripping over one or the other. "I just keep thinking, if I could find a way, then I wouldn't have to feel so…."

I wait, but there's nothing more. "So…?"

"Scared," she says.

My Sense flickers but refuses to glow. "What do you Sense?"

"Not of this," she says, her hand sweeping the dell. "Of today."

"The wedding?"

She nods, and when she looks at me, her lashes bulge with tears. "It's my wedding day," she says. "I'm supposed to be happy. But I'm not."

I'm startled by her admission, but I can't let her see. "Nerves," I mutter. "Doesn't every bride get them?"

She shakes her head. "I've spent the past week running over all the reasons I shouldn't get married. All the reasons I'm being a fool. I can tell you every shrub those baby pig-deer ate, but I can't come up with one good answer to the questions in my mind."

I have no answers either, no idea how we got onto this subject. But Miriam doesn't let my silence stop her.

"What if he doesn't really love me?" she says. "What if he's only marrying me because of our pledge? What if he's doing it to prove a point, to please Chief Warden Daniel? What if I find out tomorrow, or the next day, or the next year that I'm his burden, not his joy? Or what if I never find out?"

Her eyes beseech me. The terrible thought strikes me that she knows my secret, that she's seen something in Isaac, or in me. I swallow the thought, remind myself he's never suggested he might retreat from his vow. Never suggested he wants to. It's entirely possible he feels nothing for me anymore, that I feel in him only what I long to. *Pick up a thread*, I say to myself. *And watch it lead nowhere.*

"I'm sorry," Miriam says, tears continuing to spill. "It's

just…we barely saw each other after he joined the healers. I thought he'd forgotten our pledge. And then he told me…before I became a Sensor, he told me…."

That he no longer loved her. I've heard this story; I took it from his lips the day both of us nearly died.

"So maybe he's only marrying me because he feels guilty," Miriam rushes on. "Maybe he feels he owes it to me. Maybe he wishes"—and her last words come out a whisper—"that I *had* died so he wouldn't have to go through with it."

I'm at a total loss. I search for the right words, but all I find is anger. Anger that she's telling me this, anger that I'm the one she expects to reassure her about a marriage I wish were my own. I've never been good with people, not under the best of circumstances. That may be another reason the healer's life is not for me.

"I can't help you," I say, and my words sharpen like knives. "If you think I can, you must have forgotten who I am."

Her face quivers as if I've actually cut her. Now that I've said the words, they release a flood of others I didn't know I was carrying.

"You're a Sensor," I say. "Sensors aren't supposed to love, to marry, to know joy. You've been handed a gift no Sensor's won before, struggle and suffer as they may. My grandpa"—Aaron's beloved face flashes before my eyes, but his smile only heightens my fury—"my own grandpa hid his love for forty years, hid his daughter, hid me. I never knew my mother because her act of love led to banishment, vilification, and death. You're free to love, yet you whine about *questions*. Your questions are a slight to every Sensor who's dreamed of love and found only despair."

Miriam covers her face with her hands. Her shoulders shake, brittle with sobs. But my heart has hardened, and each tear only thickens its armor.

"Marry him, or don't marry him," I say. "Plague me no more with your schoolgirl sorrows."

She keens into her hands. The forest echoes her cries. The lightest of rains has begun to fall: I wouldn't have noticed it if not for the drops that cling to her hair like dew. A rumble in my chest thrills me with the thought of thunder.

Then all falls silent.

Miriam has removed her hands from her face and stands with her head raised, red-rimmed eyes wide. Tears branch silvery across her puffy cheeks. She spreads her fingers, wiggles them in the flow. I glance at the clearing and find the pigdeer gone.

"What do you Sense?" I whisper.

She says nothing. She won't meet my eyes.

A stirring in the ground. "Is it—?"

She nods. That's all. Without another word, we turn and flee.

The Ecosystem has awakened.

WE RUN.

Side by side, exchanging neither looks nor talk. The Ecosystem convulses around us, shaking as if wracked by chills. The tremors speed my heartbeat, rattle the roots of my teeth. I can't Sense its mind. But I can tell this is no ordinary paroxysm.

Cicatrix screech as they swarm blindly through the trees, lacking leaders or ignoring them. Bloodbirds wheel and dive, only to be snatched in midair by ghosthawks and aukpreys. These harpies tear their prey to pieces, blood showering like rain. Prowler monkeys leap wildly through the canopy, jarring branches with the shock of their landings—and then, as if the ground is just another perch, they fling themselves into the air to plunge to their deaths. It's as though the forest has forgotten its grievance against us and turned its anger inward, attacking whatever slithers or crawls or flies. It's as though the Ecosystem has gone mad.

Within sight of the village, Miriam reeling while I hobble a step behind, the trees tear themselves from the earth and fall around us.

Giant aches many hundreds of years old lose their grip and topple, their descent slowed by the closeness of their own branches. When they thud to ground at last, they throw me and my partner from our feet. We scramble to stand, but have to duck as animate branches and roots—hexlox, sickenmore, harm—lash out. Not at us: whip-like appendages wrap around each other, tugging until the trees come unrooted and collide. I watch a pair of hexlox fight over a sickenmore, each of the two trying to stuff the fifty-foot bole into their digestive pustules. If we die out here, it will be as chance victims of the Ecosystem's suicidal rage.

In our path, limbs are woven as tightly as a reed mat. Miriam and I squirm on our bellies beneath the flailing web as each tree tries to liberate itself. We're almost clear of danger when a stray branch catches her by the ankle and sends her sprawling.

"Miriam!" I call as she rises, shakes her head woozily, and resumes her flight to the village. She's made it to the sward when the tallest ache of them all, the one that's shadowed the village for untold years, collapses directly over her head.

"Miriam!" I scream.

Her face tilts upward. She sees the wall of branches descending, yet for some reason, she doesn't move. She stands rooted to the spot, eyes wide. As if in a nightmare, I watch the massive tree fall, and I know I can't reach her in time.

But then, at the final instant, she leaps aside. Nimbly, for her. I Sense nothing—I've Sensed nothing our entire run—but I see what she's done: judged the ache's descent, waited for the perfect moment to avoid its crushing weight. Her face is scratched by twig-ends, but she's otherwise intact.

"Where did you learn to do that?" I gasp as I come up

to her. I hear the beating of my own heart, and I realize the forest has gone still once more, as if the failed effort to slay Miriam was its final spasm.

"From you," she says into the silence. "I've learned so much about the methods of self-preservation."

Then she sprints across the sward, while I limp in her wake.

A WEEK AGO, the gathering hall was draped for a funeral. Today, it's arrayed for a wedding.

I've never attended a wedding before. Sensors don't. What the thinking is behind this—that public displays of love might stir improper desires, or that Sensors need to avoid the appearance of belonging too closely to the community they serve—I don't know. But while I'm no stranger to the ceremony that marks life's end, I've never witnessed the one that marks love's beginning.

Today's different. All the Sensors are here. Today, we join Sensor and healer. Today, we commit ourselves to a new road.

Sensor and healer.

Miriam. And Isaac.

He stands in front of the ceremonial hearth at the head of the room, dressed in a flowing robe I've never seen him or anyone wear, killdeer-brown and lined with black-and-white pandalion fur. Truth be told, it looks a bit dandyish on him, but that only makes it harder for me to tear my eyes away. He's done with the walking-stick, or at least, he refuses its support today. The arm he wounded in the urthwyrms' lair, however, hangs uselessly at his side, and will for the rest of his days, so I've heard. His hair has been trimmed, and—a surprise—he's grown a neat beard, a week and a half's worth of wisps along his jaw. The smile that clutches me so is subdued for the moment, a proud hint on his lips. I close my eyes so I won't have to see it, but then I realize that other eyes might be watching me, so I gaze around the room and attempt a smile of my own. If Isaac looks at me, I don't think I'll be able to continue the masquerade.

But he doesn't. Thankfully, cruelly, unforgivably, he doesn't.

Sprigs of healer shrubs—witch hazel, goldenrod, purple vetch—have been arranged in earthenware vases at the hearthside. That in itself is a major concession on the Sensorship's part, one that wouldn't have come to pass without Esther's support. Torches adorn the walls, brightening the gloom of a day that has yet to see the sun. The Ecosystem is invisible from inside the hall, but there's an unnatural quiet outside, none of the accustomed sounds of the forest having returned since the giant ache tree's fall.

This seems not to trouble the smiling audience that occupies the floor before the hearth. I know all of them by face, relatively few by name; up until recently, as a Sensor, I was kept apart from the life of the village. Twin offshoots from the crowd branch toward the soon-to-be-married couple. On Isaac's side—the left, the healers' side—stands his widowed mother, Hagar, along with the midwife Judith and the others of her order. On the right stand Miriam's parents and sister, and flanking them, at a slight remove from the immediate family, the Sensors: Esther, Judah, Adam, Ezra, Levi. The apprentices, Jarrod and Saul. The trainees, Rebecca and Esau. And me.

Chief Warden Daniel officiates, a resplendent russet-brown robe cascading over his bulk, his genial face holding nothing back. How he'll smile any broader when the marriage vows are spoken, I can't imagine.

We burned Aaron's body in this same place. Sent the smoke streaming through the rooftop vent into a starlit sky. Daniel, his mien and voice somber, officiated then as now. I'd wished to bury my grandpa in the ancient way of the healers—in the ground, where his body could join the Ecosystem he'd spent a lifetime traversing—but Daniel convinced me otherwise. Or Isaac did, speaking on Daniel's behalf. Now was not the time, he told me. Let the body of our past Chief Sensor be cremated according to custom. A wedding was the proper place for the healing of old wounds, the forging of new paths.

How readily I'd agreed with him. How little choice I'd had.

And now he stands beside Miriam, whose hair has been tussled into plaits and whose tranquil face, though scratched by the ache tree, shows no sign of the morning's torment. She's changed from the skintight shirt and shorts that all Sensors wear into an actual dress, beige-colored quetzal hide cinched at the waist to show her not-quite-woman's figure to best advantage, the token resting between her breasts. To anyone else in the room, I've no doubt she appears composed and reflective, honored to be the first Sensor to stand openly in her beloved's presence. The past behind her, all the days of her life ahead.

Only I know what she went through to get here.

By the time we fell, panting, onto the charred circle of grabgrass that fences the village, my nerves felt like an animal hide stretched thin and raked with a stone blade. We glanced behind us at a forest that seemed to have been jostled in a giant hand: trees fallen, carcasses littering the wreckage. Miriam and I had been tumbled as well, though of the two of us, I alone had trouble keeping my legs from trembling.

We rushed to find Chief Sensor Esther. As expected, she'd assembled the Sensors in our council chamber, the Sensorium. All had experienced what we had. None could make Sense of it.

"I must ask you," Esther addressed her troops. "Has any of you detected a purpose in this outbreak?"

Heads shook in unison.

"What, then?" she demanded. "What can account for this disruption?"

There was silence. At last, Levi spoke.

"Today a Sensor marries," he said, not acknowledging that the Sensor he referred to was in the room.

"The Ecosystem has never concerned itself with our celebrations," Esther replied. "Why should it now?"

Levi muttered a word about the ancient ways of the Sensorship, before Esther's eyes taught him the wisdom of silence.

"Would it not be best, Mistress," spoke Judah, "to delay the wedding until further investigation? Even if this…phenomenon has nothing to do with today's ceremony, it might be wise to explore the Ecosystem's will before proceeding."

Esther's eyes sharpened. "And when have we in this room ever bent to the Ecosystem's will? When have we consented to call it master?"

"I misspoke," Judah said calmly. "I merely meant that as it is the Sensorship's duty to protect the village, it might be best not to allow other business to take precedence until we discover the source of this extraordinary occurrence."

Many heads nodded in response: Levi's, Jarrod's, Saul's, Adam's, Ezra's. Only Miriam and I stood unmoved.

Esther turned to us, her eyes troubled. "I would speak with you two alone."

The others filed from the room, not without a reproving glance or two. At Miriam, or at me.

When none remained but the three of us, Esther sat on one of the stone benches that surrounded the central circle, gesturing for me and Miriam to join her. For a long time, she kept silent, a woman roughly the age my mother would have been. The morning's events piled on me, and I felt an unaccountable impulse to rest my head on her shoulder. I found nothing in her sharp features to make me believe she'd welcome my advances.

"I knew your mother," she said abruptly, shocking me into full wakefulness. "As one Sensor may know another. I did not like her." She said this frankly and without malice. "I thought her a fool, always running off to sport with the healers, never minding what the elder Sensors advised. I saw the danger she courted, even before her...." She waved a hand at me, and I assumed she was unable to bring herself to speak the word *pregnancy*. "When it happened, I shared Nathan's distaste for what she had done. I voted gladly, young as I was, to cast her from the ranks of the Sensorship. When she died, though I knew nothing of Nathan's part in it, I did not mourn. And when Aaron presented you as her successor, I most definitely did not approve."

Her almost-black eyes flicked from my face to Miriam's. I waited for her to resume.

"I still do not approve," she said. "For as long as our order has existed, the Sensors have formed a special class, separate from the commoners we serve. In all my years in the field, I have permitted none to touch me, much less to...." Again, a wave of her hand took the place of whatever she was unable to say. "Though I see now that it was wrong of me to blame your mother for what I did not understand, I remain unconvinced that *her* way can ever be *our* way. I know that it can never be mine."

"Begging your pardon, Mistress Esther," I said, with a formality I didn't really feel, "but why did you wish to speak with us?"

"I need to know if you Sense any reason the Ecosystem should object to this child's wedding."

Miriam's mouth fell open. It took a moment for me to find words.

"Did the Ecosystem run wild when my mother suckled me?" I asked, and it gave me pleasure to watch the Chief Sensor squirm.

"There was no such disturbance at the time," she said when she recovered her poise.

"I thought not," I said. "I sense only the ill will of the council. But that I have grown accustomed to."

Esther stood and walked to the doorway of the windowless room. Beyond her slim figure, the remaining ache trees stood motionless against a gray sky. When she returned to us, her face looked wearier than I'd ever seen.

"My mind is uneasy," she said. "I foresee that changes are coming, that the Sensorship may be swept up in those changes, if not wholly swept away. If that be so, let it be so. I do not wish to defend a dying creed. But there are many in the council who do not share my philosophy. Today's manifestation serves their desires, even if it cannot have been brought about by their devices. So I must ask again, of both of you"—yet her eyes leveled on Miriam—"whether you know of anything that explains the Ecosystem's unrest."

I glanced at Miriam, wondering if she would recount our conversation in the glade. If she would take this opportunity, perfect as it was, to voice her doubts. She returned my gaze, and knowing what I knew, I might have said her violet eyes appeared harder than usual, with a bitter edge of experience she'd not truly earned, unless she learned that from me, too. Then she addressed Esther.

"I'm marrying Isaac," she said. "I pledge my life to the Sensorship, but I cannot pledge my heart."

The Chief Sensor exhaled loudly, and for a moment, I caught a glimpse of her solitary life and mind. Then it was gone, like a whiff of smoke sucked into the trees.

"I will inform the others of your decision," she said as she rose to leave. "And I will defend you as I can. But I cannot say how effectual my defense may be."

"Thank you, Mistress," Miriam said when the Chief Sensor reached the door. Esther did not pause, and neither did Miriam look at me as she exited the room to prepare for her wedding.

And so I know why she stands still and silent, facing the congregation with neither fear nor apology in her eyes. I know why she gives herself to him today. She was a girl this morning, but she is a woman now, and the world has no power to daunt or command her any longer.

She will marry her love this day. Hers, and mine.

She grips Isaac's hand, the nerveless one whose use he lost in the borers' tunnel. He can't squeeze back, but he grins at her and mouths words I'm too cowardly to decipher. Daniel steps forward, arms outstretched as if to encompass us all, and opens the wedding with a smile.

Everything that happens after breaks my heart.

"Dearly beloved," Daniel intones in the rich and melodious cadence he's perfected in his long years as Chief Warden. "This is a time for special joy. Today we join this man and this woman in lifelong love and companionship. And today we bind our community ever more closely through the promise of their love. They stand before us ready to lead us into a better world."

The two have turned to face each other, their hands forming a bridge. Daniel smiles benignantly at them and goes on.

"Every marriage tells a story: the story of two people, the story of a family, the story of a world they build for and with each other. Today is the story's beginning, for them as well as us. But to understand the story fully, I must take you back to an earlier beginning, to a time long before any of us walked this earth. Only then may we appreciate how uniquely marvelous this day is."

My gaze is fixed on Miriam's profile. I can't look anywhere else, can't let my eyes wander for a moment to the one whose hands link with hers.

"We are told," Daniel continues, "of a time when only one man and one woman walked this earth. Their names are lost to us, so long ago did they live. We are told that the land upon which they walked was new as well, and that it was fresh and wholesome, a place of beauty and rest and repose. A paradise, to use the word we have heard from those tales. When the man and woman were hungry, they ate; and when they were thirsty, they drank; and when they were tired, they lay upon the open ground and slept, with only the trees to shelter them. No predators did they fear, no bird or beast or branch. Indeed, we are told that where they walked, all living things bowed their heads to the man and woman, and whatever the two called them, that was what they answered to from then on. It is said that the name of this paradise was *edinnu*, which in one of the lost languages means 'fruitful place,' or simply 'place.' For it was at that time the only place, just as the man and woman were its only masters, and they knew and wanted no other."

Daniel pauses, and I tear my gaze from Miriam to look around the room. Judith's eyes shine at the story he tells—but then, Judith's eyes shine on most occasions. Some others in the crowd seem rapt as well, their breath hushed to hear his words. The Sensors, by contrast, stand rigidly, expressions of doubt or hostility on their faces. I can't say I disagree with them. The world of which the Chief Warden speaks sounds charming, but the Ecosystem is no *edinnu* now, if it ever was.

Daniel smiles sadly, as if sensing his listeners' skepticism. "And yet *edinnu* was not to last. Some say the man and woman defied one of the earth's vital laws, and the land revolted against them. Others say they grew weary of ceaseless pleasure, and left in search of new lands from which to wrest a living. It is told—I know not how truly— that a single tree stood where they dwelt, a tree whose fruit provided all their wants and needs, but that tree was stricken, and they were forced to wander abroad to seek shelter and sustenance. It is said that when they left, the earth grew wild and dangerous, until even *edinnu* was covered in blight and could no longer be restored. Some tales say that the two wept to see the creatures of the land turn deadly, their former companions grow savage until they no longer recognized their true names. Others say that the man and woman themselves grew lawless and wild, and cared not for the ruin of their onetime home.

"But this much we know," Daniel says, his voice a whisper that nonetheless fills the cavernous hall. "It was their loss of *edinnu* that gave birth to all we celebrate today: marriage, family, community. While they dwelt in *edinnu*, the man and woman recognized no need for each other, for what could harm them there? When they were banished from this place of delight, only then did they bind hands and hearts to face the world together. And though we may not know it, we have lived their choice down to this day, for better and for worse. Those of us who cannot feel the grain of the earth beneath our feet or hear its voice in our ear or detect its pulse pounding in our veins, these are the ones to whom we say: marry, and bear children, and grow old together, and be a support to each other in this most perilous of worlds. But those of us who have retained a trace of what it must have been like in those forgotten days, those of us who *can* speak the language of beasts and trees, who *can* walk this earth freely and hear its voice crying in their souls, to these we say: never shall you know the joys of marriage and parenthood and community, for the last echoes of *edinnu* sound within you, and what need have you of the company of your fellow beings?

And so, when we celebrate the joining of two in marriage, there are those we do not invite to share in love's triumph. There are those we ourselves cast out, forsaking them to face the perils of this world in solitude."

My tongue dabs the corner of my lip, where I taste salt. When I blink, the flickering torchlight stings my eyes. I look at Judith, and see that tears have slid down her wrinkled cheeks, their tracks gleaming in the torches' glow. I think to brush my own tears away, but stop, knowing this will only call attention to my plight. Daniel hasn't looked directly at me once, but his words have entered my chest and taken a seat beside my heart.

"That is why," he continues, "the marriage of this man and this woman signals a new day for us all. When they speak their vows before us, they speak for all who know what it is to live in the hope of recovering *edinnu*. For none of us should live alone. None of us, be the gifts of our birth what they may, should dwell beyond the community of human love and sorrow. Look at this woman!" he says in a ringing voice, and Miriam lifts her chin and faces the crowd, keeping one hand in Isaac's, and in that moment I see what he has always seen in her, and I see that she is beautiful, strong and tender and stern, and my breath catches in my chest. "Why should this woman not share in the joys of our race? Why should the love she has to give not meet and touch the love of this man? Why—"

"Because she's a Sensor!"

A gasp leaps from me, and it's a moment before I realize I'm not the one who shouted. The sound is so close, at my ear, that when all eyes turn, I'm convinced they're staring at me. But the one who stares back is a Sensor even younger than I am, his fists clenched, his unruly red hair standing erect as the display of a fearkat about to strike.

It's Levi.

"She's a Sensor!" he repeats. "Her place is in the wild, not in some healer's hovel!"

"Levi!" Esther reprimands. But he's not listening.

"Open your eyes!" he shouts to the crowd. "Look at what comes of breaking our most sacred laws! Do you wish to face the Ecosystem without our protection?"

The congregation shifts uneasily. Whatever their awareness of the morning's events, the villagers are unaccustomed to challenging a Sensor's words, especially when those words are uttered in anger.

"Levi," Esther repeats. "You do not speak for the Sensorship here. If you persist in this spectacle, you do so alone."

"Do I?" Levi says, laughing recklessly. "You're not so wise as you think, Mistress Esther. The Brotherhood of the Sensorship stands united against this...this"—he sputters, as if seeking a strong enough word—"abomination."

Esther glances warily at the Sensors who form a line at the hearthside. To a man, they meet her eyes with defiance, and—what's more—stone knives flash in their hands. Esther's own knife has yet to make an appearance, but I've seen her draw it with a deftness that tricks the eye and mind. I clench my fingers, but my own knife is gone, relinquished to Esther on the day I gave up the hunt.

"There is no need for this," Daniel speaks from the hearthstone. His voice, smooth and reasonable, carries no hint of alarm. "It is the will of the people, Levi. The will of Miriam and Isaac, and of all who wish to see our community healed. Do not fight this, my boy. Do not bring this curse upon yourself."

Levi laughs again. "I used to listen to your speeches," he says to Daniel. "Before I joined the Brotherhood. Do you remember what you used to say?"

Daniel meets his eye, unflinching.

"*There is a time for everything*," Levi recites in a mocking voice. "*A time to be born, and a time to die. A time to laugh, and a time to weep. A time to rejoice, and a time to mourn. A time to heal, and....*" He smiles. There's the scratch of a blade. "You know the rest."

Everyone moves at once. Esther, knife in hand, launches herself at Levi, but she's blocked by the phalanx of Sensors. She goes down, and I lose her beneath their bodies. The crowd recoils. Isaac throws himself in front of Daniel to protect him from Levi's blade, but Miriam shoves her beloved with all her strength, and he stumbles to a knee on the hearthstone. I leap for her as Levi's knife, thrown wildly but with the sureness of rage, finds its home in her breast. She falls, and I catch her as her pale dress turns red. Isaac's cry is the only sound in the hushed building.

He and Daniel are stooping by my side when the hearth erupts and an urthwyrm thrusts its massive head into the hall.

I LOSE MY grip on Miriam's body as I fling myself from the tilting stone. She tumbles and rolls to a stop on the ruined hearth, where she lies gushing blood from a chest that moves just enough to show me she still lives.

Isaac's shout rises above the screams of the crowd, the screech of ruptured stone. The wyrm's head whips from side to side, slamming into Daniel and sending him half-way across the hall, where he lands in a motionless pile of red-brown robes. Isaac ducks beneath the creature's head, clutches Miriam's blood-stained form in his arms and attempts to rise, but she spills from his grasp as the stone explodes behind him and another wyrm forces its way into the room. A cry escapes me as the second monster's body lashes blindly against Isaac, battering him to the ground. The floor heaves so violently I can barely gain my feet, and by the time I do, a fissure as wide as I am tall blocks my way to where he and his would-be bride lie.

My mind reels as crazily as the room. How could we not have heard them? Sensed them? In the days it must have taken them to travel to our village, how could we not have known they were coming?

The crowd has fled, the screams of those who haven't been crushed by flying stone echoing outside the hall. I can't count the bodies. The walls shake, and I fear the roof may soon come down. With a strength I didn't know my legs possessed, I leap the chasm between me and the hearth, land in time to see another urthwyrm spit stone from its maw as it bursts to the surface. Miriam and Isaac lie unconscious, she with Levi's knife buried to the hilt beside my mother's token, he with a mammoth chunk of stone pinning his legs. Both of them are alive, though her breath has grown faint as her life's blood spills on the stone. There's movement behind the broken hearth, and I catch a glimpse of Levi's reddish hair the instant before he attacks.

The youngest Sensor but one—older only than the girl whose breast bears his blade—swings violently with a fist, his face contorted in rage. But I've fought worse monsters than he. I dodge his blow, trap his arm before it can recoil, and pull with all my might. Levi howls as the arm comes loose from its socket. Enlivened by contact with his skin, my healer's touch whispers to me how to undo the damage I've caused.

I ignore it. My hands go to his head, grip his hair to the roots, and slam his chin against my knee. Blood spurts from his mouth where he must have bitten his tongue. I hope he bit it in two. From there, it's no challenge to throw the boy face first against the hearthstone, where he collapses in a bloody heap beside the wedding couple.

Esther is gone. Daniel's corpse sprawls a room's length away. Miriam and Isaac lie precariously near the pit, their bodies about to slip into the darkness. I hear a rumble in the stone, and I know I have no time. I can save either her or him. Not both.

My heart makes the choice for me.

I KNEEL AT Isaac's side just as another concussion rocks the room. The stone that traps his legs weighs easily as much as he does, but I've no sooner gotten a grip on its jagged edges than I fling—not slide—it from him. By sheer luck, it lands on Levi, who flops like a boned tricky vulture. So much adrenaline flows through me, it's child's play to lift Isaac and drape him across my shoulders. Then I rise to survey the ruins.

Three urthwyrms have forced themselves partway into the hall, a fourth beginning to crack the floor's crust. The first to emerge has nearly succeeded in freeing its entire body, while the other two appear trapped by their own trails of destruction. I see only two Sensors standing—the apprentice Jarrod and Levi's master, Ezra—but aside from Levi, I identify only two members of the order down, one of whom, black-haired, has to be Esther. Where the other two are, I don't know. My path to the hall's sole entrance is blocked by bodies, stone, and crevices as broad as the urthwyrms' backs.

I don't let myself think about any of this. I do what Sensors do best. I run.

The floor slants beneath my feet. Fragments of stone shower around me, some large enough to crack my skull if they hit squarely. Relying on sight, not Sense, I leap past one monster's tooth-filled mouth, stoop beneath another's lashing tail. The exit appears before me, rubble piled around it but with room enough to squeeze through. I'm almost there when Jarrod and Ezra materialize to block my path.

Their faces stream with blood and dust and sweat, but their hands clench knives. Jarrod leers at me, no doubt glimpsing my fate in my eyes. He loved Rachel, the apprentice I lost to the Ecosystem on my quest to recover Miriam. When he draws back his blade, I face him with sympathy, not fear.

Then a dark shape slams into him, and his body explodes in a spray of blood. Chunks of flesh rain heavily on the stone as the urthwyrm none of us Sensed coming disgorges what's left of Jarrod and clamps onto Ezra's leg. He screams and beats its head with his fists as it carries him high into the air, bashing him against the roof. Most of his body, crushed and bloody beyond recognition, falls to the floor, only a single leg dangling from the creature's maw. It swallows the appendage in a spasmodic gulp and rears back to strike.

I thrust upward with a sharp fragment of stone as the wyrm's head barrels toward me, a blur of teeth and flesh and blood. Driven more by the monster's force than my hand, the stone skewers the head, bursting from its crown in a slop of thick black fluid. The thing has no brain, but the agony is enough to send it careening against the roof again. In the instant before it slams back down, I clutch Isaac in both arms and fling our bodies through the narrow exit. I've dragged his body and mine no more than a few feet away before the hall groans and crashes to the ground with a concussion like an earthquake.

I creep from the ruins, tugging Isaac behind me. When I stand on quivering legs, I see that nothing is left of the hall but a pile of smoking stone that pulses with the urthwyrms' movements as if alive.

Miriam. Daniel. Esther. Judith. Rebecca and Esau. All buried, all gone. Though Levi lies with them, his plan couldn't have succeeded better.

Or yes, it could. It could have taken Isaac, too.

I kneel by his side, stroke matted hair from his forehead. His face is cut and bloodied and bruised, one if not both of his legs broken. But his chest heaves, his heart beats. I haven't touched him since last week, on the day he told me of his planned wedding. When I touch him now, the familiar tingle buzzes in my fingertips, spreads up my arm. I see, as always, a glimpse of his life.

He and his bride sit in the hut they would have shared from this day forward. Their hands are clasped, their gaze locked. Her hair carries a strong scent I never noticed, a warm sweetness like honey. Her lips are parted, and her miraculous eyes fix on his with a depth of simple devotion I know I can't match.

I pull my hands away before I see any more. Then I lower my head to my arms and huddle by Isaac's side, too dazed for either gratitude or grief.

A SHUDDERING IN the stone makes me lift my head. Nothing stirs in the Ecosystem: no bloodbirds fly, no quetzals leap among the thinned branches of the canopy. The cicatrix and prowler monkeys are silent. My Sense remains mute, but from what my other senses can tell, a deadly calm reigns over all.

I wish I could say the same of the village.

The wreckage of the gathering hall rises and falls like breath as the creatures that brought it down slither beneath. Everywhere I look, broad heads fracture the pavement, nudge cottages aside as if they're no firmer than mud. The houses of the Sensors, including my own, lie beyond my sight, but I assume they're suffering the same fate. In the hall, I saw only four wyrms, though I heard evidence of more. Now I see twenty, fifty, a hundred of the things undulating over the village like parasites on a rotting carcass. The rock shifts beneath their bodies with a horrible squealing sound as of bone rubbing against bone.

I stand. The ground beneath my feet feels stable, probably because the creatures have finished their task here. I doubt, though, that they'll leave the pavilion intact for long. It seems clear that their purpose is to tear the entire village down, stone by stone.

But why?

The question gnaws at me. When I gave myself to the

urthwyrms three weeks ago, I thought I'd called a truce, a temporary ceasefire in the war that's raged between the Ecosystem and me all these years. I didn't expect that truce to hold forever, but I did expect I'd have some warning when it expired. Can it be because I've lost my Sense that the Ecosystem no longer respects our bargain? Or can it be that there never was a bargain to begin with, that it wants my life *and* the lives of everyone I know?

But if it does—and in some ways this is the hardest thing for me to understand—why did it wait so long to take them? If it could always have dispatched an army of wyrms to our village without a single Sensor detecting their approach, why didn't it do so before? And what made it do so today?

Human survivors dot the village, far less numerous than the wyrms. Many bodies must be buried with Miriam and Esther, others dead in the homes to which they resorted for safety. Some may have fled into the forest, though for the common villager, that means certain death. I scan for signs of surviving Sensors, but their skintight outfits are nowhere to be seen. That, at least, is a mercy. I have no wish to fight any other, no wish to kill. Though I'll do it if any should threaten the ones I love.

The *one* I love. All the rest are gone.

Some of the stragglers, seeing my uniform, have turned toward me. They pick their way through the rubble; luckily, the wyrms are too preoccupied with the work of destruction to bother with such puny beings. When the small crowd draws near, I face them apprehensively. They're unarmed, bloodied, terrified—but will they see me as they must see Levi and his crew, as their sworn protectors who for selfish reasons chose to rain death on their ceremony and their sanctuary?

One of the women steps up to me, a girl-child in her arms and a ragged ten-year-old clinging to her dress. The woman is small but solidly built; a cut across her forehead gives her the appearance of severity, though her eyes are gentle. I recognize her as the seamstress Leah. She can't be much older than I am, which makes it possible that the toddler, though not the other urchin, is hers.

"Mistress Sarah," she says, the unaccustomed title contributing to the pounding between my ears. "Are you hurt?"

I shake my head, then look down at my hands, steeped to the elbows in the blood of many beings. I wipe the gore on my shorts, try not to think of Jarrod's body spattering the stone. Leah's eyes tighten as if she doesn't trust my self-diagnosis, but she speaks again.

"Mistress," she says. "There are so many of them. What should we do?"

It's the simplest of questions, the one I've been asking myself. I have no answer to it. Or I do, but it's not one they—or I—will like much.

"They've torn down the Sensorium," Leah continues when I don't respond. "The Chief Sensor—"

"Is dead," I say. "Along with the Chief Warden."

"Master Aaron served for years," she says. "Mistress Esther only for a little while. The Chief Sensor is the one who serves."

"It's not that simple," I say. I don't know her well enough to confess the damage to my Sense, so I settle for the next closest truth. "I can't lead so many through the Ecosystem. You'd be sitting drakes for…well, pretty much everything."

She takes this in with a flinty expression, then stoops to hush the older of the girls, who's started to whimper. I'm suspicious enough to find her tears rehearsed. When Leah stands again, I find no self-pity in her eyes.

"If we're going to die," she says, "I'd rather die fighting. There's nothing left for us here."

"You don't know what you're saying," I respond. "It's"—I can't think how to put this, so I speak the first words that come to mind—"it's no walk in the woods out there."

As if in answer, a deafening report presages the collapse of the main archway that shadows the village thoroughfare. The lane is an urthwyrm's back, and other wyrms can be seen coiling around the few remaining homes, constricting until the stone succumbs with a succession of popping noises and falls into dust.

Leah smiles sardonically. I like her already. "It's no party here either," she says, and I like her even more.

The remainder of the refugees have reached us, maybe fifty in all. Less than a quarter of the village population when this day dawned. Yet even that number will be all but impossible to shepherd through the Ecosystem. If they were Sensors, keenly attuned to the mind of the wild, they might stand a chance for a day, a week, a month. If *I* were a Sensor in full possession of my faculties, I might be able to protect a villager or two, for a day or two. But this crew, with me as their leader, with no home to return to and no place to go, are doomed. They must know that.

Yet they're here. And they don't look as if they're going away.

"All right," I say. "We have a little time. Stay away from the wyrms, but search for anything that can be used as a weapon or to hold water. Stones, buckets, skins, anything. We'll also need flints to make fire, and as much wood as we can carry."

A man steps forward. He's Aaron's age or older, judging by his snow-white beard and hair, but his carriage is erect and his arms roped with muscle. A blood-soaked rag covers one of his eyes where he must have taken a fragment of stone.

"Mistress," he says. "I am Gideon, chief of the firestarters. Our tools are kept in the storehouse." He points across the village, to a spot that hasn't been wholly savaged by wyrms. "If ten of the strongest will come with me, we will collect the supplies you require."

"Good," I say. "But be careful. Are others wounded?" I'm not sure what I want the answer to be.

It turns out there are a few, though none so badly hurt as Isaac. Leah's gash will need to be treated at some point; other villagers have been stunned or battered by flying stone. All can walk. That's a stroke of good fortune, as the only healers left, other than the unconscious Isaac, are Caleb and Noah, fourteen-year-old twins who've been training for mere months. I could count myself as well, but I'm not ready to think about that.

While Gideon and his assistants rush off to scour the ruins, the twins make the rounds, binding wounds and fixing slings as best they can. That other survivors may lie hidden in the rubble, no one says. That leaving them to die in order to save our own lives is not the first decision I want to preside over, some in our party must suspect. They watch me, waiting to see what choice I'll make, what kind of sacrifices will mark my regime at the outset.

Again, Leah comes to my rescue. Her wound's been covered with a strip of hide that wraps her head like a bandana. Resting the babe against her hip, she prods the other child in the back until the girl steps to my side.

"We've all suffered losses," Leah says, her voice soft enough it could be for my ears alone. "These children lost their parents. As for me…." She shakes her head, then raises her voice so all can hear. "We'll follow where you lead, Mistress Sarah."

"It's just Sarah," I say, as the murmur of Leah's words passes through the crowd. I take the little girl's hand in mine. My healer's sense ignites at our touch, and a lifetime of hurt leaps from her to me. I realize as never before that no matter what I do, I'll carry these deaths with me for the rest of my life.

Which, at present, it strikes me might be mercifully short.

A CHORUS OF shouts interrupts the salvage operation. I leave the ten-year-old with Leah and hasten to the site of the voices, on the far side of the stone heap that was once the gathering hall.

When I draw near, I see that there's a hole at the border of the rubble, deep enough to hide all but the heads and shoulders of the people who've climbed inside. Two bodies lie on the pavilion, and though they're too covered in blood and dust for me to tell who they are or if they're alive, I'm close enough to see from their clothes that they're Sensors.

My heart doesn't know whether to leap or fall. The workers pass another body across raised arms, and I'm seized with an even stronger mixture of hope and dread when I realize from its small size that this figure, also dressed as a Sensor, must be either Rebecca or Esau.

I break through the crowd, rush to the lip of the hole. Another body's emerging from darkness, and this time, I glimpse enough of her face to know that it's Rebecca. When the workers lay her carefully beside Esau, I see that both children are breathing, though fitfully. The unnatural position of Rebecca's legs, however, suggests an injury to her spine. On closer inspection, I see that she's wet herself, though I hold out hope that that was merely a fear response. My fingers give an anticipatory tingle, as if I could heal her from where I stand. As if I could heal paralysis no matter how close I come.

"Are there any more?" I ask an unfamiliar woman near the edge of the pit.

"Mistress Sarah," she says, as if surprised. "We've found the hearth, but it's too tight a fit to dig any deeper."

"Don't," I say. "It could cave in. Get everyone out of there."

She frowns, but immediately passes my order to her coworkers. They've no sooner climbed from the hole than, disobeying my own instructions, I leap in.

It's dark as night inside, and as cramped as the woman said. The ground quivers with the movement of the urthwyrms far off, but I feel none of the stronger vibrations that would indicate one directly below. Groping forward on hands and knees, I make contact with the softness of flesh. When my hands close around the victim's shoulders, my healer's touch provides me the best news I've gotten all day: it's Judith, and she's alive. My fingers give me the bad news next: she lies beneath a pyramid of stone blocks, and I fear that moving them might bring the whole structure down.

A flint scratches behind me, and Gideon's bearded face emerges from darkness as his torch flickers to life.

"Easy, now," he says.

With his light, we determine that Judith's not completely trapped. Gideon gives a call, and two of his assistants enter the pit to help us wiggle the elderly midwife free. The firestarter waves his torch around the confined space, but there are no more bodies to be found, no more maneuvering room to search for others. I quickly see why.

Where the hearth used to be, a twenty-foot wide hole descends into the deeper darkness of underground. Gideon lowers his torch within this second hole, but if there's a bottom, we can't find it. This must be the tunnel one of the urthwyrms dug: it plummets straight down, and with the creature's mining ability, it could be hundreds of feet deep. Anyone else who was in the vicinity of the hearth—Miriam, Esther, the remaining Sensors—must have fallen into the abyss, the surrounding stone collapsing over their collective grave to make any further searching impossible.

It doesn't shock me to learn that Miriam is truly gone. Quite likely, she wouldn't have survived the wound from Levi's knife. But that doesn't change the fact that, should he wake to discover that I rescued him and abandoned her, Isaac will never forgive me.

"Mistress Sarah!"

The voices meet my ears at the same moment a tremor in the stone jars my body. Gideon offers a hand as I scramble backward, and though I'm surprised that someone of his generation would break the ages-old taboo against touching a Sensor, I take it. Perhaps because I'm surrounded by so many injuries, my healer's gift seems to have caught fire, and the clasp of his hand sends signals down my arm that tell me his covered eye is gone. He's fortunate the stone shard that took it from him stopped short of his brain. It came close.

We emerge from the hole to find a fleet of wyrms headed in our direction. Their slick black bodies rear high above the pavilion, crash down like fallen timber. Each time a wyrm lands, the ground shakes beneath our feet, and the mound behind us shifts. The creatures are slowed by all the piled and broken stone, but it won't be long before they plow or chew their way through. Even if there were a chance of finding more survivors, the time to fly the village has come.

"Carry the wounded," I tell Gideon and his crew. "Be careful not to jostle Rebecca. I think her back is broken."

The old firestarter's single eye blazes. Handing his torch to an assistant, he strips off his shirt and gently wraps Rebecca before lifting her in his powerful arms.

"Take care of the children," I instruct Leah and the others. "We're going to cross the sward and stop at the edge of the forest. Don't let anyone set foot into the trees. And don't touch the leaves, not even with the tip of your finger. They'll make you so dizzy you won't be able to stand."

Silently, they obey. The unsteady way everyone's moving makes it seem as if they've already succumbed to ache leaf venom and can barely keep their feet. By the time I hoist Isaac over my back and give the signal to depart, the wyrms have come so close I can see the multiple rings of teeth within their mouths.

We troop across the circle of charred turf that's separated us for time immemorial from the Ecosystem's wrath. Now the protective ring is humped and rutted by the wyrms' passage, and I have to lead the survivors in a wandering course to avoid weakened ground. When I reach the sward and set foot on living grass, a momentary hope flutters in my chest that I might receive some Sensation from the earth, but it's a hope without cause. I could be standing on grabgrass, which camouflages itself to mingle with its harmless counterpart, but my Sense can't tell the difference any more than my eyes can. I move as quickly as possible with my burden, avoiding the trees that fell earlier in the day, hoping that any grabgrass I disturb will be too slow to ensnare me. Behind me, the villagers match my pace as I zigzag over the sward.

We're lucky. Either I've chosen a safe path, or the grass lies dormant for the time being. Either way, the entire body of us reaches the edge of the forest without mishap.

The bearers lay the wounded where I designate, on bare ground that appears to my eye as innocuous as any the Ecosystem affords. A downed sickenmore rests nearby, its roots waggling feebly but its telescoping limbs lacking energy for the attack. Having laid Isaac beside the others, I approach Gideon, who cradles Rebecca's damaged body. I wonder if he has children and grandchildren of his own, if he lost them today. I reach out and touch the unconscious girl's forehead, and instantly, my healer's power confirms what I feared. She might live, but Rebecca will never walk again.

"Mistress Sarah," Gideon says. Tears flow from his one eye to trickle into his beard.

"It's just Sarah," I say, and that's the last thing I can say.

A woman gives a cry, and I see that it's Rebecca's mother, who's only now realized that her daughter lives. She flies from the pack, followed by her husband, a man little older than Leah who now looks as if he's seen seventy years. Together, they converge on Gideon and weep with joy at their daughter's survival, grief at her broken body.

I turn from their reunion to face the village. The wyrms have overrun the remains of the gathering hall, their bodies covering it in such numbers the stone is all but hidden. The movement of their black bodies is intricate, a twisting and weaving dance, but if the pattern means anything at all, I'm unable to decipher it. I watch as the weight of the monsters drags the heaped stone downward, watch as the force of gravity pulls the surrounding pavilion toward the immense hole the hundreds of wyrms create in their descent. It starts slowly, but soon, the ruins of the village are tumbling into the hole like an avalanche. I stand with the survivors as the earth collapses inward, forming an emptiness as broad and deep as the lives we all lived.

"Mistress," Leah breathes. "Sarah. What are we going to do?"

I haven't begun to think of an answer when the village gives a final groan and melts from view, and only the devouring land remains.

I FACE AWAY from the smoking crater to find some sort of quarrel in progress. Raised voices. A scuffle. Not the best omen for the newborn community I've led into the boundless wilderness.

Fifteen or so villagers are involved, the bulk of them trying to get past four who've formed a line to block their passage. A single woman seems to be holding the line against the unequal odds: she shouts, gesticulates, shoves anyone who confronts her. She's a big woman, tall and brawny, and I'm not the first Sensor to have remarked on the peculiarity that she gave birth to a daughter so small and frail.

It's Rachel's mother.

Her name, I recall, is Dinah. I look for her husband, Ephraim, but can't find him. That can only mean he's dead. The two were inseparable, and I remember Aaron telling me they were loath to let Rachel join the Sensorship. Overprotective, my grandfather said at the time. Prophetic, it now appears.

I halt, remembering the painful meeting in their home little more than a week ago, when I stumbled through an apology for letting their only child die on the journey that recovered Miriam. They sat in silence until I was done, then ushered me out of their home without a word. I knew at the time that my advances were doomed, Jarrod having met with the grieving couple days before. I don't know what was said at that meeting, but Dinah won't want to see me now any more than I want to see her.

Still, it can't be avoided. I take a deep breath and march toward the scene of the commotion.

"You'll not touch them!" Dinah is saying to the crowd. Her arm's drawn back as if to take a swing. The few others on her side seem less than happy about where they've found themselves, but Dinah's presence holds them in place.

"They're killers," one of her challengers, a man I believe is named Amos, says to her. "They have no right to be here."

"They're Sensors!" Dinah shrills, and the others fall back, as if reminded of the magic of that title.

I'm close enough now to learn what they're fighting over. The two Sensors who were first to be rescued from the downed gathering hall sit propped against tree trunks behind Dinah's line, alive but too weak to defend themselves. One, I see to my dismay, is Levi, his arm dangling where I tore it from its roots, his face bloodied and bruised. The other is the apprentice Saul. His condition seems better than Levi's; at least, his eyes don't wobble and his head doesn't loll. He's a boy of only fourteen, and before today, I'd have said that his master, Judah, was less devoted to Nathan and Levi's faction than some of the others. But after what I witnessed in the gathering hall, there's no telling where his allegiance lies.

"What seems to be the trouble?" I say in what I hope is a calm voice.

Dinah looks startled to see me. Her demeanor,

however, straightaway turns dismissive. "Nothing we can't settle ourselves, Mistress."

I face the man who exchanged words with her. "Amos?" He nods. "Is there a problem?"

"Only that these two deserve death," he says. "The one killed Mistress Miriam, and the other, well, he didn't exactly stand in the way, now did he? But according to these here—"

"My daughter was a Sensor!" Dinah cuts him off. "She gave her life to rescue your Mistress Miriam. And you dare accuse *me*, when it's you who's lusting to shed a Sensor's blood!"

"The only blood shed was shed by that boy!" Amos rages.

"A righteous blow!" Dinah screams back. "To preserve the sacred Brotherhood of the Sensorship from pollution by—"

"Enough!" I say. I've never heard such fanatical loyalty from a villager, though I've encountered its like from Nathan and his followers. It was he who insisted that my mother be cast out of the order for the crime of bearing me, he who wounded her in the field and left her for the Ecosystem to finish off. He who, now that I think of it, first used the unfamiliar title Dinah has adopted, the Brotherhood of the Sensorship. But much as I might sympathize with her for everything she's suffered, I can't allow her to be the death of us all.

"None of you has ever set foot in the Ecosystem," I say to the warring sides, Dinah's and Amos's alike. "You think you can stand here and shout at the top of your lungs, and nothing will come of it but hurt feelings. You don't realize that the Ecosystem is listening to every word you say. The angrier you get, the louder your pulse sounds in its ear. The heat radiating off your skin is drawing it to you, telling its creatures that you're too wrapped up in your own passions to heed their approach. If you spill a drop of anyone's blood," I say to Amos, "the bloodbirds will swarm, and they won't be choosy about where the blood came from. And if *you* care so much about Sensors," I add, turning to Dinah, "then listen to what one tells you, and drop this squabble before the forest feasts on everyone here, including a group of blameless children."

Dinah's face contorts. It's possible that mentioning dead children was a low blow. "You don't command us, Mistress," she says.

"Fine," I say. "Then follow the Sensors you're partial to. One of them's an apprentice, and the other's nursing a concussion and a badly dislocated shoulder. See how far you get with the two of them in charge."

That silences her. For now. I'm not naïve enough to think I've heard the last of this.

She steps aside and lets me approach Levi and Saul, though she continues to stand guard as if I might decide to kill them myself. The thought's in my mind, but it's no more than a thought. The trouble isn't merely that shedding blood will attract the Ecosystem, nor that I can't start this journey by taking lives. Much as I hate to admit it, I need Levi. He mustn't learn how shaky my Sense is, but maybe I can find a way to use his Sense without him suspecting.

I squat in front of him. His arm twitches uselessly,

and his eyes won't focus on my face. "Do you know who I am?" I ask.

"Sarah," he says sullenly. His voice betrays how badly his tongue's swollen. "The cur."

"Let's start again," I say. "With you not calling me names and me not reminding you of what you did today. Do you know where we are?"

"The Ecosystem."

"And do you know why we're here?"

He looks confused. "Urthwyrms. The village isn't safe."

"The village is gone," I say. "Along with more than half the people who used to live in it. We're all that's left."

He looks around wildly, his eyes taking way too long to catch up with the movement of his head. "They'll never make it."

"Not unless we help them," I say. "I can fix your arm, and maybe heal the head wound. But I'm not about to attempt either unless you agree to do as I say."

"Make me," he slurs.

I'm preparing a response when Leah and Gideon force their way through Dinah's group to stand beside me. Truth be told, Dinah is pretty much alone by now; the others, as I thought, have little heart for her war. Only fear of the Sensorship kept them in line this long.

"You're outnumbered," I say to Levi. "Not to mention very poorly regarded by the majority. They were about to kill you before I stepped in."

"A true Sensor doesn't fear death," he says, but his eyes say otherwise.

"A true Sensor defends his people," I say. "You failed that trust, Levi. I'm offering you a chance to make amends."

His answer is to spit bloody saliva at me. Except, with his swollen tongue, it mostly dribbles down his own chin. I grit my teeth and suppress an impulse to strangle him and be done with it.

"Let me show you," I say. "That arm's got to hurt."

"Don't touch me!" he shrieks, his expression very close to actual panic. In keeping with Sensor orthodoxy, he'll bury a knife in any living creature he's got a disagreement with—human or otherwise—but he won't allow even the gentlest of touches to relieve his torment. I could pity him, but I'm not in a pitying mood.

"It won't heal on its own," I say. "Or it will, but it'll heal wrong. You'll never be able to use it again."

"Better that," he says, "than suffer defilement at hands such as yours."

"Very well," I say. "You've made your choice."

Gideon offers an arm to help me stand, but the last thing I want is to show weakness before Levi and Saul, so I rise—not too unsteadily, I hope—on my own.

"You'll be placed under guard," I say to Levi. "No one will harm you, but if I catch you spreading your poison, that might change. The same goes for you, Saul," I say to the apprentice. His eyes widen in innocence, but I'm not buying it. "Our only chance for survival is to stick together."

"You're all going to die together," Levi snarls, but I ignore him. I'm walking away to arrange his guard when his final words send a shiver down my back.

"A true Sensor," he says, enunciating each word carefully, "would have known she was standing on a patch of grabgrass."

THE SUNLESS DAY is dipping to night when I hold a conference with my lieutenants at the edge of the forest. I'm sure it would be better for everyone, emotionally speaking, not to camp within sight of the gaping pit that used to be their home. But the Ecosystem remains somnolent, and so long as that interval holds, there's time for the villagers to rest and become acclimated to the brand new world they'll have to enter soon.

My first order of business is to take a headcount. There are sixty-seven of us, more than I'd thought, which is both a good and a very bad thing. Almost everyone who was standing in the vicinity of the hearth is gone: Isaac's mother, Miriam's parents and little sister Naomi. Of the twelve children in our company, seven are orphans, including the girls Leah rescued, who go by the names of Huldah and Zipporah. Add to that three villagers past the age of sixty—not counting Gideon, who's hale as a man half his years—plus a woman fairly toppling over with child. Among the rest, teens and adults, we have a variety of useful professions: threshers, firestarters, stonemasons. We also have a scheming Sensor and a cook—Dinah— who can't be counted on not to lace whatever food we catch with hemorrhagic herbs. Which, I'm sure, the aforementioned Sensor would be only too happy to point out to her.

The tally of the wounded is no more heartening. Leah's cut and Gideon's injury have been treated by the twins, who were fortunate enough to salvage a few witch hazel leaves from their pouches. I saw the old firestarter's empty socket when they removed the bloody patch; his pain must be exquisite, but his face might as well be carved from wood. More worrisome is Judith, who awoke badly disoriented, suffering from a head wound or worse. I probe her forehead with cautious fingers, but nothing penetrates the fog that's descended over her mind.

Isaac's condition is even more critical. His broken leg was set by either Caleb or Noah—I can't tell the two apart—but he remains unconscious, having made no motion, no sound, during the operation. His closed eyes, I see when I come close, don't move in dreaming. I suspect a coma, but I know of nothing to recall him from it. If he doesn't wake soon, I might try a deep scan, if only to locate the damage I can't undo.

And then there's Rebecca. She's unconscious too, lying with her parents by her side. They wanted to move her, help her sit up, but I absolutely forbade it. Her legs, long for her age as mine were when I was a child, have been arranged by her mother in unnaturally straight rows like twin sticks waiting to be picked up by children at play. In all the times I've glanced over at her, I've yet to see them so much as twitch.

None of this, however, may matter in the end. Feeding a group this size will be almost impossible, even if I break my vow and try my hand at hunting. Esau has awakened, but he's useless to me, huddling with his parents and pressing his hands against his ears when I try to talk to him. I remind myself that he's only nine, and nowhere near ready to hunt. The very young and very old will need food and water sooner than the rest, plus I'll have to teach everyone how to dispose safely of their wastes. In the case of almost-two-year-old Huldah and a few others, bowel and bladder mishaps are inevitable. And regardless of these individual issues, there's the overriding fact that I've hand-delivered the Ecosystem the largest banquet it's enjoyed in centuries, and it's only a matter of time before it sharpens its claws for the feast.

"We'll need fire at all times," I remind Gideon, who set up a ring of torches around our campsite before I had a chance to tell him to. "Given our numbers and the amount of noise we're bound to make, you can't let the torches go out for a moment, especially at night. I'll leave it to you to figure out the best system for making that happen, but you mustn't let it fail."

"It will not fail," he says, and I believe him.

"We'll also need water," I say. "Lots of it. It'll have to be fresh—drinkable—and it'll go bad quickly, so we'll have to replenish it on a regular basis." The realization that I won't be able to detect impurities makes me fretful, and I wonder whether Levi's grabgrass taunt was simply that or whether, concussion or no, he's divined the sorry state of my Sense. "We can boil water to eliminate the dangers, but we'll need plenty of containers to transport it."

"Will these do?" Leah asks, and holds out several beautifully stitched bladders, constructed, it seems, on the spot from superfluous items of clothing. My favorite is the one she designed from a charmeleon-hide jacket, which retains the rainbow coloring of the beast it came from.

"You're a miracle worker," I say. "But how'd you know?"

"I've never walked in the Ecosystem," she says. "That doesn't mean I've never thought of what I would need if I did."

"Perfect," I say. It strikes me that I couldn't have found sturdier deputies if I'd scoured the village for days, and these two practically fell into my lap. "But you'll have to make more. Enough for everyone except the littlest children to carry."

"I'm sure I can convince people to part with unneeded garments," she says, with a rather saucy wink that makes me realize which garments she's talking about.

"There are many techniques for surviving in the Ecosystem," I change the subject to cover my embarrassment. "Ways to walk, ways to breathe, things to do and avoid doing. Some I can teach you, but others will be hard for anyone but a Sensor to duplicate. Which isn't to say you might not develop some degree of Sensitivity now that we're out here," I add, remembering Isaac's flowering on our previous trip. "Unfortunately, the Ecosystem's behavior has been highly erratic today, so some of my knowledge—about its normal routines and the strategies for evasive action—might not apply."

They take this in silently.

"The most important thing," I continue, "is not to panic. The Ecosystem thrives on fear—produces fear, really, so it can target its victims. We're a big group, with children and elderly and wounded, so we'll be moving slowly, which might make us less conspicuous. But we can't move *too* slowly, because we can't risk being spotted before…."

"Before…?" Leah asks.

I swallow. "Before we get where we're going."

Her eyes dance. "Which is?"

"I was going to tell you—"

"Mistress Sarah?"

I look up and find that Amos has approached. "It's just Sarah," I say in exasperation, though I'm relieved to be spared Leah's request for the moment.

"Miss Rebecca is awake."

"That's wonderful!" I glance over and see her lying as she was, blinking in the light of Gideon's torches. "Where'd her parents go?"

"She asks for you."

"I'll be right there." I rise, stretch stiff legs. Every step I take makes me painfully aware of every step Rebecca never will. "No one leaves camp," I say to Gideon and Leah. "Not even to use the bathroom. Dig a hole instead." I don't wait for Leah's response before hurrying to Rebecca's side.

Her eyes rise as I come close, and her lips form a tentative smile. Aaron always said the girl looks like a miniature me, not only the long legs but the high cheeks and forehead. Her skin's a shade darker than mine, probably because of my grandmother, a woman I've seen only in a vision, whose skin and hair were pale as moonlight and whose eyes were blue as a blurjay's feathers. Even with Esau being two years older, Rebecca easily pulled ahead of him in every race I made them run. Now she wiggles her shoulders uncomfortably, trying to make the rest of her body change position on the rough ground.

I sit beside her. "I'm glad you're up."

"My head hurts," she says. Not crossly, just stating

a fact. "And my back. It feels like someone keeps pinching me."

"I can get you some blankets," I say. "That might make it feel better."

"Okay."

She's silent, as if waiting for me to do what I said. I fumble, try to speak. "Would you like me to...."

"Sarah." Thank grabgrass, she's never felt the need to *mistress* me. "Why can't I move my legs?"

I look around for her parents, find them at the far side of Gideon's fire ring, standing with another group of grown-ups. All of them childless, many newly so. "What did your mother and father say?"

"They won't tell me," she says, and now she does sound cross. "They said I need to rest and get better. When I asked them to help me sit up, they said you told them not to. That's when I called for you."

I consider what to tell her, decide to tell her all, though in terms a seven-year-old will understand. "You hurt your back. There's a"—I can't remember if we've covered the nervous system in our Sensor lessons—"there's a thread that runs down your spine, and it's how your brain talks to your body. If the thread gets...cut, parts of your body won't be able to hear your brain telling them what to do."

She nods solemnly, wide-eyed. "A stone fell on my back," she says. "That must have been what hurt my spinal cord."

I almost laugh, I feel so much like crying. "It must have been."

"And will it get better?" she asks. "Like your legs?"

"It's...." I reach out and brush hair from her forehead.

The touch of my hand against her flesh rekindles what I felt when I touched her before. "Our bodies can fix themselves sometimes by making new parts to replace the parts that got hurt. But the thread—the spinal cord—can't fix itself like that."

Her eyes fill with tears. Or maybe they don't; I can't see through my own. "Then I'll never be able to walk?"

"I don't think so, dear one." The expression startles me, though it's what comes naturally to my tongue. Likely it's the name her own mother spoke to her, and it's made its way to me through the touch of my fingers against her skin.

"But how will I," she chokes, "how will I be able to come with you if I can't walk?"

"We'll carry you," I say. "As long as we have to. Maybe we can find a way to...to build something to help you. Crutches or...or a chair...." Her tears fall harder, and I realize what a mess I'm making of things. "I'll carry you myself, Rebecca. Every step of the way. I promise you."

"I'll grow up," she says. "I'll be too big for you to carry."

"You'll never be too big for me to carry."

"I'm scared, Sarah," she says.

I'm scared too, I think. Not only of the Ecosystem. Is this to be my life from now on, surrounded by hurts I can touch but not heal, grief I can feel but not mend? "Come here, Rebecca."

I move close, stroke her hair, hold her body so delicately it's as if I'm holding her heart in my hands. As my skin warms to hers, I'm bombarded by images of her life—not memories, for some are too early for her to have remembered, others little more than distant dreams that may never come true—but fragments, pieces of who she is, communicated to me the way my Sense, when it was whole, communicated the lives of things around me. As when I first learned to exercise my Sense, the fragments come too rapidly, in too hopeless a tangle, for me to find the right one, if right one there is. "Can I tell you a secret?"

She nods, blinking tears.

"When the urthwyrms attacked me," I say, "they didn't hurt just my legs. They hurt something that's even more a part of me."

"What?" she whispers.

"My Sense," I say. "It's not working anymore. I can't Sense the Ecosystem like I used to, like I was teaching you how to. It feels like…like the cord that binds me to the world has been cut. And I don't think it's going to heal the way my legs will."

She takes this in. Her breathing is calmer, though her tears soak my shoulder.

"So I'm going to need you to help me," I say. "To *be* my Sense, the way I'll be your legs. We'll be like," and I try a joke, poor as it is, "a two-headed hydra bird."

"Esau's older," she says, sniffling.

"I don't want Esau," I say. "I want you."

She looks up at me, and her eyes, though luminous, are almost dry. I consider telling her that this has to be our secret, but I don't want to alarm her. She was always a sensible child, and I count on that now. "Rebecca," I say, "what do you Sense?"

She stills, her eyelids fluttering as if she's going into a trance. That's unorthodox, but it's always been her way. I hold myself motionless so as not to interfere, and as she sends filaments of Sensation into the world then draws them back to her, it feels for the briefest of moments as if some small portion of her power enters into me. That tenuous spark illuminates the world below, a living world where roots and normal-size worms and the invisible lives that ultimately claim all life multiply in abundance. Her eyes don't open fully, but her hand darts to the loose soil beside us—loose, I realize, because something's burrowing underneath.

She pulls it out. A mammal, little larger than the child's hand that holds it, with pinkish skin and a prickly shell covering its back. Its front paws are adapted for digging: they're abnormally large, with long, curved nails that face its tail. The thing has no eyes, but its nose wrinkles as it detects itself being kidnapped from its underground lair.

Rebecca holds her catch out to me. "There are lots of them. They're digging a circle around where we're sitting. If we let them finish, the ground will collapse."

I hoist the squirming monstrosity. I've never seen its like, but that's not surprising: the Ecosystem births new atrocities to harry us from time to time. "Do you know what this is called?" I ask.

She cocks her head, concentrates. "Molusk."

"No," I say. "Supper."

And we share a smile.

WE MOVE OUT the next morning.

The molusks proved not only abundant, but laughably easy to catch. I can't say as much for how they went down, but our stomachs are full. We've bludgeoned an additional hundred or so of the devious little monsters and stuffed them in Leah's sacks for later eating. They'll go rancid quickly, plus we've little water and the torches are burning low, so we can't stay here.

I've been up half the night trying to educate our camp on everything there is to know about staying alive in the Ecosystem. I lecture them in shifts of ten so each group has time to sleep while I instruct the others. *Tread lightly*, I tell them, demonstrating the moves as I talk. *On the balls of your feet if you can manage it. Don't stand still for long. Breathe shallowly and evenly, through your nose if possible. No talking except when necessary, and then only in a whisper. If you get into trouble, don't scream, don't struggle. Calm yourself and call for help. Most birds won't attack unless blood's already flowing, but mammals are a different story. Stay out of long grass and avoid stepping on bushy plants. And watch out for the trees, especially the ones that seem to be watching you back….*

When I'm done, I fall into fretful sleep, knowing that I've not come close to covering everything. My dreams consist of me sinking into a hole in the ground while I shout over and over the list of all they still don't know.

The new day dawns as cloudy as the one before, with just enough light to show me that my lieutenants have risen early and prepared the others while I slept. Leah's given out assignments so each person over the age of ten knows who and what they're responsible for. Gideon, as much a wizard with wood as with fire, has constructed stretchers for the most grievously wounded. One goes to Judith, who's lapsed overnight into a childlike state, querulous and unfamiliar with any who attend her. She watches with fearful eyes while I touch her forehead, my fingers tracing a map of a mind undone: the pieces that no longer fit, the ones that are gone altogether. Though I can detect the damage, I can determine neither the cause nor the cure.

The second stretcher is occupied by Rebecca, whom Gideon has strapped in place to keep her as still as possible. Two of his assistants carry her while her parents walk on one side and I on the other, supervising. But that's not the real reason I stay close: she talks to me in a coded language we made up last night, feeding me what she Senses. It's little more than a variation on the child's game "scary or safe," but to the appearance of anyone not in the know—Levi and Saul, who walk ahead under guard, being my main worry—I hope it appears to be my instructions, not hers, that steer us clear of snares. A Sensor in sync with the Ecosystem can disappear from its mind, move through the dense web of its consciousness without stirring a single strand. Everyone else is a bug caught in the web: kicking, struggling, luring the web-maker to the kill. This is not the time to admit I'm as much a bug as everyone else.

I remember what I told Isaac once: my Sense is my breath, without which I'd die. If it's truly gone, I wonder what air I'll breathe in its place.

The third stretcher belongs to him, though unlike Rebecca, he's anything but still. He's not woken, but late at night he began to thrash about, similar to what I witnessed on our previous trip when he was suffering from histeria poisoning. I've scanned him, thinking another infection might be working its way through his blood, but I detect nothing except his restlessly turning mind. It's intact as Judith's is not, yet a shadow seems to have fallen between us, blocking me from seeing beyond. Having accustomed myself to discovering so much—too much—every time I touch him, this new manifestation worries me. But every time I press harder, his distress increases, and I have to pull back for fear of causing him further harm.

We creep forward through the day, under a darkened sky that makes the forest feel more like dusk. To avoid spreading us too thin—which would prevent Rebecca from Sensing all the snares someone might stumble into—I've arranged our numbers in a series of circles, with Gideon's tireless torch-bearers on the outside, able-bodied adults and teens in the middle, and children and wounded at the core. In consequence, our movement is something like that of a snailsnake, not only in pace but also in the way we elongate to slip between trees, then relax into our normal shape once we're through. Rebecca reports that the Ecosystem remains torpid, as if it's having as much trouble recovering from yesterday's calamity as we are. But that could change at any time, and it could decide to sic something far more lethal than a colony of molusks on us.

I itch for speed. But it's one of many things I'm not going to get.

Out of the corner of my eye, I'm aware of Leah watching me, as if she's trying to figure out what's driving me so. She hasn't repeated her question from last night, for which I'm thankful. If she knew what I know—and what I don't—she might not be so considerate.

Here's what I know: three weeks past, when Isaac, Miriam, and I nearly died in the Ecosystem following an urthwyrm attack, someone rescued us. Rescued us, treated our wounds for a week or more, and returned us secretly to our home. It couldn't have been someone from our village, because no one there had any idea who our deliverer might be. Though I'd never dreamed this might be so, though the man who held the knowledge of our people's history—Nathan, Conservator of the Sensorship—told us we were alone in the wilderness, there must be another village sufficiently close to the lair of the wyrms for someone to have found us before it was too late.

Here's what I suspect: my grandfather knew of that village. The day he died, I touched him and saw the truth he'd kept from me all my life: the truth that he *was* my grandfather, having produced a child—my mother—with the woman of pale skin and blue eyes. A woman like that must have come from elsewhere; in my village, all are born with brown skin and dark hair—sometimes, as with Levi, tending to red. My mother, whose brown eyes were sprinkled with blue, carried hints of her ancestry from this second village; my own eyes, which bear a faint trace of hers, confirm that connection. Given the hazards of the Ecosystem—the fact that few Sensors, my mother being the notable exception, had survived even a single night beyond our village walls—my grandfather couldn't have traveled far to reach the home of his beloved. So my grandmother's village must be the place from which our rescuer came: a village far enough away to remain undetected, but close enough to be reached in a few days' journey.

Here's what I definitely don't know: where it is.

I've chosen to retrace the steps that Isaac, Rachel, and I took on the journey that recovered Miriam. It leads eastward through the forest, then downhill into swampland—the site where Rachel died, but where, fortunately, the dominant lifeforms are so terrified of me from our last encounter, they should let even a company our size pass unmolested. From there, the trail crosses desert beneath which the urthwyrms' tunnels lie. I remember the way well enough, and if I were walking it on my own, I could make it in less than a week. At the rate we're going, it'll be more like three. At the end of which, we still won't know in which direction the other village lies.

But it's the best chance we have. The only chance we have. If there's another sanctuary of stone close by, we might reach it. If there's none, or if it's not where I hope it is, we're as good as dead.

I don't say that to anyone. I push them as hard as I can, and I try not to let the thought of failure enter my mind.

And yet, I have to admit that my fear and urgency are leavened by something more complex, something far from excitement but not so far I can't feel it in my chest, taste it on my tongue. Had our village survived, a time would have come for me to set out on this journey anyway—to learn my history, to meet my mother's people, to discover the true scale of the world. My grandmother's village, I've imagined since I became aware of her, might be a village of healers; how else to explain my mother's gift and my own, my rescuer's ability to cheat the death that awaited me and Isaac in the urthwyrms' lair? I'm not ready to tell anyone this, but if I long for speed, it's not only because I hope to save my village. It's not even because I hope to save the boy I love.

It's BECAUSE I hope to save myself, too.

BOOK TWO
SWATH

*Man is indeed a rare animal, having but
a precarious hold upon this land.*

—H. G. Wells, "The Empire
of the Ants" (1905)

Judith dies before dawn. She slips away from us while we tend her in the night, her breath growing shallower, her mind dwindling and dimming. Caleb and Noah wait at her bedside along with me, but they're as helpless as I am: though they've picked up a bit about roots and herbs, can clean a cut or set a limb, Judith's mysterious ailment is beyond them. Maybe they're lucky. Unlike me, they can't feel her life drifting beyond their reach, don't have to wonder why their hands are unable to hold on.

But I'm being unfair to them. The two weep by Judith's body. She was the oldest of their order, the one who taught them everything they know. And now she's gone.

When weak daylight shows the aged midwife's resting face, I rise and adopt a businesslike tone. "We can't burn her," I say to Gideon, who's stood near through the night. "Torches are one thing, but there are too many trees here to risk a bonfire. We'll have to put her in the ground."

"Mistress?"

"Bury her." I've given up on correcting his form of address; he's too old to get used to calling me by my first name. "We'll have to dig a hole and place her body inside, then cover it back up."

He frowns. For a man accustomed his whole life to funeral pyres, burial in the earth must seem an act of disrespect, as if I'm suggesting we discard Judith like a piece of baggage too inconvenient to carry. But I know, because Isaac told me, that this old healer custom was never meant to be taken that way. It was meant as a way of completing a life lived in the Ecosystem's hands, closing the circle as much as can be.

"We'll dig the hole deep," I say. And then, though I know it's a lie: "Nothing will touch her."

Gideon nods, and keeps nodding, his beard bobbing as his head does. He takes up one of his innumerable tools—this one a shovel for digging firewells—and follows me to the safest spot I can find, relatively free of vegetation that might object to being uprooted. He sinks the stone blade of the shovel into the moist earth, and I listen for the sound of the Ecosystem's cry as its flesh is sliced. But there's nothing; my Sense is silent. I look to Rebecca, who mouths one of our code expressions: "It doesn't hurt." To anyone else, she might be describing her own condition. To me, there's another translation: the Ecosystem remains dormant here.

"I'm glad," I mouth back, and step to Gideon's side.

The other firestarters have gathered around their chief, each of them employed with some digging or cutting tool. They're all strong men, in their teens or twenties, but none can keep up with Gideon, who's a blur of bronzed skin and white beard. He attacks the ground as if he's furious with it, and maybe he is; hasn't it swallowed our whole village, and isn't it about to swallow a life he thought it had spared? I lay a hand on his arm, feel his anger, but something else as well: he and Judith were playmates as children, might have become more if their separate duties hadn't driven them apart. Neither of them, I realize, ever married. I feel his grief, his pain, but I can no more heal it than I could save the woman he loved.

"I'm so sorry," I say, and squeeze his arm. He nods again before returning to work.

In time, I judge the hole deep enough to protect Judith from aboveground scavengers. Gideon climbs out, refusing the hands his crewmembers offer. He brushes clods of mud roughly from his arms, then reaches for Judith. No one interferes as he raises her from the ground and turns to me.

The others have gathered behind him. They all look at me, waiting. I wish I could remember the healers' song I learned from Isaac before we burned the body of Rachel, but without him, its words and melody escape me. The twins stand by, shamefaced, as much at a loss as I am.

"Judith brought most of us into the world," a voice says, and I find Leah standing by the gravesite, wearing the headscarf that covers her wound. "She was there when we drew our first breath, when we gave our first cry. She helped our mothers through the pain of birthing us, and she watched over us as we took our first turn at the breast. It's only fitting that we give her back to the earth we wouldn't have known without her."

Gideon bows his head, and everyone does the same. Everyone, that is, except Dinah and her favorite Sensor, who stand aloof, glowering at this further violation of the old laws. When Gideon has lowered Judith's body into her grave and climbed out unassisted once more, I remember one of the things Isaac did at Rachel's funeral, and I take a pinch of earth between my fingers and sprinkle it on the corpse. Gideon follows suit, then his crew, but everyone else hangs back. When it's plain they don't intend to join us in the ritual, the old firestarter doesn't wait for my signal to begin filling the grave back in.

I walk from the gravesite. My legs feel weak, and it seems as if I float above the ground. I sit shakily and watch Gideon, who's in no hurry to finish the job. If he emptied the hole like a man possessed, he fills it as if it holds the rarest of treasures.

My own thoughts take only one direction: Judith is gone. Isaac might be next.

Leah drifts over to join me. "Are you all right?"

"I'm fine," I say. "Thank you. For what you said."

"You're most welcome," she says. "You and Judith were close?"

"Not really," I say. "She helped me when I got hurt. But she spent most of her time with the healers, and I…."

She nods, then unexpectedly pats my hand, too quickly for anything to be conveyed from her to me. "Considering how small our village was, I'm always surprised by how little we knew about each other."

"Did *you* know Judith well?"

She shakes her head. "She delivered me, so I'm told, and would have tended me if I'd gotten with child. But that, I'm afraid, has never been my pleasure."

One mystery about Leah is cleared up. She's right, though: I know so little about her, about anyone. I'd always thought that was because I was kept from others, trained in seclusion for fourteen years. Can it be that we all face such seclusion, each in our own way? "What's it like?" I ask. "Being a seamstress?"

She tosses her head. "The less said, the better. I wanted

to be Chief Warden once, until I discovered I lacked the most important qualification for the job."

"What was that?"

"The small matter of my sex," she says, smiling.

I'm taken aback by her frankness. "A woman has never served?"

"Not to my knowledge," she says. "But come, how many Chief Sensors have been women? Mistress Esther was a rarity, and thanks to our friend"—she jerks a head at Levi, whom I really shouldn't let hobnob with Dinah—"her career lasted only a matter of days."

"Nathan believed that women were too weak to serve," I say. "He hated my mother for disgracing the order. Levi might have hated Esther for the same reason."

"If I can offer a word of advice," Leah says, "I'd be less worried about what Levi thought of Mistress Esther, and more concerned about what he thinks of *you*."

I glance again at where Levi, Dinah, and Saul have congregated. Before we set out yesterday, I gave orders to the guards to keep the three apart, but apparently those orders have been forgotten in the wake of Judith's funeral. I find myself oddly reluctant to leave Leah's side to restore discipline. "Do you think they'll try to...?"

"Not while you have the upper hand," she says. "But tread carefully, Sarah. As carefully as you'd tread the Ecosystem. The majority will follow you if they think it means safety, but not if they think it means further loss."

I let her words sink in. "I shouldn't have insisted on burying Judith."

"You shouldn't have let them think it was your idea

alone," she says. "They're all wondering what will happen if they should be next. If you'll decide to bury them, too."

"I never thought of it that way," I say. "I just thought… well, we couldn't take a chance of setting the woods on fire. And I didn't want her carried off by a pack of jekylls."

"I don't blame you," she says, giving my hand another quick pat. "You've trained to be a healer, yes?"

"Barely," I say. "I inherited the gift from my mother, and I learned a few things from…from Isaac. But I don't know how to do much with what I learned. Did you ever train?" I ask, a bit too eagerly.

"I trained from age five to stitch and mend," she says. "There's hardly a man, woman, or child in the village who hasn't worn my handiwork. Do you know what I learned in all that time?"

I shake my head.

"I learned that you can dress up people's bodies all you want," she says. "But it's their hearts that suffer the worst slights, and that need the most care."

She's right, I know she's right. But I don't know how to do what she wants of me. "Who did you lose?" I ask, and hope I've not gone too far.

Leah stiffens, then relaxes and smiles. "It would take a lifetime to tell you. So," she holds out her hand, "why don't you see for yourself?"

Tentatively, I reach for her hand, feel it enfold mine. She's got strong hands, Leah does. I close my eyes, focus on the warmth of her skin against mine, the tingling that follows. I wonder if it'll always feel this way when I touch another, or if, as with my Sense, I'll learn to control it in time. For now, though, Leah's life opens before me, in a flood of images that threaten to carry me away.

I see her as a child, walking hand in hand with a girl her age, though taller and slimmer. I see them grow up together, fiercely attached to one another though their lot in life—Leah's apprenticeship as a seamstress, the other girl's as a potter—should drive them apart. No matter how exhausted they are at day's end, they seek each other after dark, find each other in places only they frequent. There, they disclose each other's secrets, including the one secret no one else knows. And they hold each other, more tightly than they held hands when they were children. They look into each other's eyes, and when the other girl smiles, Leah's lips meet hers, smiling in return.

I jerk away from her grasp, my eyes opening to the image of the actual Leah sitting before me. "You...." I can't finish the thought. "You and she were...."

"Sick," she says. "That's what our parents wanted us to believe. But I tell you, Sarah, our bodies needed no healing. Only our hearts suffered, for they were kept apart, when they should have been one."

I'm shaking. I can barely control my voice. This is too much—too much to know about her or any other. "But you...you *couldn't* be together. The ways of our people...."

Leah's brow lowers. "That's what everyone told us. Are you so sure those ways are right?"

My stomach roils at her words, the images I saw. I never dreamed of such a thing, never thought it was possible—not in the Ecosystem, and not among our own kind. "Why are you telling me this?"

"Because you need to know the lives you're dealing

with," she says. "When you were a Sensor, you had one set of priorities. Hide. Stay in control. Strike fast, then move on. But I've heard you talking to Rebecca. You're not a Sensor anymore, are you?"

Numbly, I shake my head.

"Then you have to let that part of you go," Leah says. "People aren't like the Ecosystem. If you want to heal us, you have to learn what truly ails us."

She rises and lays a hand on my shoulder. I'm still trembling, but I don't shake her off. I let one last image flow from her to me, and it's so clear in my mind that when she speaks, it's as if I'm hearing the words of the girl she was as well as the woman who stands before me.

"Beulah was my all," she says. "My everything. When you find that person, it doesn't matter what form she takes. It doesn't even matter," and her eyes flash at me, "if he belongs to someone else."

Then she leaves me, walking off to supervise the others as they break camp.

A SECOND DAY's march passes without sunlight, and without the Ecosystem registering our presence. A family of warhogs trundles by in the forest darkness, fat sow and squealing progeny, but they're unaccompanied by the territorial boars. I check in with Rebecca, who tells me the Ecosystem stays sluggish, its mind distracted and diffuse. It fusses sometimes—that's her word—as if a burr has slipped beneath its planet-wide skin. But as far as she can Sense, there's no concentrated anger, nothing to suggest it's targeting us, tracking us.

We bed down in a forest glade ringed by towering ache trees. Far as we are from the site of our village, some of the trees have fallen, so what we witnessed two days ago wasn't a local phenomenon. Though I really should be catching up on sleep, I stay awake to scan Isaac. In the torches' glow, I lay a palm on his forehead, try to plumb the life within. He's hot and clammy, but that's the extent of what I can feel. I wonder if what Leah said is so: that I won't be able to reach him, much less cure him, until I accept the truth about him. Until I admit that Miriam was his true love, and that if he does awaken, he'll choose a life alone rather than dishonor their bond.

A life alone. Like Leah's.

Leah. And Beulah. I don't know what to make of it, and I've avoided her this day, as she has me. When I was a child first discovering the ways of the Ecosystem under my grandpa's tutelage, every new thing under the sun announced its name, just as Daniel said was the case in *edinnu*: I had only to become aware of a life form's presence, and what it was called flowed to me without conscious thought. But what do I call Leah? I have no name for what she is.

I look over at her, sleeping peacefully in the torch-light. I wish I'd not reacted as I did earlier in the day, wish I'd not shown her the disapproval she's known all her life. *Can* it be wrong, to love as deeply as she and Beulah did? So deeply, I suspect, that Leah wouldn't have gotten out of the village if not for some sacrifice her beloved chose to make?

Daniel's words from Miriam and Isaac's wedding day return to me: *None of us, be the gifts of our birth what they may, should dwell beyond the community of human love and sorrow.* And Esther's: *I see now that it was wrong of me to blame your mother for what I did not understand.* Our village's leaders are gone, and I'm nowhere near ready to take their place. But I have to start somewhere.

I lean down to kiss Isaac's forehead. He shivers, though not from my caress. When I've left him, I seek the spot where Leah sleeps, lay my body beside hers. With hesitant fingers, I reach out and touch her shoulder. She sighs softly. Before the tingle has a chance to reveal any more of her secrets, I turn from her and settle on my side to sleep.

THE MORNING SHOWS me two things I'd begun to doubt I'd see again: rays of sunlight struggling through the cloud cover, and Isaac awake and sitting up in his stretcher.

My heart leaps at the sight of him, and I wonder if my touch from last night might have healed him. Though to be honest, he looks terrible: hair unruly, face gaunt, the beard he grew for his wedding much longer and more tangled than I'd expect from a few extra days' growth. His lips move without words, and he glances about the camp anxiously. Looking for Miriam, or for something else he's lost.

When his eyes fall on me at last, I try a smile. I'm met with a scowl that freezes the smile where it started. I can't tell if he's angry, or just confused. Either way, I decide that everything else can wait.

"Get the others ready," I tell Gideon, who as usual has appeared at my side just when I need him. "I'll be with you in a moment."

He nods and hollers for his crew. I try not to look at Leah, who stands with arms crossed and head cocked, an enigmatic smile on her lips.

I sit at the foot of the stretcher. Isaac's eyes follow my movements with a wariness that's not like him. They're bloodshot, I can see from up close, but they don't wobble like Levi's. If anything, they seem more focused and intense than I remember.

"Isaac," I say. "How are you feel—"

"Where are we?" he cuts me off, his voice a harsh croak. From disuse, I tell myself.

"We're in the Ecosystem," I say. "Two days' march from the village."

"What are we doing here?"

I proceed as delicately as I can. "At your wedding… the wyrms. Do you remember?"

"I remember." His voice is flat. "And where's Mimi?"

His nickname for Miriam. "She's…." His eyes bore into me, lacking any of the gentleness I used to see in them. "She's gone, Isaac. The wound from Levi's knife, and the wyrms…. The gathering hall collapsed, and people were trapped inside. She—"

"I don't believe you."

"It's true," I say. "I wanted to save her, but—"

"You're lying," he says. "You wanted her to die. You always wanted her to die."

I'm stunned, not only by his words but by the fierceness in his voice. I tell myself he's wrong, that I would have saved Miriam if there'd been enough time; I envied her, but I never wished her dead. Yet the objections I might make falter when I look at his blazing eyes. I wish I could touch him, comfort him, but his anger fills the space between us.

"Isaac," I say, as calmly as I can. "I know how much this hurts—"

"You know nothing!" he shouts, loud enough that heads turn in our direction. "You're glad she's dead, you and Levi…. You didn't have the guts to do it yourself, so you left it to him!"

I retreat before his fury. He looks around wildly, and seeing Levi across the campsite, he tries to push himself from the stretcher. But with his palsied arm and bound leg, he's helpless; he falls back, his head striking the ground. He curses me bitterly, words I've never heard him use. Words of recrimination and loathing I might have expected from Nathan or Levi, not from him. Never, ever from him.

"You killed her!" he screams. "You should have died instead! The Ecosystem should have taken you, like it took your cursed mother!"

He tries to rise again, succeeds in getting into a sitting position. His good arm, the one that retains his thresher's strength, flails so violently I'm afraid he'll strike me by accident. I hold out my hands to fend him off, to plead with him, but the next thing I know, Gideon and Leah have flown to my side, the twins just behind. The old firestarter wrestles Isaac to the ground, and much as he struggles, he can't break free. His curses echo against the trees as Leah helps me up and walks me away.

"You'll pay for this, I vow! You'll pay…."

Leah wraps her arms around me and pulls me close so I don't have to hear his words, don't have to see his face twisted in rage. The twins converge on him, and though I can't tell what they're doing, I hear his voice weaken, remember the times he used a healer trick on me to induce unconsciousness. His hands were so gentle then, I barely felt their touch.

"The hex take him," Leah mutters. "How dare he?"

I can't bear to watch any further, so I surrender to Leah's arms and bury my face in her shoulder.

My throat raw from unshed tears and my ears ringing with Isaac's curses, I know I'm in no condition to lead the day's march. But when Leah offers to take my place, I wave her off. I've shown enough weakness this morning to last a lifetime. And if I don't do something, I'll spend the entire day replaying the accusations that fell from the only lips I've ever kissed.

He sleeps again under the influence of the twins' healing spell. Gideon's tied him to the stretcher, and that's probably for the best, as he's started thrashing again. They're treating him as if he's lost his mind, and maybe that's true; when I touch his forehead with shaking hands, I feel nothing but darkness. The thought that he lashed out at me in madness hurts no more or less than that he did so in hatred. I can't convince myself he'll recover from the one any sooner than the other.

We set off eastward, toward a sun we can no longer see beneath a thickening blanket of clouds. Within a league or two, we reach a clearing in the woods where I call a halt to check in with Rebecca, who thankfully slept through my fight with Isaac. She's regained some feeling in her back where previously there was nothing but prickles. Her legs, however, remain as insensate as the day we left.

When I ask her about the Ecosystem, she grimaces.

"It's starting to hurt a little," she says. Translation: the forest is awakening from its two-day stupor.

"What about farther east?" I ask. "Safe, or scary?"

Her face screws in concentration. "It feels like... before."

"Before?"

"When the wyrms came," she says. "That morning."

I squat by her side. Her eyes are squeezed shut, her forehead tight. "Do you Sense something?" I ask.

"My head hurts," she says in a constricted voice. "I could Sense its mind yesterday and the day before. Now all I can Sense is...darkness. Like...like vines have covered things over. I can't see through them."

"Vines?"

She nods. "Black vines. Or a web. They're...getting closer."

"Where?"

"Everywhere," she says. "They're everywhere."

I glance over my shoulder. There's nothing to see, and no matter how much I strain, nothing to Sense. But this sounds too much like what Miriam reported the morning of the wedding—too much like what *I* keep feeling every time I scan Isaac—to be a coincidence. "Try, Rebecca," I say. "Try to focus on where the vines are. I need to know."

She wiggles her head against the stretcher, seeking a comfortable position. If we make it through this, we're going to have to develop a better way to transport her—anything other than having her lie flat on her back all day. Her eyes flutter as always, but her face, far from taking on the placid look of a Sensor finding her place in the world, contorts in pain. I'm about to remind her to relax when she opens her eyes with a gasp.

"I can't," she says. "It's too dark. I can't."

"Rebecca...."

"I can't!" she snaps. "Leave me alone, Sarah. It's not my fault you can't Sense anything anymore."

I open my mouth to reply, but her parents cluster defensively, her mother stroking her hair and shushing, her father holding her hand. For once, Rebecca lets them baby her. The two glare at me until I back off.

When I do, I nearly collide with Saul.

The apprentice looks horrified to face me, probably from what he saw me do to Levi in the gathering hall. With everything that's happened today, I'm surely not glad to see him. "Where are your guards?"

"Levi sent me," he says, as if that might earn him my favor. "He wants to know why we stopped."

"I must have missed the part where I report to him."

"He's Sensed stirrings in the Ecosystem," he says. "I guess you have, too?"

I don't like the way he says that. "Tell him we'll resume as soon as I get the groups in order. If, that is, he can wait that long."

I shove past him. I haven't gotten far when he calls out, "Mistress Sarah."

That's enough for me to spin and stamp back. "Don't call me that, Saul. You don't respect me *or* the title, so don't pretend otherwise."

"Sarah, then," he says. "I need to talk to you."

"I already told you," I say. "We start when I give the orders."

"It's not that." He looks down at his feet. "Levi doesn't know why I really came over here. He'd probably kill me if he did."

I draw close to him, speak in an undertone. Hopefully, if Levi's watching, he'll think I'm confronting his assistant. "What is it?"

Saul looks up, and the fear in his eyes is no counterfeit. "He and Dinah are crazy. They've been talking, and he convinced her the village needs to be punished for letting a Sensor marry a healer."

"Did Levi say something like that to Isaac?" I ask, half-hoping he did. It might explain why Isaac went wild.

Saul shakes his head. "I don't think so. But he's preparing a trap. Not just for you. For the others."

"How does he expect to trap seventy people?"

"It's not everyone," he says. "Only...the ones on your side."

I glance across the clearing. Levi lounges under guard, Dinah standing nearby. He looks perfectly at ease; he's even laughing. It's not hard to tell why.

His guards are laughing, too.

"The funeral," I say. "Judith's funeral."

Saul nods. "Levi got Dinah to start spreading the word that you're under a curse, which is why you didn't care about Judith's body. And, Sarah...."

Whatever he has to say can't be worse than what he's already said. "Out with it, Saul."

"He knows you're using the little girl to Sense things. And Dinah's been telling everybody."

I'm wrong again. It *is* worse. "Do they believe her?"

"Some do," he says. "Others are waiting to see."

I let my eyes roam from Levi to the villagers who mill about the clearing, awaiting my orders. If only I knew how many are having second thoughts. Amos, Gideon's fire-starters, Rebecca and Esau's parents…. Is anyone still on my side? "Why the sudden change of heart, Saul?"

He bites his lip. "Levi scares me. I don't want anyone else to die."

I watch his eyes, try to judge how truthful he's being. I decide I have no choice but to trust him.

"All right," I say. "We can't keep talking like this or he'll know. Go back and tell him what I said about moving out. And keep an eye on him. Report to me if you learn anything new. But don't come straight to me. Talk to Leah or Gideon instead."

He nods, turns to go. Levi has risen from the ground and is stretching his arms and legs, gazing across the open space between us.

"Be careful," I tell Saul as he scampers off.

Levi catches me looking at him, and his lip lifts in a mocking smile. His eyes aren't wobbling anymore; they're as focused as ever, as focused as Isaac's were. The rude gesture he makes in my direction shows me that his arm—the one I nearly tore from his body—has recovered its normal range of movement. How that's possible, unless one of the twins has turned against me too, I can't say.

The only chance this day could get any worse is if we take a wrong turn into a den of terror wolves. I'm not ruling it out.

I MEET BRIEFLY with Gideon and Leah before we resume our march. If I was concerned about trusting the two of them, I shouldn't have been. Leah touches my arm and looks at me with compassion, while the old firestarter growls a threat about what he'll do to anyone who tries to take advantage of Mistress Sarah. I've felt teary since this morning's fight with Isaac, and their loyalty brings fresh droplets to my eyes.

At Gideon's suggestion, I assign two of his most reliable firestarters to handle Levi and Saul. Leah assures me that Amos is unshaken in his anger at the red-headed Sensor and his associates, so he gets the unenviable task of watching Dinah. Leah also volunteers to gather information on who's with us, who's against us, and who's somewhere in between. She waves gaily as if attending a party before heading off to chitchat with the rest of the survivors.

With Gideon's help, I reorganize the groups in case unhealthy alliances have sprung up, give each group a specific task, make all responsible for moving us toward our destination as fast as we can go. When we start off again, I set a harder pace than before, urging parents and other adults to scoop children into their arms, relaxing the outside boundary of our caravan so we can travel faster. We eat on the move—some honeysickle berries Rebecca finds, which are edible so long as you slice off the sickle-shaped spur that holds them to the vine—and skip our customary late-day break. Leah circulates the while, gabbing when possible and speaking in confidence when necessary, and I marvel at her easy manner. From time to time, she swings past to whisper a few tidbits.

"It's nowhere near as bad as Saul made it sound," she reports on one of her passes. "You had the ill fortune to pick two of the village's worst cowards as guards, but most of the others remain steady. Dinah's having the best luck with parents who lost children. Stay strong—more to come."

She squeezes my arm and is off.

Evening falls. As near as I can judge, we've covered as much ground in a single day as we did in the previous two. That's still too slow—we've yet to come upon the rocky divide in the forest that precedes the swamp—but, in combination with Leah's favorable news, it does make me hope that we can reach our destination before Dinah and Levi recruit too many to their side. No one's carped about the pace I set; in fact, if I judge the company's mood right, they seem more than usually resolute, maybe because the new routine has given them confidence I know what I'm doing. If only I could keep myself from glancing toward Isaac's stretcher, where his rigid posture and straining face bring the morning back to me with enough force to make my cheeks burn with hurt and shame.

Before choosing a spot to bed down, I teach Rebecca how to detect inorganic matter in the Ecosystem: search for a blank space in her Sense, something not there. She rewards me for the time spent on the lesson—and, knowing her, pushes herself to make up for the morning's fit of pique—by finding a perfect spot, a broad clearing that's been nibbled to bare dirt by a passing herd of jackalasses. For the first time, we can sleep without piling atop each other, and Gideon can set his ring of torches without fear of catastrophe from stray sparks. I ask Rebecca about the black vines, but she's uncharacteristically cagey.

"I'm not sure I really Sensed them," she says. "I was tired this morning."

I consider pressing, but decide against it. "Let me know if they come back," I say. "Sleep well, little hydra bird."

She gives me a smile and falls asleep almost before I've risen from her side.

I check in with Leah, who reports that all is quiet. I'm determined to sleep soundly in order to rouse the others for another forced march, so I try to shove everything from my mind: Isaac, Levi, Rebecca's vision, our still unknown destination. I must be more exhausted than I realize, for my eyelids flutter as I rest my gaze on the motionless form of Gideon, his beard outlined by firelight at the edge of our campground. I'm not sure the old firestarter has slept at all since our journey began.

I've no idea how much time has passed when I hear a voice whispering my name. "Mistress...I mean, Sarah."

I'm awake instantly; that much of my Sense remains. There's a moon tonight, though it's having trouble find-ing its way through the clouds. What little light escapes shows me a shadowy figure kneeling by my bedside, who resolves himself into Saul. The apprentice cups a hand to his mouth and speaks softly.

"I couldn't get away before," he says. "Levi's asleep now, but...."

"This had better be important, Saul."

"It is. Levi and Dinah were talking earlier. They—"

"I've watched the two of them all day," I say. "They haven't come near each other."

"They use hand signals," he says. "They made them up in case you separated them."

"And what have they been saying?"

"That their trap is ready," Saul says. "Or will be soon. I couldn't—"

"How is this useful to me, Saul?" I ask. "You say their trap is ready—or might be—but you don't know what it is. How do I know I can trust you?"

Poor as the light is, I see his pout. "I thought I'd warn you now, instead of waiting until they spring it on you. Wasn't that the right thing to do?"

"I suppose so," I sigh. "But what do you expect me to do about it?"

His mouth opens to answer me, but nothing comes out.

Or that's not entirely true. His eyes widen, and an instant later, a stream of fluid erupts from his mouth. It hits me squarely in the face, stinking of bile, the moment before he collapses on top of me.

"What in Sense's name—" I shove his body from mine, watch it roll and flop onto his back. From there, he begins to thrash against the ground, more violently than ever Isaac did. Yellow froth bubbles from his lips, and his eyes, I see to my horror, have blackened and bulged beyond his face, more like a frogbull's than a human being's.

I leap to my feet as a scream rends the night. Its source is immediately evident: another member of our camp, this time the teenage firestarter whom Gideon assigned to take first watch, has fallen and is repeating Saul's performance across the clearing. I dash to his side, find his face so swollen its features are swallowed by puffy flesh.

"Awake!" I cry. "Awake! We're under attack!"

Figures blur in the darkness. Gideon's beard glows like a second moon. The rest of his crew responds to the sound of his voice as he takes up the alarm. My eyes seek the spot where Levi went to bed. I find his guards slumped over in a sitting position, but no sign of Levi himself.

"It's Levi!" I shout to Gideon. "He got away!"

Without a word, the firestarter grabs a torch and disappears into the forest.

"Gideon!" I yell after him, but he's gone.

I'm brought back to camp by the sound of another scream. This time, when I turn to locate the victim, the moonlight shows me something streaking across the glade too fast for my eyes to identify. Another streak, like a shining trail of light, flashes before me, and another member of camp screams and falls.

"Everyone down!" I shout. "On the ground! Don't give him a target!"

I'm obeyed, by most. Others run about in confusion, and each time the light flashes across the clearing, someone screams, falls, and pitches wildly against the ground before lying deathly still. I run to the nearest victim, find her body bloated to the point that the seams of her clothing have torn, exposing flesh the consistency of toadstools. More roughly than I might have done if I had any hope she was alive, I flip her over, then over again, trying to find the weapon that struck her.

But there's nothing. No blade, no arrow, no mark. It's as if she was felled by a beam of light.

"Sarah!" It's a thin cry, and though I can't find her in the melee of running and flailing bodies, I recognize the voice: Rebecca. She, at least, is alive.

"What's happening?" I shout to her, too panicked to remember I'm not supposed to panic.

"Poison arrow frogs!" she calls back, but that's no help, because I've never heard of such a thing, never Sensed it in my life.

Something burns my fingertips where I touched the woman's corpse. I raise my hand before me, see a viscous liquid glistening in the moonlight. Some kind of acid, maybe. I don't have time to think it through.

I'm too busy screaming.

I fall to the ground as pain consumes me, spreading with lightning speed up my arm to my chest, my neck, my face. I writhe against the hard dirt, as helpless as a warhog tormented by the abscess-producing bites of grossquitoes. The hand that touched the poison curls into a claw, and my fingers swell so rapidly my nails vanish into my flesh.

My eyes are closing, or else my cheeks are sealing over them. The forest flickers with beams of light, and I see, as if the slits that have become of my eyes are helping me to pinpoint the killers, small bright spots of color darting from tree to tree. The screams of my companions echo strangely in my ears.

Someone drops to the ground beside me. I feel hands on my shoulders, realize the person is alive. They shake me, call my name. The voice is too distorted to recognize.

I try to tell whoever it is not to touch me, but my tongue won't form words.

It's too late. My helper screams upon contacting the venom, and the hands fall away. I try to lift myself, try to crawl, try to call for help. I can do nothing.

This is the Ecosystem you've known all your life, a foggy voice speaks in my ear. *It's not Rebecca's black vines, not Levi's ambush at all. It's the thing that has always killed us. The thing that will always kill us.*

The beams of light have vanished. The screams have given place to the sobbing of a child. I try once more to rise, but my body is too weak, and I fall face down, just as my stomach clenches and vomit gushes from me. I'm barely able to turn my head to keep from drowning in the sticky pool. The moon emerges from the clouds, and the glade is flooded with its glow. I wish I could shut out the sight, but my swollen cheeks won't let me.

And so my eyes, my wretched eyes, are forced to see.

I KNOW THIS doesn't happen. But I see it nonetheless.

Bodies lie everywhere. Some may be alive. Others are surely not. Some belong to children. Some belong to adults, who've covered the children's bodies with their own in an attempt to shield them. They've succeeded only in smothering them. The fallen are barely human, full of lumps and bags of hanging flesh like hexlox pustules. I can't find Isaac's stretcher, can't tell if Leah and Amos and the twins are among the dead.

A black shape appears at the edge of the clearing: two, three. The shapes slide into view between trees, and I would gasp, if my throat were supple enough to make a sound. They're urthwyrms, black and shiny, ribbed by moonlight. Something moves on their backs, something slips from atop them to land nimbly on the ground.

People. Three people. One astride each wyrm.

They wear strange clothes: white robes without sleeves, cinched at the waist and hanging to mid-thigh. One, I see, is a man. His hair is long, his skin the brown of our village. His face is lined by strokes of moonlight. The other two are younger: a boy and a girl in their teens, he with pale skin and hair like I've seen in my vision, she with pinker skin and flowing hair the bright red color of a flamingull's feathers, with long legs to match. They don white gloves and fan out across the clearing, each moving to the nearest victim. They clear toppled bodies, free trapped children. Then they move on to the next, and the next.

My gaze is drawn to the man. He strides to the source of the sobbing, and I see that it's Rebecca, alone in her stretcher, the bloated bodies of her mother and father sprawled on the ground at either side. The man stands in such a way that I can see nothing but his long hair blowing in the night wind. But I can hear his voice, deep and mellifluous as the wind itself.

"Child," the man says, "why do you not rise?"

"I...I can't," Rebecca chokes out her answer. "I can't walk."

"Indeed not," the man says. "You were meant for running."

He kneels at her side, removes a glove and reaches out his hand. I want to scream at him not to touch her, but the only sound that emerges from me is a strangled sob, bubbling in my own vomit. If the man hears me at all, he ignores me.

His fingers touch Rebecca's forehead. He bows his head and holds still, though I can see his shoulders rise and fall in deep, easy breaths. Time passes without my knowing its length. Then the man lifts his head and climbs to his feet.

"Now rise," he says, holding out his hand.

Rebecca takes it, and steps from her stretcher as smoothly as if the past three days were a single night's dream, and the morning has come.

THE MAN FINDS me lying in my own filth, too weak to move. He steps to my side with Rebecca's hand in his, stoops, and touches my forehead with his gloved hand. There's no miraculous recovery as in her case; if anything, the pressure of his fingers makes the pain increase. Having ascertained that I'm alive, he calls his teenage companions, and the two strap me onto his wyrm. My mind moans at their touch, but my mouth can't expel the sound from my throat.

"This one seems worse than the others," the red-haired girl says to the man.

"She is pureskin," he answers. "Handle her with great care, Angelica. Let nothing unclean touch her before we reach the Cathedral."

"Yes, Gabriel," she says, before draping a cloth the color of their garments over my body. I can tell it should be soft, but it scratches like a fell-cat's claws.

A sudden jerk signals the wyrm's movement, then it settles into a smooth, undulating rhythm. The clearing filled with bodies vanishes, and the moonlight is blocked by the leafy canopy. Between the wyrm's rocking motion and the torment of its slimy skin pressed against me, I throw up so much as we glide through the night that I feel as if my stomach has followed its contents onto the forest floor.

Dawn has broken by the time we roll to a stop. My eyes, the only part of me that can move, look straight upward at what must be a mountain, a colossal spire of rock splitting the gray sky above the tallest of trees. But the spire is too perfect, sculpted in a pylon shape that rises level after level, narrowing as it goes. It's a structure of some kind, a building crafted of stone. I search my memory for anything comparable, recall the Conservator's lessons about the civilization that existed before the Ecosystem's rise, the towers built by the people of that time. Such towers haven't been known for eons, Nathan said; the Ecosystem tore them all down. Yet here one stands, and I lie in its shadow.

The man named Gabriel dismounts from his wyrm, and his teenage assistants busy themselves to free me from whatever holds me to the living transport. They lay me on cool stone that I can feel through my wrap; Angelica tucks a corner of the blanket over me and offers an encouraging smile. With the coming of daylight, I see that others are strapped to the wyrms, people I barely recognize through their badly mottled faces. One has Leah's compact body and soiled headscarf; another could be one of the twins. Isaac is nowhere to be seen. With his white beard and single eye, Gideon should be easy to spot, but I can't find him either. I try to count the bodies the two assistants unload, but the act of calculation is too much, and my spinning head produces yet another fruitless attempt to void the emptiness inside me.

Gabriel lowers himself to peer into my eyes. Now that I see him in the gray light of another clouded dawn, I can tell that he's not as old as Judith or Gideon, but he's at least the age my mother would have been. There's something in his face that seems to stoke a memory, though I can't say what. He gazes at me keenly but not unkindly, then reaches out an ungloved hand. I stiffen, or would if I could move. My eyes, I'm sure, widen in alarm.

"Don't be afraid, Sarah," I hear a voice, and my eyes rove to Rebecca, who's come up behind the man, walking with such serene assurance it's as if she never lost a step. Seeing her healed and whole would bring fresh tears to my eyes, but I seem to have lost the ability to cry, too.

"Your wounds are not fatal," Gabriel says to me in his flowing voice. "I can relieve your pain for the moment, but true healing will take much longer."

So saying, he touches my forehead with the tips of his fingers. I tighten inside, expecting a repetition of the excruciating pain, but instead I feel warmth radiating from his touch, and with it, a retreat of bodily agony. The feeling flows outward from the point of contact, a series of widening ripples that touches first my eyes, then my cheeks, my lips, my neck and shoulders and chest. I blink, and realize I've been unable to do so all this time. My lips tingle, then they're free to move, though they feel rubbery and uncoordinated. The sound that comes from my throat is little more than an animal whimper, despite the intention of words that lies behind it.

"Rest, child," Gabriel says, placing his palm against my forehead. My eyelids grow heavy, and I struggle to remain awake. I watch through half-closed eyes while others dressed like our rescuers emerge from the base of the tower: men and women with shades of skin I've never seen, from deep umber to palest gold, with hair worn in curls and waves and ringlets, eyes that take their color from the sky, the trees, the earth. They carry stretchers totally unlike the crude constructs Gideon pieced together from sickenmore branches and molusk gut: theirs are fashioned of ornately carved and polished wood piled high with blankets and bolsters whose whiteness dazzles my eyes. Gabriel lifts me gently and lays me on one of these thrones.

"Welcome, daughter of Sarah," he says. "Welcome to the City of the Queens."

I've no chance to ask how he knows me, for the drowsiness becomes too much as I settle into a softness I've never imagined in my more than seventeen years of stick and stone. I fall asleep to the sound of Gabriel's voice leading the others in a chant whose words are strangely familiar but whose meaning I can't grasp.

I WAKE IN a bed even more lavish than the one that bore me here. It's so soft my body sinks into it, so white it might be woven of moonbeams. The covers breathe an intoxicating fragrance new to my nose: sweet and warm and relaxing, defying my best effort to find a comparison. I could lie here forever, languidly stretching and nuzzling against the blankets that swaddle me, even if it's all a dream.

But if so, it's a dream in which all pain has fled my body, a dream in which I *can* stretch with arms returned to their normal shape, nuzzle with cheeks no longer swollen like rhubhard bulbs. I turn my head in the direction the light falls, see a patch of hazy sky through a tall arched window of stone. I must be in the mountain-building, the one Gabriel called the Cathedral. Reluctant as I am to leave this blissful bed for even a moment, I'm curious to know what lies outside. I prop myself on an elbow and lean out the window.

Or would if something didn't bonk my forehead. There's an invisible barrier between me and the outside, a hard but clear substance within the window frame. I tap a finger against it in several places, discover that it fills the space as far as I can reach. I'd say it's the closest thing to a miracle I've encountered if not for the fact that, within the past night and day, I've met people who ride urthwyrms and watched a man heal paralysis with a touch of his hand.

In this City of the Queens, miracles seem as common as cicatrix in the world I just left.

Though I can't extend my head outside the window, I press my nose against the enchanted barrier and let my eyes take in the view. Treetops parade to the horizon, and when I look straight down, my stomach flip-flops at the incredible distance to the pavement below. I must be somewhere near the peak of the Cathedral, hundreds—or could it be thousands?—of feet up. In all my life, I've left the ground only twice to climb trees, and on neither occasion did I reach a height of more than fifty feet. Being this high makes me feel both exhilarated and dizzy, like a fledgling bloodbird on its first flight. I lie down again, where the dreamy bed reminds me I'm positively surrounded by miracles.

For long moments, I float in sweetly scented luxury, letting my mind float along with my body. On a second glance out the window, I find that other buildings surround this one, nowhere near as tall but equally impressive, built from slabs of squared stone each of which is as large as a whole house in my former village. Ruling out a dream, there's no conclusion to draw but that this is the village I was seeking: the village from which my grandmother, and perhaps my rescuer from the earlier urthwyrm misadventure, came. It's not where I thought it would be—if I haven't lost all sense of direction, it lies southeast of the glade where we were attacked—but it is relatively close to the village of my birth. How I missed Sensing it when I searched the Ecosystem before setting out after Miriam is a mystery, until I remember that the City of the Queens is made of stone, and stone shows as blankness to the Sense.

Last night's attack—assuming it was last night—might have been a stroke of good fortune, guiding us to a place we'd never have found on our own.

I've no sooner thought that than my reverie is sliced by guilt, and I come crashing back to earth. Here I am, wallowing in endless comfort, while the swollen bodies of my companions lie rotting in the forest. Where are Rebecca, Leah, the others? What of Isaac and Gideon? Saul is dead for sure, as are the firestarters who guarded Levi, along with Rebecca's parents and the woman whose body I touched. But how many more?

I flounder in sheets as I attempt to climb from bed. An earthenware platter on a bedside table crashes to the ground, its contents—fruit and nuts—spilling across the floor. When I finally untangle myself, I see that I've been clothed in the white half-robe of the city's residents, and my heart lurches at the thought of my healer's token. A moment of frantic searching reveals that it's there, in a lined inner pocket. My feet land on stone, much smoother than that of our village, and laid in a pattern of interlocking diamonds. I'm busy looking for a way out when the wooden rectangle leaning against one of the walls pivots open and I realize it's a door. The one who enters is Gabriel.

He nods courteously when he sees me on my feet. "I came to check on your condition. It appears that you are fully healed."

"Thanks to you," I say, my voice stiff from discomfort and disuse. "I wanted to find out about the others."

"Your friends are well," he says. "Those we retrieved from the glade."

"And how," I falter, "how many is that?"

The pleased expression leaves his face. "We could not save all," he says. "Those pierced by the frogs' venom died instantly. Those, like yourself, who were merely touched by it we were able to heal. There is a cost to healing, a price to be paid. Sometimes, that price is too great for us."

"Please," I say. "How many?"

"Counting yourself, we have brought twenty-three to the City of the Queens."

I sink, or fall, into the bed, holding myself in a seated position with an effort. Twenty-three people. Of the nearly two hundred who were alive less than a week ago, only twenty-three are left. "What did you do with the dead?"

"We feared they might introduce contagion to any who handled their flesh," he answers. "We burned their bodies where they lay."

After all this death, it hardly seems to matter, but I ask, "One of the women in our company was pregnant. Did she live?"

"She did, and was delivered of her babe three nights ago," he answers. "A girl-child, as healthy as the mother."

Three nights. I've lost at least three nights while I recovered. "And Leah," I say. "Is a woman named Leah alive?"

Gabriel nods. "She was felled in the glade when she touched the venom that struck you down, but she is fully healed. She asked for you this morning."

One by one, I request the names of the survivors. There's Rebecca, of course, and both Caleb and Noah. Dinah. Huldah and Zipporah. A number of the firestarters and other adults and teens, along with more than half of the children. Amos, however, is dead, as is Esau, along with his parents. Neither Levi nor Gideon was brought to the City of the Queens, though a search of the surrounding woods took place on reports of a man, or more than one, being spotted there two nights ago. I save for last the one name I can least bear to think of losing. "Was there a boy named Isaac? He was sick, in a stretcher. The venom might not have hit him."

The sorrow that overtakes his face gives me my answer. "Alas, he was not among those we saved."

So he's gone. Unlike Gideon, for whom I hold out hope that he might have survived when he left camp to chase after Levi, Isaac couldn't have escaped the glade on his own power. It seems so long since I've known he was lost to me—though in reality, I can measure our relationship in weeks—I thought his death might not hit me so hard. But it does. I cover my face to catch the tears that trickle down my cheeks, and before I know it, my body shakes with the force of a sorrow it seems I've held inside my entire life.

Gabriel sits beside me. To my surprise, he wraps an arm around my shoulders and pulls me to him. I should push him away, but my body is no more my own than it was the night in the glade.

"The boy named Isaac," he rumbles against my ear. "He was a favorite of yours?"

I'm nowhere near ready to reveal all that Isaac was to me. The thought that our last conversation was filled with so much bitterness, that I'll never be able to tell him I'm sorry or see him smile again, feels like another shot of venom to my heart. "That's personal."

"I crave your pardon," he says. "I mourn with you for

the friend you have lost. He would have been welcomed to our city."

The way he says that makes me lift my head to search his face. He gazes back at me steadily, yet I see a hint of pain in his eyes. "Did you...know him?" I ask.

"I met him once before," he says. "In the lair of the urthwyrms, where it took all the ingenuity of my own courier to free him. Him, and the companion who would otherwise have shared his fate."

I leap back, not in anger but in shock. "Then it *was* you! You're the one who saved me and...and Isaac, and Miriam...." The thought makes tears flow again. "You saved us all, and I let them both die."

He touches my cheek, and I feel the warmth of his healing power. I wish it could stop the tears, soothe the deeper pain.

"These losses could not have been prevented by you," he says. "Yet if you would honor your friends' memory, you can help me uncover the true cause of their death. Will you promise me that, Ruth?"

There are a thousand questions I need to ask before I can promise him anything, but his final word replaces them all with a single one. "How do you know my real name?"

"I knew it before you were born," he says. "I was first to hear it spoken from your mother's lips. In all the years since, it has been my fondest wish to meet the daughter of Sarah."

I look intently at his face. What is the familiar thing that dances just beyond recall in its contours? I've seen my own face so seldom—in water, in dreams, in Isaac's eyes—I don't recognize it in another. Then he rests a hand on mine, and it's as if everything that seemed mysterious about this place falls away.

"My daughter," he says. "It is time you learned the truth."

I WALK WITH my father through the hallways of the Cathedral, and he tells me that everything I've ever believed is a lie.

Or just about everything. He stops short of saying that the world outside the tower windows isn't actually there. But he comes close.

"You have been taught that the entity known as the Ecosystem has existed, virtually unchanged, for thousands of years," he begins.

"Tens of thousands."

"Nothing could be farther from the truth," he says. "We can date the Ecosystem's rise with certainty, and we know that it is less than two centuries old."

I open my mouth to utter an objection, but he talks on.

"We also know that the Ecosystem has experienced several bursts of enhanced mutagenic activity in that brief timespan. The first such episode gave rise to the entity in its original form. The most recent period ended some eighty years ago, after which point the Ecosystem remained relatively stable until the past week's outbreak."

I nod, try to look intelligent. A group of city residents passes us in the hallway, all wearing their white uniforms. Despite the common outfit, I'm struck as before by the variety of skin colors, hair styles, eye shapes. How can such people walk the earth, when my whole life I thought that my village was the pattern for all of humanity?

My father has paused in his lecture, and is watching me stare at the others. When I give him my attention again, he nods as if he knows what questions have passed through my mind. "The City of the Queens was once a university, Ruth," he says. "A training academy for the young, as well as a research facility for the advancement of scientific knowledge. A particularly important facility from our perspective, as it was here that the experiments that spawned the Ecosystem were conducted. Its archives are extensive, and are consulted by all who wish to advance their understanding of the past."

I wish I could respond, but so much of what he says—*university*, *research facility*, *scientific knowledge*, *archives*—is beyond my experience. I address the only part of his discourse that sticks. "Please call me Sarah. That's what everyone calls me now."

He nods again. "It will take time to get used to that," he says. "For me, there is only one Sarah."

He holds out a hand and ushers me through one of the swinging wooden doors. I wonder why, given our fairly extensive practice with woodworking, my own village never thought to place such barriers at our doorways to keep out the elements.

The room we enter is larger than the one in which I woke, and whereas that one was plain, this new room is elaborate beyond my wildest fancies. The floor is composed of many small, colored stones, cool to my bare feet. I realize as I walk on them that they form an image: a bird I've never seen, with widespread wings of red and orange crafted to look like flame. The ceiling is wooden, but I'm abashed to have compared my own village's woodcraft to this: beams and arches crisscross in lines too complex for me to follow the overall design, while the whole is whittled with spirals and grooves nearly dizzying in their intricacy. On the walls, brightly colored panels hang, each depicting some fantastic animal: a four-footed beast with a single horn sprouting from its forehead; a thing like a lizard standing on two powerful legs but with two puny arms dangling beneath a toothed maw; a creature that resembles a pandalion except everything about it, from its hide to its eyes to its flowing mane, is the same tawny gold color, not the black-and-white pattern of the robe Isaac wore on his wedding day. When I come close to these images, I realize that they're woven of thousands of tiny colored threads, a miracle of workmanship that—even if we'd had the materials—would have taken my village months if not years to construct. What kind of place is this, where people are at luxury to build beauty into the floors and ceilings and walls of their homes?

My father lets me inspect the room for as long as I please. But that's not long; I find it wearying to stare at all this wanton prettiness, angering to think that while my people scratched out a living from bare rock, others lived close by who could have showed us an easier way. So many have died—my mother, my grandfather, Miriam, Esther, Daniel, Judith, Isaac—knowing nothing of this other world. I face the man who brought me here, and I can't help the anger from bubbling into my words.

"Why are you showing me this?" I ask. "What good

are these"—I wave an arm at the animal likenesses, having no name for any of them—"after all we've lost?"

"That is the pity," he answers, with sorrow in his eyes. "Or, I should say, the great tragedy of our being. It was a terrible fate that divided us, that forced your village—once mine—to live as it did. None of us can undo the damage that was done, but I can tell you how it came to pass, that we might strive to ensure it never happens again."

He places a hand on my arm and leads me to a pair of wooden chairs that stand beneath tall windows along one side of the room. Like everything else, the chairs are fashioned as much for beauty as for use. We sit, and while he resumes his speech, I warily lean my elbows on the platform of wood that juts above my lap.

"Students once sat where you do," he says. "They listened while their teacher—their professor, as the teachers of that time were called—discoursed from the podium." He points to an upright block of wood standing at the front of the room. "It may be that the professors would have done better to sit among their pupils. But I am no professor, and I sit here now to speak to you, my daughter, Ruth"—he smiles fleetingly, as if his face is unaccustomed to the action—"Sarah, to tell you of things long past."

He reaches across the small space between us, takes my hands in his. In all the times he's touched me, I have yet to receive a glimpse of his life, either because I'm still weakened by the frogs' venom or because, as my grandfather did until the very end of his days, my father has figured out a way to block my sensitivity. When he looks at me with his so familiar-yet-unfamiliar eyes, I face a wall, not a window.

"The City of the Queens arose following the original onslaught of the Ecosystem," he says. "With the bitter knowledge those first survivors reaped from the events that took place here, they learned a degree of humility, and pledged themselves to accept their reduced role in the Ecosystem's grand design. Thus was born the line of queens, the title given to the healer-women who demonstrated this new path. The first queen of the city was named Dominica, and she taught her people much of humanity's altered place in the Ecosystem, as well as helping us to understand and control the new powers that had been given to our kind as if in recompense for all we had lost. You will learn of these things too," he says to the question forming on my lips. "When the time comes, you will meet Queen Celestina, newly crowned this past month. But for now, it is enough for you to know that the bargain of Queen Dominica has preserved us for nearly two hundred years, in this very place, without threat of harm from the Ecosystem at our door."

I nod, realizing as he says this that I've yet to see any of the defensive mechanisms—the charred circle, the firewells, the threshers—that were maintained with such care in my village.

"Dominica never married, but she gave birth to three daughters," my father continues. "Three girls, each with a different sire, to carry on her legacy after she was gone. From the first two daughters, Demetria and Delphina, all of the queens who have ruled this city are descended. But through the line of the third daughter, Divina, a rupture occurred within our community that has never healed."

He rubs his eyes wearily, then returns to his tale.

"Long after Queen Dominica's death," he says, "a faction arose that rejected the peaceful path she had charted. Never great in numbers, these dissidents dreamed of striking a blow against the Ecosystem, repaying its outrages with attacks of their own. They called themselves *Sensors*, and spoke of a power they named *the Sense*: a power of grievance and retribution without which, they said, none could truly master the wild. Their teaching might have been dismissed as folly, and their society—the Sensorship—might have died out with its founders, had not Divina's sole daughter, Delilah, claimed common cause with them. Never a queen herself, Delilah was put forward by the Sensorship as a claimant to the throne. A bloody revolution was averted by the queen at that time, Leonida, daughter of Demetria. The result was that, eighty years ago, the Sensors and those citizens who followed them fled the city with their would-be queen, and vowed never to return."

"That was when they founded the village?" I ask.

"It was," he answers. "There might have been women of queenly blood among your neighbors, but now that the village is no more, we may never know."

He casts his eyes down, and I think of queens walking the village of stone, unaware of their lineage. Women like Leah, perhaps, whose freedom to live and love as they pleased was taken from them by forces beyond their awareness.

"The society founded by the Sensorship pursued a life of forced privation," my father goes on. "Alone in their village, isolated from their history and their people, they gave free rein to their core philosophy: that warfare, not

reconciliation, was the true state of being between humanity and Ecosystem; that only the power of the Sensors was
equal to waging this war; and that, as individuals supe-
rior in kind to all others, Sensors must be shielded from
human contact lest it corrupt their abilities. By some mad
logic, they decreed that it was only those who bore the
characteristics of their queen, Delilah"—he touches my
hand, then his own, our skin a common brown—"who
were worthy of preservation. In the early days of their
village's founding, five men who called themselves the
Brotherhood of the Sensorship took it upon themselves
to weed out any who differed from their ideal form. Their
leader, a man named Malachi, oversaw a reign of terror
that resulted in the loss of many lives."

Malachi. Chief Sensor before my grandfather. He'd
always seemed particularly frail and wizened to me, and
now I understand why: he must have been close to a
hundred years old when he died. But I never would have
thought him capable of the horrors my father describes.
"If the Brotherhood founded the village," I ask, "why was
it administered by a Chief Warden? I'd never even heard
of the Brotherhood until recently. And I've never heard of
anyone named Delilah."

"That is a mystery we have not been able to unravel,"
he says. "From those few who escaped the Brotherhood's
wrath, the city heard of great disruptions in the Ecosystem,
cataclysms similar to those we have witnessed of late.
Some said that Delilah, the lost queen, died defending her
village from these tumults. All we know for certain—and
this from failed attempts to provide relief to our com-
rades—is that the Brotherhood responded to the crisis

by transforming itself into an army with rules of absolute authority and obeisance, strict habits of discipline, and intensive training in the martial arts. Toward that end, they apprenticed a corps of children to serve as an armed militia in case of conflict with the city. Most of these recruits were born in the village, having never known the City of the Queens. But the eldest of their number was a ten-year-old boy named Aaron."

"Aaron?" I say. "You mean my grandfather?"

He nods.

"But you said they left eighty years ago. That would make him—"

"Your grandfather was much older than you suspected," he says. "He enjoyed strength and vitality far beyond the common state, but he had reached his ninetieth year when he died."

He falls silent while I take this in. The idea that the Sensorship is less than a hundred years old, not many thousands as Nathan taught, makes me feel oddly adrift, as if I've discovered that I live on a planet other than my own. From the age of three, all my training was dedicated to propositions I believed to be ancient teachings, the only teachings that had enabled human beings to withstand the Ecosystem for hundreds of generations. To learn that the Sensors' violent creed was only one of many possible ways leads me to wonder if the Conservator knew the truth, or if he was merely parroting what he had been taught. He was only in his fifties when he died; it's possible that, like me, he'd been fed a lie since childhood.

But Aaron knew the truth. He knew what Malachi and the Brotherhood had done to their own people. And he never told me. "Why did the Sensors take people like Aaron with them? Weren't they worried the truth would get out?"

"They had no choice," my father says. "Given their vow of chastity, the Sensorship needed others to perpetuate their ranks. As a safeguard, they took only those who were most loyal to their teaching, including your grandfather's parents. These families were sworn to secrecy, and held that secret throughout their lives. In time, fear of the Ecosystem—and of the Brotherhood—kept all but the Sensors from venturing beyond the village, and so the secret was secured."

"My grandpa was a Sensor," I say. "He could have told everyone the truth."

His face turns more than normally grave. "Your grandfather's part in this tale is perhaps the strangest of all," he says. "When Aaron departed the City of the Queens, he left behind a playmate, a girl three years younger than himself named Seraphina. For the ten years following the exodus, he trained to become a Sensor, and was installed at the end of that time to lead the corps of younger recruits. By some occurrence in the field—the nature of which we do not know—he was drawn to return to the city of his birth. There he met his old friend, now grown to be a woman. For the many years that followed, he came again and again to the city, as often as he could, though that might be but once every two years. From that chance beginning, your mother was born, the child of Aaron and Seraphina. The rest of the story—"

"I know the rest," I say. "My grandmother died in childbirth, and Aaron brought their daughter back to the village. When she turned three, he began training her as a Sensor. And when she died, he did the same with me." I swallow, hating myself for saying this, but feeling it all the same. "Which means he lied to both my mother and me every day of our lives, and chose for us a fate he could hardly stand himself."

My father looks at me, and I realize I'm much less a wall than a window to him. "There will be time to learn more of these things," he says. "But there is one last part of the story that you must know now."

He gestures for me to join him at the room's windows. Through the invisible barrier—my father calls it *glass*, and warns me it's as sharp as desert glassgrass if broken—we look out at the Ecosystem, which seems peaceful enough when seen from afar. Maybe it's always peaceful this close to the city.

"The disorder that led to the destruction of the village was unforeseen by us, either in its advent or its severity," he says. "When we realized the extent of the threat, we set out on our wyrm-mounts, risking conflict with the Brotherhood in hopes of recovering any who might survive. But it was with your safety that I was most concerned."

"Me?" I say. "Because I'm your daughter?"

He nods. "That, and more. Your grandmother Seraphina was no common resident of the City of the Queens. From an early age, she had been identified as pureskin, possessing an unusually strong connection to the Ecosystem. At the time your grandfather reunited with the friend of his youth, she was being trained to assume the mantle held by her mother, Leonida, queen of this city."

Nothing he's said rattles me quite like this. "But then I'm...."

"Indeed," he says, and bows his head. "You are pure-skin like your mother, and your grandmother before her. You trace your line through Demetria to Dominica herself. You are of the blood of queens."

I visit Leah in her room. I consider telling her I'm roy-alty, but decide she'd never believe me.

I hardly believe it myself. That's one reason I seek her company. After everything my father told me, I crave the normalcy of talking to someone from my own village, even if she's someone I've known less than a week.

She runs across the room the instant she sees me, and enfolds me in a hug. I hug back, which seems the most ordinary thing in the world, though in fact it's close to a first for me. Sensors don't hug. The word for what Leah is strikes me so suddenly and simply, I can't help laughing, because it's a first, too. *Friend.*

"How are you feeling?" she asks, and that makes me laugh even harder. She holds me at arm's length, inspects me with concern.

"I'm fine," I say. "Really. I feel just fine."

"Oh, Sarah," she says, her face crumpling, "I heard about Isaac."

"It's okay," I say, and force a smile. "We've lost so many. Not only Isaac, but Judith, and the children, and… and Beulah. That's why we have to…."

I don't find out how I planned to finish that. She holds me, and I hold her back, and our cheeks grow wet with each other's tears.

Afterward, we talk of other things. Simpler things, I'd say, except nothing is simple anymore.

"I wonder if I'll get to meet Queen Celestina," Leah says.

"Do you want to?"

"Yes and no," she says. "Honestly, it sounds very intimidating."

"No more intimidating than meeting me," I say, and Leah looks at me strangely. I add: "I'm sure she'd love to talk to you."

"Not likely," she says with a snort. "Have you walked around the Cathedral? I feel like a flame ant surrounded by a race of giants. All of them rushing around with their heads in the clouds, and me scurrying back and forth trying not to get stomped on."

I smile back at her, but say nothing. I feel the same way.

"I have to admit, though, it's exciting," she says. "In a city ruled by a queen, what isn't possible?"

Her eyes are shining. I don't want to spoil her daydreams, but my father's history lesson has made me wonder about my place here. The tale of Leonida and Delilah suggests it can't be a healthy thing for two queens to inhabit the city at once.

"Come with me," Leah says, holding out her hand. "I want to show you something."

We leave her bedroom and walk through the corridors of the Cathedral. Everything is made of stone, though the walls are hung with pictures—Gabriel calls them *tapestries*—like the ones in the teaching room. There are also enormous flights of stairs that lead from one level of the building to another, far more than the one or two steps my village managed at our best. These seemingly endless stairways sit within sloped corridors called stairwells, which Leah is exuberant enough to use as an echo chamber. I join my voice with hers; it feels good to hear our laughter rebound as if we're among numbers of our own kind once more.

It's a long walk before we reach the base of the Cathedral. No one has told us we can't come and go as we please, and no one we pass looks at us suspiciously; in fact, they hardly look at us at all. We link arms and stroll out onto the vast stone pavilion on which the building rests, and though my supposedly pure skin doesn't register any images from Leah's life—due to damage from the frog venom, I'm convinced by now—I do feel the comfort of having a companion at my side.

"Take a look," Leah says.

I look where she points, and find an immense body of water spreading before us, so large I think it must be a swamp or a lake. But it's perfectly circular in shape, and bordered by stone all the way around, so it must be yet another thing built by the miracle workers who founded this university. People in their gleaming tunics amble around the circumference of the manmade lake, alone or in pairs. Out on the water, I see other shapes floating on the surface, something like lilith-pads except large enough to hold two people as they scud back and forth. At my side, Leah squeezes my arm.

"I saw it from the window on my side of the Cathedral," she says. "I didn't want to come down without you. Look, Sarah."

I follow her finger again, and see that some of the

strolling couples are holding hands. A girl with brown skin walks with a golden-haired boy; elsewhere, a couple who share the same shade of skin lean close to share a kiss. What's more remarkable than this open display of affection is that though many of the couples are boy-girl, others are single-sex, two boys or two girls. No one shies from these pairings, no one stares at them—except, possibly, me. When a girl I identify by her bright red hair as Angelica draws close to her dark-skinned partner and accepts the other girl's kiss, what shocks me most of all is the smile that finds its way to my own lips. Leah squeezes my arm again, and I need no healer's power to feel her joy.

"You see?" she says breathlessly. "What isn't possible?"

BEYOND THE POOL, far from the Cathedral, there's a hilly expanse of bright green where I go to be alone. The walk's good for my body, which aches from everything it's been through; the destination is good for my heart, which feels pretty much the same. Paths paved with stone meander through the green; trees shade the paths; wooden benches beckon if I grow tired. I've figured out why no one worries about me wandering off: in the City of the Queens, nothing that lives poses a threat. Trees are of benign species I've never known—oak, cottonwood, hemlock—while grabgrass, where it exists, leaves human feet untouched. Birds of prey circle high as always, but never dive to the attack. In some way my father won't yet tell me, the power of Queen Celestina tames the Ecosystem in her city.

The place where I visit has one truly peculiar feature: row upon row of polished white stones poking up from the ground. They've been laid in a pattern too complex for my eyes to understand, curves and loops and diagonals it would probably take a soaring bloodbird to unravel. From time to time, I see people approach one of the stones, stand before it for long moments, lay their fingers on its surface. They talk to the stones too, in quiet voices I can hear but not interpret; before they go, many leave offerings of flowers at the stones' feet. Hesitantly at first, then more boldly once I realize this is not only accepted but expected of those who come here, I examine one or another of the stones to learn what attracts visitors to them. There's not much to see, just plain white faces with strange scratch-marks chiseled into them. I stand by the stones anyway, silent, leaving no flowers, bowing my head sometimes in imitation of the others I see do the same.

There's a deep dell in this place where the stones are newly laid, the dirt around them upturned and moist. I've seen no other visitors in this section, found no flowers. I've counted the stones, which number exactly forty-four, laid out in four neat rows of eleven each. They're somewhat smaller than the norm, and their surfaces are smooth, lacking the scratch-marks I've found on the others. They look lonely, which is why I'm drawn to them again and again. I wish I could say a word to ease their sorrow, but every time the beginning of speech arrives on my tongue, I swallow it down in embarrassment. Why talk to stones, when they can't hear or answer?

In time, it comes to me what these stones are for. And it comes to me that this is what my own village could never afford, never allow. It makes my heart hurt to count so many, though it lightens my spirit ever so slightly to know that the people of this city have laid a monument to strangers they never met, strangers who, if not for the mischance of eighty years past, might have been their neighbors and friends.

I've seen visitors kneel before the stones of this place. I do so myself, resting my bare knees carefully on the ground. My Sense, as ever, is mute, but my other senses respond to the softness of the grass, the freshness of the earth. I'm reminded of the funeral of Rachel, a funeral attended only by me and one other. I don't know which stone is his, but I hear his voice as if he's right beside me. Not his last words, the ones he threw at me in madness or malice. Instead, I hear the words of the song he sang, fragments of verse I'd forgotten until this moment. Fragments, I now know, that must have been passed down from this city to our village:

*Rest in the lap of Earth, our mother, of Earth
far-spreading, very kind and gracious.
May she guard your footsteps upon the
distant pathway.
Move softly, Earth, and do not press him
down: give him easy access as he approaches
the end.
Cover him as a mother wraps her garment
about her child.*

I lower my head and close my eyes to trap the tears. Aloud, I speak the vow I would have spoken if I could. I'm answered only by silence. I rise and depart the place, not looking back. The next time I come, I'll bring flowers.

Now that I'm fully recovered from the frog attack, I spend most of my time out of doors. Beautiful as the Cathedral is, its beauty can be overwhelming. The grounds on which the tower rests are no less lovely, and the delight I feel at coming so close to the Ecosystem without fearing its vengeance is something I can't express, not even to my new best friend, Leah.

Today, we sit by one of the many gardens that keep the city supplied with food. I'd been puzzled by the lack of meat on my table, the absence of hunters returning from the forest with bulging kill sacks or streaming carcasses, but now I know why: nothing is consumed here that has brain or heart or lungs. That makes me think of what Miriam said to me on her final trip into the Ecosystem, and I wish she could have lived to see this place.

Some of the gardens aren't for food but for the medicinal plants used by the healers. I recognize only a handful, but Caleb and Noah, who've joined me this morning, are jealously eyeing an abundance our village never knew.

"There are many methods of healing," explains our tour guide, Michael, the pale-haired boy who accompanied my father and Angelica that night in the forest. Add to my list of new words the color of hair he and my grandmother Seraphina had in common: *blond*. "Some methods involve the application of extracts and ointments, others the manipulation of bodily energies. Surgical procedures are possible with the assistance of biofeedback techniques and acupuncture in place of chemical anesthesia."

Most of this goes over my head, but I hazard a question. "What about healing by touch? Can anyone do that?"

Michael's eyes flick toward my father before he answers. "Very few."

"But those who can," I press him. "Is there a limit to what they can do?"

"There are always limits," Michael says. "To live in concert with the Ecosystem, one must accept the sacrifices."

"I see," I murmur, though actually, I don't. I glance over at my father, find him studying me. There are many things I've wanted to ask him the past several days—about my mother, about his healing powers—but I haven't found an opening. Any doubt that he's truly my father has been erased; thanks to the reflective squares called mirrors that hang in the rooms, I see more of his face in mine every day. But that doesn't mean I feel close enough to him to probe his secrets.

Michael's about to lead us to the next garden when Rebecca skips up to our group, dragging her own new best friend, Zipporah. The littlest Sensor is adjusting remarkably well to life here, though Leah tells me she wails for her parents at night. Out in the vibrant gardens, though, she's all smiles. I've meant to probe her about the black vines she Sensed the day of the frog attack, but as with the unasked questions for my father, I've been too busy recuperating and learning the ways of the city to find the time.

Today's not going to be the day either. Michael's boyfriend Luke, who wears the modified white tunic of the

city guard, appears with a report of another guard's training accident, and Michael excuses himself to check on the
injured trainee. With Angelica absent due to her blossoming love affair, that leaves my father to continue the
tour, and he seems disinclined to do so. We wander over
to the pond, where the girls play while Leah watches the
babies, including Huldah, who seems to have accepted her
as surrogate mother. Of the twenty-three who survived, all
but Dinah have begun to explore the City of the Queens.
Leah, who apparently knows everything about everybody,
insists that the woman is fully recovered yet refuses to
leave her room. Though I'm not eager to deal with Levi's
co-conspirator again, I understand that the mind's healing
may lag behind the body's.

"Sarah," my father says of a sudden as he steps to my
side. "I need a moment of your time."

I give Leah a look, but she only rolls her eyes. The
gentle pressure of my father's hand leads me back toward
the Cathedral, Rebecca's excited cries fading into the distance. I expect to mount the stairs to the teaching-room,
but instead, my father directs me to a stairwell that leads
downward, exiting into a corridor below ground level.
Torches in brackets along the walls light these windowless
regions, but in other respects the area looks the same as
the rest, a broad central hallway with many closed wooden
doors along its length. Even with the firelight, the air is a
bit chillier than above. My father stops before a door at
the end of the corridor and lets my arm go.

"I know I have kept much from you, Ruth," he says,
slipping up with my name as he does from time to time.
"There are some lessons you are not ready to learn, others

I am not ready to teach. But I ask you to believe that I do not keep these things from you without good reason."

"Okay," I say, not sure what else to say.

"Michael spoke truly when he described the limits of our powers," he goes on. "We have built the City of the Queens on the knowledge that was housed in this university, adding our own measure under the queen's guidance. But as you know from recent events, our understanding of the Ecosystem remains far from complete."

By *recent events*, he means the death of my village and most of its inhabitants. I merely nod in response as he takes a torch from the wall and leads me into the room.

It's much larger than any of the rooms I've visited before, nearly a corridor in itself. It's much less flashy, too, built of featureless stone with torches lining unadorned walls. In some ways, it reminds me of the gathering hall from my lost village, though the ceiling is far lower than the vault of that place. There's one further aspect of the room that reminds me of the hall—in particular, the final time I was there.

Stretched along the floor to its full length of thirty or more feet lies the body of an urthwyrm.

Not, I realize at once, a living wyrm. This one has been opened up by axe or blade, the layers of its rubbery skin peeled back and pinned to the floor with ropes and rings. That gives me the opportunity to observe the wyrm's innards, muscle and blood vessels and nerve fiber, all snaking along the tube-like gullet that is a wyrm's main reason for existence. My father walks me close to the dead beast, and my nose wrinkles at the prospect of rot. But there's no scent of corruption, nothing but a sharp briny smell that seems to penetrate not only my nostrils but my eyes as well.

"This experimental subject is the latest of many," my father says as he holds his torch above the carcass to provide a better view. "For years, I have labored to understand the workings of wyrms, and in some respects, I have succeeded. Did you know, for instance, that urthwyrms possess so great a power of regeneration that, when a living wyrm is cut into segments, each is able to develop a complete, independent nervous system within less than a day?"

"I seem to remember something like that," I say, thinking of the multiplying monsters that attacked me in their underground lair.

"You need not wonder, then, at the recovery of the child Rebecca," he says. "She was healed of her injury by the same power that animates these wonderful creatures. My own role in her healing involved nothing more than channeling the wyrms' power."

"That's a lot more than nothing," I say. "How did you take control of their power? Was it inside your body? Your hand?"

He shakes his head. "This is something you will not understand until you have been trained in the healing arts. But as pureskin, surely you appreciate the power that may reside in a simple touch. Even now, were I not monitoring my reaction to your power, you could reach inside and find what ails me."

My skin shivers at his words, and when I turn my concentration to the space between us, I feel what he's describing: an invisible wall, like a sheet of glass except more elastic, that separates me from him. I prod at it with mental fingers, but it doesn't yield. "What ails you, Father?"

He smiles slightly at the sound of that name, but his eyes are turned inward as he broods over the body of the behemoth.

"The wyrms of this city are domesticated," he says at last. "On the orders of Queen Estella, late mother of Celestina, we bred them here, housed them, cared for them. In return, they have given their bodies to us as mounts, revealed their secrets to the healers. When you and the boy—Isaac—were trapped in the wild wyrms' lair, we set out on our couriers to rescue you. And yet, their recent rampage took us all by surprise, and our efforts to understand what drove them to these acts have failed. They have run wild like their kin, and except for the very few we have ridden for years, we can no longer reach them."

"Do you mean," I say, "that the wyrms that destroyed my village came from *here*? From the City of the Queens?"

He nods, his face tormented.

"But how?" I ask. "How is that possible?"

"We have reason to fear that the Ecosystem has entered a period of change more virulent than any before," he says. "The Sensors among you are blocked from reading its will, are they not?"

"Rebecca could Sense its mind to some extent," I say. "But much of it was…clouded."

"As it is for us," he says. "There are life forms in the Ecosystem that did not exist as little as a week ago, creatures such as the spitting frogs whose venom, once it enters the body, we are powerless to treat. We have brought what specimens we could find to the city for analysis, but we have been unable to discover their origins or properties."

I consider telling him about the black vines Rebecca described in her vision, but I don't want to add to the worry I see in his face.

"At present, the city appears secure," he continues. "But we cannot say how long this may last. For the past eighty years and more, we have devoted all our wisdom to adapting to the Ecosystem as it is. I do not know what will happen should it become foreign to us again, as it did in its beginnings."

"And you think I can help?" I ask.

"I would not request more of you than you are prepared to give," he says. "And yet, my heart tells me that your coming here is a chance we cannot afford to miss. Now that you are healed, I must ask you to lend your strength to ours."

"I'll do anything," I say. "Whatever you want. Just say the word."

His face relaxes for the first time since we entered the room. "The blood of Dominica is strong within you, my daughter," he says. "I will set you a task worthy of a queen."

"What is it?" I ask, imagining another journey into the wild. My tired body reacts instinctively against the thought, yet I'll do it if I must.

But once again, my father surprises me.

"To understand the Ecosystem in its fullness," he says, "one must consult the archives. And so you must learn to read."

I'VE FACED FLESH-EATING urthwyrms. Been pursued by homicidal Sensors and poisoned by spitting frogs. Watched the boy I love stand on the hearth beside the girl he loves. And listened as my father gave me news of that boy's death.

But learning to read is the hardest thing I've ever done.

It's maddening. And pointless. Angelica or Michael—the two trade off as teachers—lead me to an airless room in a building they call the library, where they remove thick, leathery boxes from the shelves. They lay the boxes—the books—in front of me, then open their covers with a puff of dust to reveal thousands of skin-thin sheets. The dust makes my eyes water. When I wipe the tears away, I find that the sheets—*pages*, I'm told they're called—are covered with thousands of ant-like squiggles, similar to the scratches on the burial stones or the marks on the clay tablets that only a few people in my village, like Daniel, could understand. These marks are called *letters*, Angelica tells me the first day, and they're supposed to form different words, but I'm at a loss as to how they can do that when they all look the same.

"They're not the same, Sarah," she says, pointing to a list of letters. "Just look at the first two. The *a* is a little ball with a short stick coming down from the right side, and the *b* is a little ball with a long stick going up from the left side."

"What's this one?" I ask. "The one that looks like a tent?"

"I thought they all looked the same."

"Most of them do," I grouse.

"That's a capital *A*. All twenty-six letters have two forms, capitals for the start of sentences and names, and lower-case for everything else."

"There are *two* of these things?" I ask, horrified.

"Yes," she says. "And you have to learn to recognize them both."

"Oh, Sense," I sigh.

I return to my room when the Cathedral's shadow grows deep and the torchlight shines from its windows. Leah asked the night before if she and Huldah could move in with me, and I happily agreed. She rests with the little girl on a low cot beside my bed, though the moment she gets a good look at me, she has me lie face-down on the bedspread and tries to rub the tension from my shoulders.

"It's torture," I tell her. Now that I'm healed from the frogs' venom, Leah's touch makes images from her life—most of them involving Beulah—flow peacefully into my mind. "I'd rather he sent me out into the Ecosystem."

"He must have some reason," she says.

"He'd better," I answer. "I've already lost my Sense. What am I supposed to do when I lose my mind?"

The next day, I return to the library, where Michael continues my letter lessons. He's created palm-size pages with a single letter printed on each one in an oily black substance called ink. By the end of the day, he's flipped so many of these miniature pages so fast, my swimming head can hardly tell the difference between the right side-up tent of a capital *A* and the upside-down tent of a capital *Y*.

Or, actually, I realize as I lie in bed and listen to Leah's soft snores from the cot beside me, I can. The letters are burned into my consciousness, and the only thing I can hardly do is sleep while the strange symbols flicker on and off through my mind.

Angelica, who returns the next morning, seems foul-tempered as she yanks books from the shelf—I assume because she'd rather be with her girlfriend—but brightens when she discovers my progress. "It took me a whole week to learn my ABCs!" she says. "And I was only five, when it's supposed to be easier."

"Sensors have really good memories," I say.

"Plus you're pureskin," she says. "Maybe that helps, too."

I allow myself to revel in my triumph for approximately two blinks of an eye. That's the point at which Angelica spoils it with a new lesson. "Now that you know your letters," she says, "you need to learn the sounds they make."

"I didn't hear them making any sounds."

"Not out loud," she says, giving me a look as if I'm either stupid or pretending. "Each letter stands for a sound in speech, or sometimes more than one sound. So, for example, here's the word *tree*," and she points to a string of four lower-case letters in the book we're using. "The *t* makes a *tuh* sound"—she kind of clucks—"the *r* an *urr* sound"—she growls—"and the two *e*'s an *eee* sound"—she finishes with a squeal. "So it's *tuh-urr-eee, t-r-ee,* tree.

But an *e* can also make an *eh* sound or an *uh* sound, and sometimes, when you have a single *e* at the end of a word, it's silent."

"Then why's it there?"

She blows red strands from her forehead. "I don't know, Sarah. It just is."

The lessons continue. By the end of the week, I've learned to sound out a hundred or more short, simple words, which earns me Angelica's lavish praise and Michael's more measured approval. He's a better teacher than she is, not only because she alternates between being crabby and gabby but also because the way she pronounces the sounds often misleads me into saying each one separately, whereas Michael makes sure I blend them together. I grudgingly admit that it's kind of interesting, how marks on a page can correspond to sounds, which in turn correspond to the words we use to designate things. But I fail to see how my being cooped up in this room is going to help us survive the changes taking place in the Ecosystem. I know the names of many things out there, but that doesn't mean they can't kill me.

I'm happy, therefore, when instead of either of his assistants, I find my father at the table when I arrive the following morning. Maybe, I think, I've learned enough reading to be ready for whatever else he wants me to do.

I'm badly wrong, though. He merely wants to hear me read. I try to hide my disappointment as I go through the list.

"Tree. Book. House. Bird. Woman. Man. Sky. Earth…."

"It's *earth*, my daughter," he corrects. "Not *eee-art-huh*."

"I knew that."

"Good," he says. "Continue."

I reach the end of the list without further correction. I look at him expectantly, but all he does is nod.

"I will call for Angelica to continue your lessons," he says. "Michael if she is…indisposed."

"But—"

He lifts an eyebrow.

"Why do I have to learn to read?" I blurt. "Why can't you just tell me what happened?"

"That will not do," he says. "You must learn the history of the Ecosystem by yourself."

"I don't see what difference it makes," I mutter.

He studies me for a long time. That's another thing they do differently here: tell time. They have elaborate objects called *clocks*, wood-and-glass boxes full of threads and pulleys that operate things they quaintly call *faces* and *hands*; these, they say, measure time with much more precision than the reckoning of sun and shadow I've known all my life. But with the daily reading, I've had no chance to learn this new system.

"You wish to know of your mother," he says at last.

I sit up at this unexpected turn. I've wanted to ask since the moment we met. "Can you tell me about her?"

"I can do more than that," he says, and reaches out a hand. "I can show you."

I take his hand, and feel the familiar tingle as the barrier between us falls. Images crowd my mind, moments from a time before I was born. I see him as a boy, walking with a young man I recognize as Daniel. The two talk easily about the Ecosystem, Daniel telling my child-father about the corps he's building to promote the healers' way. I wonder how Daniel learned of the healers, how he picked up bits of their songs, their ceremonies. I receive no answer to that question, for a new image rises in my mind: my father as a teenager, training to become a Sensor while working secretly with Daniel to recruit others to the healers' cause. Our resemblance is even stronger in this younger Gabriel, or Abraham as he was known then: I see where I got my hard jaw, my high forehead. But it's not until the next image flashes into my mind that I see where I got my eyes.

From my mother. Sarah.

She's a teenager herself, two years younger than Abraham. They sit side by side in the Conservator's hut—not Nathan, but the man who preceded him, whose name I don't know. Nathan is one of her fellow apprentices, a muscular youth who sits sulky and silent on Abraham's other side. By contrast, my mother seems fidgety, her long legs twitching, her bare heels smacking the stone floor. It's not long before I see the reason for her impatience: she longs to be out in the field with the boy who will become my father. As apprentices, both of them dance around their feelings, neither of them willing to break the taboo. It's only when she becomes a Sensor, two years after his own investiture, that she makes the first move: out in the forest, beyond the eyes of the village, she tracks him, meets him, kisses him. It's then that he confesses his work with Daniel, and though it's another nine years before the girl-child named Ruth is born, it's at that moment that my mother sets herself on the course that will claim her life.

My eyes have filled with tears, but my inner vision remains sharp. I see my mother big with child, see Abraham touch her one last time before he flees the Sensorship's wrath and loses himself in the Ecosystem, only to find himself again in the City of the Queens. I watch him haunt the village over the three years that remain to her, watch him skirt its edges but never dare reveal himself to the woman who plays with her child on the pavilion of stone. When she dies, I see one thing I don't expect: he searches for her body in the tunnels of the urthwyrms, but, finding no trace, he swears a vow to uncover the secrets of these most powerful yet mysterious dwellers of the earth's deep places. I see him in the underground room of the Cathedral, brooding over the bodies of the monsters supplied to him by Queen Estella, burying his pain in the discovery that though they stole his beloved's life, they can restore it to others. His face grows lean and hard and weathered—he seldom smiles—but when, years later, he emerges from his den, he is selected as chief of the healer corps, a man who knows the Ecosystem better than anyone except the queen herself.

The vision falls dark as the barrier reasserts itself. I open my eyes to see my father's grave face, softened the slightest bit by his memories. I touch his cheek, and though no more images flow from him to me, I feel as if I know his life—and hers—as well as I ever will.

"She was seeking herbs for the village healers on the day she died," he says. "Medicine found deep in the forest, far from aid. I know that it was Nathan's bow that wounded her, but I cannot help thinking that her death was my doing. Had I never joined my life with hers, she might be here today. But then," he says, "you would not be."

I can't speak, so I simply nod, and when that's not enough, I lean forward to kiss my father's lined cheek. My lips come away moistened by his tears.

"You ask why you must learn the Ecosystem's history for yourself," he says. "I could tell you that history, as I could tell you your mother's, but would not the telling lack the power of the seeing? I was not alive in those days, so you cannot see the Ecosystem's rise through me. But you can see it through the eyes of those who *were* alive, and who recorded in these pages what they saw."

I look around me. I've never thought of books that way; I've been too focused on letters and sounds and words to realize that what these dusty relics contain are the *lives* of people who walked the earth long ago, people who wrote what they did in hopes that someone like me would survive to read their record. I can't bring them back, but maybe, I can use their words to save Leah's life, and Huldah's, and Rebecca's, and even mine.

"Do you understand, my child?" the man once named Abraham asks.

"Yes, Father," I say.

And I return to my reading.

AT THE END of two weeks, I read my first complete book. It's called Seeds of Change, by a woman named Jen. Its cover, brightly colored but creased and scarred, shows a girl kneeling in a grove of trees and cupping a miniature tree in her hands. The girl's skin is a darker shade of brown than mine. Her name, I learn, was Wangari. I think about this long-ago girl who planted seeds, and I remember what Daniel told me about the seed he kept with him, waiting for a time he could plant it and watch it grow.

Angelica tucks long hair behind an ear and leans over me as I read the book word for word. She doesn't correct me a single time, though I have to sound out dozens of words that refer to places and things I've never heard of. I'm a bit edgy, not knowing which face she'll show me today: the one that snorts at my mistakes, or the one that beams at my successes. When I look up at the end, she claps and smiles.

"Let's try more like that one," she says.

She hands me book after book, all of them with pictures as well as words on every page. There's one called Out of School and Into Nature, about a girl who spent most of her time in the forests and fields, the way I used to when I was a Sensor. There's one called The Tree Lady, about a woman who planted trees just as Wangari did, except this woman had pale skin and red hair like Angelica's. There's another simply called Rachel, and I'm drawn to that one because the cover shows a little girl looking at a bright orange-and-black butterfly, and though the girl's skin is pale as the skin of the Rachel I knew was not, I wonder if the two might have had anything other than their name in common. I struggle with this one—many of the words are long and unfamiliar—but when I'm done, Angelica treats me to the broad smile I've seen her bestow only on her girlfriend.

"I think you're ready for something a little more challenging," she says.

She brings me a book called Girls Who Looked Under Rocks, and though there are a few pictures sprinkled throughout its pages, there are hundreds of words each page. I look at my teacher, aghast, but she smiles encouragingly.

"Just read the chapter about Rachel," she says. "I'll be here to help."

I read. I learn more about Rachel, whose other name, I knew from the first book, was Carson. I read about the book she wrote called Silent Spring, which I can only assume has to do with the predators that spring so silently at us from their hiding places in the trees. I remind myself that her book was written a long time ago, when there weren't any predators like that. Angelica stands ready to help me sound out words I don't know, and there are so many of them, I can't get through it without her assistance. When I'm finished, she suggests I read it again, all by myself. I do, and it not only goes faster but makes much more sense this time. By the end, though, I'm exhausted, dry-mouthed and bleary-eyed, and Angelica tells me I've done enough for one day.

"You're the fastest learner I've ever seen," she says. "We'll pick up where we left off first thing tomorrow."

That surprises me, as she's never worked consecutive days before. We put the books away and leave the library, and I'm surprised a second time to learn that evening has fallen. Angelica takes a deep breath and shakes out her hair, which is so long she sits on it when we're in the library.

"Freedom!" she says. "Reading is wonderful, but that place gets stifling after a while. I usually take books out to read at home."

"You can do that?"

"Of course," she says. "You don't think the students who used to go here spent all their time in the library, do you?"

We cross the stone courtyard to the Cathedral. Angelica can't get over how fast a learner I am.

"I keep wondering if it's because you're pureskin," she says. "You know, with a special aptitude for picking up information."

"Or maybe it's just because I'm smart."

She laughs, the sound echoing around the courtyard. Late walkers stop and smile at her; I get the feeling everyone knows Angelica's laugh. We climb the stairs together, and she walks me to my room. I'm hoping Leah will be there—I don't think she and Angelica have been formally introduced—but when I open the door, the room lies in darkness.

"She must be out with Huldah," I say. "They like to spend time at the pond."

"Don't we all," Angelica says, glancing around the room and smiling in a distracted way that makes me think she's meeting her girlfriend later tonight. "Is Huldah yours? I mean, did the two of you adopt her or something?"

I'm not sure what to make of the question. "She's… well, her parents died when our village was attacked. Leah took her in."

"And the three of you live together?"

My puzzlement deepens, but I try to answer. "Only here in the city. It's hard with so many…strangers. Hard to meet people, I mean."

"I see," she says. "So you and Leah…."

I wait for her to finish, but she leaves my friend's name hanging in the air. "Yes?"

"Nothing." She gives me another smile; her teeth, unlike mine and everyone else's from my village, are straight and white. "See you tomorrow. First thing."

"See you." I watch her walk down the hallway, red hair swinging. I wish I knew what she was talking about, but my brain feels stuffed from all the reading.

Leah returns with Huldah shortly thereafter, back from a walk. The little girl's eyes are red from crying, so I assume Leah took her out to settle her, not to socialize.

"I'm going to go crazy if I don't find something else to do around here," she confirms my hunch after she finally manages to sing Huldah to sleep. "Something with someone who doesn't throw an epic tantrum every time she hears the word *no*." She sighs. "What about you? Any exciting news?"

"I read a book," I say, and tell her about it while she braids my hair—to keep her fingers busy, she says. I don't say a thing about Angelica, though when I go to bed, I lie awake a long time, the words of the books I read mingling with my teacher's in my mind.

Angelica's waiting for me at the library the next morning—another surprise, since she's been late every other day except the first. Her hair is piled atop her head in an elaborate configuration I have no words for, and there's something more than usually sweet in the scent she leaves as she flits around the room. She keeps touching her hair, and finally, I get the idea that I'm supposed to say something about it.

"I like your hair," is the best I can come up with.

She smiles. "Yours is nice, too."

"I guess." Leah showed me the result of her labors in the mirror last night, and she did a decent job, considering what she had to work with. It's nothing like Angelica's, though. "Why no books?" I ask, nodding at the bare table.

She claps her hands. "I have a special present for you."

She darts to the shelves and pulls a book free. When she approaches the table, she moves slowly, holding the book in both palms and placing it in front of me with exaggerated care. I take the book in my hands. Its faded green cover is nibbled at the corners by time, with gold capital letters imprinted on the green: SILENT SPRING. I look at Angelica, who smiles.

"She lived close to where we are right now," she says. "In a town called Springdale."

"Is that why she wrote about things that spring?"

She laughs. "She went to college near here, too. A college only for girls. But that one didn't make it through the Ecosystem. This is a first edition that somebody salvaged from their collection."

"Oh."

She sits, and a wave of sweetness washes over me. "Take as much time as you need. I'll be right here if you have any questions."

I open to the book's first page. There's the title again, with Rachel's name and a black-and-white drawing of a nest with four eggs. The pages feel extra thick as they move beneath my fingers, and they carry a musty smell missing from the other books. The first page has its own title, A Fable for Tomorrow, and there's a drawing of what the world must have looked like in Rachel's time: level fields sprinkled with small square houses, sparse clumps of trees, a branch with flowers in the foreground. I look at Angelica. "What's a fable?"

"A make-believe story," she says. "One that teaches a lesson."

"So this book isn't true like the others?"

"It's true," she says. "It's hard to explain. Just read and we can talk later."

I lower my eyes to the page. There are so many words, I'm momentarily flabbergasted, forgetful of where I'm supposed to start. Then I find my place and read:

"There was once a town in the heart of America where all life seemed to live in harmony with its surroundings. The town lay in the midst of a checkerboard of prosperous farms, with fields of grain and hillsides of orchards where, in spring, white clouds of bloom drifted above the green fields...."

I settle into the rhythm of reading, and though some of the words are new to me, I don't ask Angelica for help. I read about the wonders of this town in the heart of America, though I don't know what or where America is. I think it must be something like the City of the Queens. Then I read about a deadly sickness that crept over the land, and I think of the black vines and Daniel's story of *edinnu*. I read of the shadow of death that settled on the forests, the fields, the hills. I learn that the birds stopped singing, and the plants died, and the animals, too. The final sentences make me stare as if in recognition, though they don't entirely make sense to me: "No witchcraft, no enemy action had silenced the rebirth of new life in this stricken world. The people had done it themselves."

I stop and lift my eyes to Angelica's, which are a shade of green far more striking than the book's faded cover. "Rachel's not talking about the Ecosystem, is she?" I ask.

She shakes her head. "She died almost a hundred years before its rise. But I think she saw some of the signs."

"And she tried to stop them," I say. "That's why she wrote this book."

"I think so."

"But she failed," I say. "The book didn't stop people from"—my eyes flick down to the page—"doing it themselves."

"That's not what books are for," Angelica says. "Books like this try to warn people, but people usually choose not to listen."

I close the book. My fingers tremble. It occurs to

me that's another reason Rachel might have called her book Silent Spring: because though letters make words that make sounds, the sounds are silent unless somebody hears them. "What was it like growing up in the city?" I ask Angelica.

She looks taken aback by the question, but I'm no less so by her answer. "Hard. There was food scarcity off and on, depending on the Ecosystem's mood." She makes a face. "And if I never see another chamber-pot, it'll be too soon."

I consider telling her about the joys of pit latrines, but decide against it. As it turns out, she doesn't need my input to continue the conversation.

"The hardest part was the training," she says. "I was identified for the healing profession pretty young, and Gabriel's a really tough teacher. There wasn't much time for, you know, normal stuff."

I've no idea what normal stuff is, so I'm as silent as the spring.

"But when I turned sixteen and passed my practical exams, he eased up on me," she says. "More freedom, you know? Which was all I really wanted in the first place."

"But didn't you," I say, and fumble my words, "didn't you want to help people? Isn't that why my father...why Gabriel wants me to learn to read?"

She cocks her head and looks at me for a long time. Then she smiles, and though I'm still waiting for an answer, Angelica's smile is so infectious I can't help smiling back.

"Keep reading," she says. "You're probably at the point where you could read inside your head, but I like listening to the sound of your voice."

I nod and plunge back in. Reading inside my head seems too much like staying silent.

Hours pass. Yes, hours: I've figured out enough about clocks to follow the progress of the one on the wall. I read about many things that are brand new to me: the obligation to endure and the right to know and the elixirs of death. I get completely lost at that point, because even though there are illustrations, the concepts make no sense to me. I'm beginning to wonder again why my father wants me to learn to read—this book isn't about Rachel's life after all, much less about the Ecosystem; it's about hidden things that happened even though she warned about them—but I keep going until I'm not really reading anymore, just making sounds, as foreign and nonsensical as the voices of the Ecosystem have become to me.

Angelica listens quietly the whole time.

When I can't take any more, I close the book and look up at her, expecting I don't know what: another smile, praise, correction of the many hundreds of words I'm sure I've said wrong. Maybe an answer to the question she never answered. Instead, she does something that totally throws me.

She leans across the table and kisses me.

I stiffen at her touch. It's not that her kiss is unpleasant—in fact, of the two kisses I've had, I'd say hers is the better, her lips softer than Isaac's, her breath fresher, her technique making me realize he was almost as much of a novice as I am. I catch images from her life, the succession of girls she's kissed, including her latest girlfriend. One image refuses to take solid shape in my mind; it's a bright blur, as if Angelica is blocking me, though less expertly than my father did. I'm glad when, a few ticks of the clock later, she pulls away, our lips coming unstuck with a soft smacking sound.

"Um," I say.

"I'm sorry," she says. "I didn't mean to shock you, or anything."

"It's not that," I say. "It's just I thought you were courting—"

"Lavinia? We broke up two days ago. That was only a fling, anyway."

I don't know what a fling is, but I suspect Angelica's covering something up; when her lips touched mine, I felt sadness in her, and I wonder if the decision to end their courtship was Lavinia's, not hers. But I don't have the words to ask her that.

"I figured you and Leah weren't exclusive," she rushes on, cheeks coloring. "I mean, you told me last night you were looking to meet new people."

"I...." At last I realize what she's talking about, and I'm flooded with embarrassment. "Leah and I aren't... I mean, I'm not...."

Angelica reddens even more furiously. "I'm so sorry," she says. "I just assumed...."

She jumps to her feet and circles the table to where the door is. She's about to open it when she turns back to me.

"Your father didn't ask me to teach you to read," she says. "Michael's the teacher around here. I volunteered. Not because I was interested in you. Okay, I'll admit that was part of it." She smiles awkwardly, unable to meet my eye.

"Then why?" I ask.

"Because I've heard the way he talks about you," she says. "And I thought, if it couldn't be me, at least I could help. At least I could be part of it."

She raises her eyes, and for the first time since I've known her, the sadness shows in their sparkling depths.

"Read as much as you can," she says. "It gets pretty technical, so if you have any questions, you know where to find me."

Then she exits, her sweet scent lingering in the air.

I RETURN THE next day worried that Angelica will be waiting for me, but the room's empty. In place of her is a stack of books, all of them thick like Silent Spring. Warily, I step closer to the pile and read the note lying on top:

Just the pages I've marked. Come find me if any questions. I'm sorry again. Love, A.

I sit, heart pounding. I didn't read anything yesterday after Angelica's kiss; I tried, but my thoughts were in too much turmoil. I didn't sleep, either. I tossed and turned all night, wishing I could talk to Leah, feeling for some reason that I couldn't. When I left for the library this morning, I had a speech prepared, one that I hoped wouldn't hurt Angelica's feelings or add to her embarrassment. Now, I sound out the lines to the empty room, the words no more than shapes on my lips.

I like you, Angelica. I really do. As a teacher, and a friend. But I've only kissed one other person in my entire life. I didn't know about girls kissing girls until I met Leah. And even though the boy I loved is gone, I can't think of giving my heart to another. I don't know if I'll ever be ready for that....

That's as far as I get before I start to feel as if I'm reading from a book, and I close my mouth and turn to the actual books Angelica has selected.

The one on top is huge, but fortunately, she's marked only a few pages for me to read. It's called On the Origin of Species, by a man named Charles. Or Darwin; I'm still unsure what to make of people with two names. There's a picture inside of a man with a huge white beard like Gideon's and strange black clothing like nothing I've ever seen, which must have been what people wore when Charles was alive. From the look of things, that was a very long time ago: his book is the oldest I've read, its cover crumbling and its pages smelling of poisonous mushrooms. The part Angelica wants me to read has to do with how creatures come into being through a process Charles calls *natural selection*. He's talking about the creatures of his own day, but I assume it's the same now. If so, that would explain where things like poison arrow frogs come from, though it wouldn't explain how they've appeared so quickly. From what Charles says, the process is very slow, taking thousands and thousands of years.

Angelica has anticipated my question, because the next book in the stack, by a man named Stephen, tells me that sometimes creatures come into existence in relatively short spans of time. Still, by *relatively short*, Stephen is talking about centuries, not days.

I turn my attention to the next two books, which Angelica has marked: *Read together!!!* They're by a woman named Elizabeth and a person named Bill, who could be either a man or a woman judging from the unfamiliar name. The marked sections are about a period of time called the *Anthropocene*, which I'm sure I'm mispronouncing but which seems to have been just before the rise of the Ecosystem. What Elizabeth and Bill tell me is that human beings became so powerful during the Anthropocene that instead of creatures coming into existence, most of them began to disappear. The title of Elizabeth's book gives me a name for this: *extinction*. She and Bill tell me that there have been five periods of mass extinction throughout earth's history, including the one that killed the upright reptiles pictured in that first room I visited with my father. But in the Anthropocene, they say, a sixth extinction happened, killing almost every animal and many of the plants that were alive at the time—not the horned beast from the tapestry, which was only a fable to begin with, but birds and fish and insects and mammals like the tawny pandalion that was called, simply, a lion. If things kept disappearing at that rate, Elizabeth and Bill predicted, pretty soon there would be nothing but people left on the entire planet.

I rise to stretch my legs and to work the creepy feeling from my chest. My head is spinning from all the new ideas, including the idea that life on earth is not thousands but billions of years old. Though I've always known about the period of human dominance that came before the Ecosystem—the Conservator talked about it all the time—reading it from the point of view of people who lived through it is different. It's like standing beside them as they watch things die, wanting to warn them what's coming but knowing they can't hear my words. Like reading inside my head—which, it dawns on me, I've been doing most of the day. I definitely liked it better when Angelica was there to hear me. But thinking about her makes me lose focus, so I force her out of my mind and reach for the final book in the stack.

It's different from the rest, much stiffer but not as thick. There's no title or author's name on the outside, or anywhere else; when I open the hard black cover, I find sheets of paper held in place by rings made of what my father said is called *metal*. Most peculiar of all, where the other books were printed in neat letters that Angelica told me were produced by machines—another concept I'm not sure I grasp—the writing in this book is faint and sloppy and hard to read. Remembering Michael's flip cards, I realize that someone wrote this book in ink, which must have faded over time. I bring my nose close to the first page and, in the flickering light of the room's torches, I read.

> *mutagenic process advancing at exponential rate —*
> *attempts at control ineffective*
> *in light of worldwide infrastructure/systems failure,*
> *electronic data storage unfeasible*
> *attempting to preserve record for survivors — should*
> *there be any — by compiling to best of ability all*
> *known data on A. impunita infestation*
> *no doubt much lost already as sites go dark*
> *safe locations identified include the following research*
> *facilities, government depositories, and private*
> *storage vaults…*

After that, there's a long list of names, filling page after page. I know they're names because they start with capital letters, but none of them is the slightest bit familiar to me.

I take a deep breath and let the handwritten letters blur beneath my eyes. This, I realize, is what I've been building toward all along. Learning letters and sounds, reading books written for children, graduating to harder books under Angelica's eye—all of that was meant to prepare me for this nameless book, a book unlike any other because, where the ones that came before helped me to understand the Ecosystem, none of their authors foresaw its rise. But *this* book—whoever wrote it didn't need to imagine the coming of the Ecosystem.

They lived through it.

I flip past the list. The pages that follow are covered from top to bottom with scribbled sentences lacking capital letters and punctuation, full of words I think are new to me until I realize I'm misreading the messy letters. Still, plenty of words *are* new, and that makes the reading painfully slow. But gradually, as I turn page after page, I realize what this book is talking about.

It's a strange thing, the last thing I would have expected in a book detailing the dawn of the Ecosystem. It's the story of one creature that went extinct during the Anthropocene, a creature that had existed for a hundred million years beforehand. A small creature, but one that was so important to the world, the people of that time grew very worried when they realized it was dying out and wouldn't last much longer.

It was a creature with the same name as one of the first letters I learned. A creature called a *bee*.

THERE ARE NO bees in the Ecosystem. There are monsters I learned to call vampire bees, night-flying terrors that feed their young a sweet, sticky substance spun of the blood of their victims. There are winged insects, including horrornets, whose stingers can pierce bone. But of true bees there are none.

According to this book, there used to be many. The pictures clipped to some of the pages—*photographs*, Angelica told me they're called, but they're another mystery I don't have time to investigate—show me what the bees used to look like. There were honeybees, carpenter bees, sweat bees, dung bees, and my favorite, the little fuzzy black and gold balls called bumble bees. They existed everywhere on earth, in numbers too great to count. And then, mysteriously, they began to die off.

People had many theories why. They blamed everything from pesticides—poisons they put on their fields—to tiny spider-like things called mites, which some people believed got into the beehives and killed the young. Taken together, people gave the bees' disappearance a name: *colony collapse disorder*. And they fretted about it, because bees were pollinators, and without them, lots of plants had trouble growing.

Much as I hate to do so, I have to take a break at this point to read about pollination. In the Ecosystem, plants reproduce by touch, by projecting seeds through the air, by parasitic infection. But in days past, I learn from a picture book my teacher has helpfully left behind, many plants relied on pollinators, creatures that carried seeds from one plant to another. It all sounds strange to me, how plants needed animals to spread their seeds: bees, butterflies, fast-flying birds called hummingbirds, which look like huntingbirds except without the long, dangerous beaks. But apparently, that's the way it was.

When bees died, plants died. When plants died, food dwindled. The people of that time tried other methods to pollinate the plants they ate, but nothing worked. When they realized that the bees were close to extinction, so close that bee-hunters could roam an entire prairie without hearing the buzz from a single hive, they decided that if they couldn't save the bees, they would have to do the next best thing. They would have to make their own.

I get thoroughly lost at this point in the story. So many of the words, from *genome* to *adaptive variability*, make no sense to me, and the handwritten book doesn't explain what they mean. I have to search for other books, something that, thankfully, Angelica has left instructions on how to do. Following her hand-drawn map, I discover that our reading room holds only the smallest fraction of the library's collection; the entire building, three levels high, is crammed from floor to rafters with books. I roam through this maze of reading material, using the map to determine which books are in which areas, but always having to read the first few pages of many books before I find the best one. I'm frustrated more than once when a book I want is too swollen from water or rotted with mold to read. It's a solid week before I have a firm enough grasp on the subject to return to the handwritten book—a week I barely see my room, and then only to flop down exhausted yet unable to sleep, my mind in a whirl. I speak not a single word to Leah in all that time, leaving the room long before she wakes and returning long after she falls asleep. No matter how much I read, I'm desperately aware that every day I take to educate myself on the Ecosystem's origins is another day for the current Ecosystem to slip farther beyond my grasp.

But I do learn. About a man named Gregor, or possibly Mendel, who studied pea plants. About other people—*scientists*, they called themselves—who gave the name *genes* to the things Gregor hadn't been able to see. I already knew about invisible things in the Ecosystem, things that break down dead matter and make you sick from consuming spoiled food or water. I'd never have guessed that, inside these things as inside all things, there are even tinier things that shape our bodies. Genes are what gave my grandfather his brown skin, my grandmother her blue eyes. When you mix them, you get results like my mother and me: brown skin a shade paler than the norm, brown eyes with specks of blue.

When the scientists, using tools so complex I don't waste time learning about them, mixed genes, they got bees. New bees. Better bees. They had a name for their creation: *Apis impunita*, the invincible bee. These were the bees they released to re-pollinate the world.

Because by that time, even if they'd been able to bring back the extinct bees, those bees wouldn't have been good enough. Too many plants had died. *Apis impunita* had to be fast, and strong, and cunning. It had to spread quickly, avoid predators, target some plants while ignoring others. To make it that way, the scientists had to mix in genes from other animals: faster-flying insects like dragonflies and moths, sneaky creatures like rodents. To make the bees *want* to spread as fast and far as possible, they had to mix in genes from naturally aggressive creatures: snakes, pigs called warthogs that were slightly smaller and less heavily spiked than our warhogs, sharks, chimpanzees.

And people.

Reading this part makes my head throb. I imagine bees with human faces, bees wielding knives and spears. I learn quickly that such thoughts are crazy; according to the photographs, the new bees looked more or less like the old, if a little bigger and better armored. But I can't help thinking of these invincible bees, designed to spread far beyond the range any normal bee would dream of, as my ancestors: Aaron and Malachi and the other members of the Brotherhood, people who colonized new territory and built a new home for their queen. A home they were prepared to fight, and even kill, to defend.

And, in a way, that's exactly what these bees did.

It's a good thing there are no bees left. If there were, one would surely fly into Leah's wide open mouth.

"So these beads…" she says.

"Bees."

"These bees spread all over the world? Why would they do that?"

"Because that's how they were made," I say. I'm bristling with nervous energy, anxious to tell someone what I've discovered. I rushed off in search of my father as soon as I finished the handwritten book, but he wasn't in his chambers or laboratory. Leah was my next best substitute for the news I bear, but Leah hasn't spent fourteen hours a day for the past three weeks reading. "The scientists figured the bees would stop once they reached certain limits. But the bees weren't smart enough to know what the limits were. Or maybe," I reconsider, "they were *too* smart."

Huldah, sleeping in the cot beside the bed, chooses that moment to fuss. I have to wait while Leah rises to check on her, but it's nothing; a moment's rubbing of her back makes her settle, and my friend returns to her chair by the window, where the uniformly gray sky mirrors the clouds that have been forming in my mind all day.

"You were talking about the…sign tests?" she says.

"Scientists," I correct her. "The people who made the bees. Once the bees were let out, they spread everywhere.

Now that I think of it, it's possible they realized they'd be harder to stop the farther they went."

"But," Leah says, "then why are there no bees left? You did say there are no bees left?"

"Because they mutated," I say. "Changed, along with everything they came into contact with. The other thing the scientists didn't realize is that these bees didn't just spread seeds from one plant to the next. They spread their *own* seeds, their own genes. They fertilized plants with bee-genes, and the plants changed as a result."

Leah shakes her head. "You lost me again."

I stew for a minute, trying to remember how all of this started to make sense to me. "Think about the two of us," I say. "Your skin's darker than mine. Why?"

"Because…" she says doubtfully.

"Because of my grandmother," I say. "The genes for her pale skin mixed with the genes for Aaron's brown skin to produce medium-brown skin. It's why children look like their parents: they get their parents' genes."

"I know *that*."

"Well, it's the same with the bees," I say. "They gave plants their genes, which made the plants more…more bee-like. So the plants—"

"Could fly?" she ventures.

"No," I say. "At least, not all of them, and not all at once. The most important thing the bees gave to other creatures are what scientists call *hive-genes*. Genes that made them part of the bees' hive, their family. You know how wasps live in hives, and all of the wasps act together to defend the hive and collect food for the young?"

"I guess."

"That's because they're what scientists call *eusocial insects*," I say. "Most insects just do their own thing and go their own way, right? They only come together to mate. But eusocial insects develop a lifelong connection to each other, a *hive-consciousness*. It's like," and I cast about for something it's like, "it's like how friends can guess what the other is thinking or feel what the other is feeling. Except in the case of a true hive-consciousness, it's thousands and thousands of insects all thinking and feeling the same thing at the same time, and working together in the best interests of the hive."

"I get it," she says. "But what's that got to do with the Ecosystem?"

"That *is* the Ecosystem, Leah," I say. "Once the hive-genes spread far enough, the entire planet became effectively a single mind, a single consciousness. Every organism on earth linked together, thinking as one, ready to defend the hive. And while this was going on, mutations as a result of the unstable hive-genes were producing all kinds of creatures that had never existed before, and these new species were coming into being in an incredibly short period of time, years or even days instead of the millennia it usually takes."

I say all of this in a rush, and I look to Leah for confirmation that she's understood. But it's obvious she hasn't; she's smiling for my sake, but she's as lost as I was that first day in the library. More lost; all I had to do was learn my ABCs.

"We got them, too," I say.

"Beg pardon?"

"The hive-genes," I say. "They entered into people,

and changed us like everything else. In a way, they saved us, because without them, we wouldn't have developed the Sense."

Leah's face lights. "So Sensors are…."

"People with an extra strong connection to the hive," I confirm. "They can read the mind of the Ecosystem because they're *part* of that mind. All people are, actually. Not just Sensors."

"But then," she says, "why doesn't everybody have the Sense?"

"It's possible everybody does," I say. "Or at least, a degree of it. Remember I told you our first day in the forest that villagers can develop the Sense? There's not much consensus about this, because the scientists studying the Ecosystem died before their research got far. But some of them theorized—believed—that to express a true link to the hive-mind, a person would need a certain concentration of hive-genes. Below whatever the threshold is, you'd be connected to the hive, but you wouldn't be aware of the connection or able to do anything with it. Prolonged exposure to the Ecosystem, though, seems to activate latent genes, giving common people partial access to the mind of the hive."

Leah works this over for a while. "So we're insects?"

"Kind of." I remember the time I told Miriam and Isaac that we were bugs to the Ecosystem. I was trying to scare them. "I'll be honest, though. I still don't know why my dad wanted me to read all this stuff. It's obvious that what's happening now is similar to what happened when the Ecosystem first rose. But knowing *that* it's happening doesn't help me to understand *why*. And it's not like I have all the time in the world to figure it out."

"I certainly hope you're not asking me," she says, smiling. "My mind's as common as they come."

She holds the smile, and her eyes dance as always, but I catch the tone. For what must be the hundredth time, I wish I were as connected to my fellow beings as I am—as I was—to the hive. "I could teach you to read," I say. "If you're interested."

"Not much point in that," she says. "Unless your father needs an expert on hemlines."

"It's not just him," I say. "If you knew how to read, you and I could...could talk about these things, and maybe you could help me...."

She dismisses the idea with a toss of her head. "I've had my fill of people patronizing me since we came to this place," she says. "I don't need my best friend to start, too."

"I'm not patronizing you," I say. "And I thought you were meeting other people. At the pond, or...."

"The places where girls like me go?" she says. "I discovered pretty quickly that no one wants my sob story to interfere with their oh-so-perfect lives."

"Why didn't you tell me?" I ask. "I could have—"

"Could have what?" she says. "Kissed my boo-boo to make it all better?" She shakes her head. "I did try to tell you, Sarah. But you were too busy with your books and your bees to listen. Or to see what was right in front of your face."

The silence that follows is thunderous. I try to remember anything Leah said or did in the past three weeks to let me know what she's been going through, but she's right:

I've paid attention to nothing but my own thoughts in all that time. I'm grateful when the silence is interrupted by a knock at our bedroom door.

I'm less grateful when the head that appears through the crack sports long locks of bright red hair. "Am I disturbing anything?" Angelica asks.

"We were just talking," Leah jumps in before I can answer. "Sarah was telling me about all the fascinating things she's read."

She smiles, but Angelica either doesn't notice or is too wise to take the bait. "Queen Celestina's called for an audience with you," she says to me.

"A what?"

"She wants to meet you," Angelica translates the queen-talk. "She needs you in her council chamber right away."

I look to Leah, but she shoos me with the back of her hand. "Go. Give my regards to the queen. I'll be here with Huldah."

Angelica ducks out ahead of me. I glance into the room before I exit, but Leah's seated beside the sleeping child's cot with her back turned. My own statement of a minute ago comes back to sting me: *friends can guess what the other is thinking or feel what the other is feeling.* What's it been like for Leah, cooped up with a not-quite-two-year-old in a city of strangers while my mind traversed the world?

"I'll be back soon," I say, but she doesn't respond. I don't blame her. My words sound false even to me.

ANGELICA'S HALFWAY DOWN the corridor by the time I leave the room. I run to catch up with her long strides. "What's going on?"

"One of the scouting teams returned with a member of your village," she says. "At least, we think it is."

My heart leaps. "Was it a boy with—"

"It's an old man," she cuts me off. "Long hair, big white beard. I didn't get a good look at him."

Gideon. "Is he hurt?"

"Your father's checking him," she answers. "Celestina insisted on having you there when he's finished."

We match strides down the stairs and across the courtyard—or, to be precise, I take an extra stride for every three of hers. The building we're headed for isn't one I've visited; it stands alone some distance from the rest, a structure I would have called enormous if I hadn't seen the Cathedral first. This new building's stone sides are carved into fancy pillars and arches; a tower rises to a sharp point from its roof. My father told me that there's a bell inside the tower, and on celebration days, when the queen presides over ceremonies to commemorate Dominica's triumph, she has the bell rung. I wish I could hear it, but my companion's hurried strides and knitted brow make it clear this is no day for celebrating.

We reach the short flight of stairs before the building's

front entrance, arched double doors with metal fashion-
ings that curl like vines across their surface. Angelica holds
a hand out to stop me from climbing the stairs, not that I
was about to without her say-so.

"First: I wanted to say I'm sorry again," she says. "You
don't know how crummy I feel about...misreading you."

"Angelica, I—"

She waves me off. "Second, maybe I'm not supposed
to tell you this, but Celestina is a very young queen. She
was rushed into service when her mother died, and some
of the healers believe she wasn't fully prepared for the job.
She's undeniably powerful, but also prickly. Don't cross
her, Sarah. She won't like that."

"I wouldn't dream of it," I say.

"You don't have to dream of it," she answers. "Your
lineage is bad enough. If she suspects that Gabriel brought
you here to take her place, things could get ugly."

I'm shocked by her words. "*Is* that why he brought
me here?"

"He hasn't said," she mutters. "But if I were the bet-
ting type...."

"Why didn't he tell me any of this?"

She regards me narrowly. "You don't know Gabriel
like I do. He would never directly challenge the order of
the queens. In fact, if you weren't of queenly blood, he
wouldn't be asking for your help, daughter or no daughter."

Her face is flushed, almost the color of her hair. I
can tell she's actually scared, and the thought of Angelica
scared scares me. "I thought *my* village was bad," I say.

"It's not your village," she says. "And it's not the city,

either. It's people. You read about *Apis impunita*. Where do you think they got all that hostility and suspicion from?"

I take a deep breath, the way I used to when I needed to calm myself in the Ecosystem. I remind myself that I'm not here to serve the queen, and I'm certainly not here to *be* the queen. If I have to hold my tongue to stay on her good side, I think I can manage that.

Angelica studies my face, nods. "Make sure you don't stare. And remember to call her *Your Majesty*. And curtsy."

"And what?"

"Just follow my lead," she sighs before pulling open the doors.

We enter a dark hallway poorly lit by candles in tall metal stands. The floor has a soft feel, almost like grass, but when I look down, I see that it's a faded material the color of blood. Ahead of us, rows of wooden benches bathe in the muted light of multicolored glass windows, the first of which depicts a woman with mournful gray eyes and skin the hue of an earthenware pot. She's reaching out toward other people who lie on beds or on the ground around her. I look questioningly at Angelica, who speaks in a whisper.

"Queen Dominica," she says. Her whisper is gathered up by the vaulted ceiling and sent back at us. "The first."

"You mean…?" I whisper back.

"Yes," she says. "The very first. They say she healed thousands in a single day, though personally, I think that's a bit of a stretch."

She grins, and I'm glad to catch a hint of the old, bold Angelica. She continues to narrate as we proceed between the benches under the eyes of other glass women.

"Those are the three sisters," she says, pointing to the

next window. Three young women stand side by side, all of them wearing long dresses and veils over their hair. The first has a complexion somewhat paler than her mother's, while the second and third are successively darker. "And over there is Leonida"—she gestures at another window depicting a woman in a white dress, with unnaturally pale skin surrounded by a glowing halo of yellow hair—"who, of course, was queen during the unrest with Delilah and the Sensors. She ruled for over sixty years, which means she was pretty much a crone by the time she was done. Though word has it she was quite the spitfire."

"The what?"

Angelica rolls her eyes. "Anyway. Delphina's line took over when your grandmother died. There's Estella"—she points to a window that's only partially finished, with some of the pieces missing so I can't make out the woman's face. "She ruled for twenty years, up until a month ago. Celestina took over then."

"Where's her window?"

As she's done before, Angelica gives me a look as if I'm purposely playing dumb. "The windows are unveiled on the first anniversary of the queen's death. So the rest of us can worship her for perpetuity."

I look away, thinking about how my grandmother—and mother—might have had their own windows if not for the history Angelica talks about so glibly.

This carefree Angelica vanishes once more when we reach the platform at the end of the corridor. She takes the two steps to the top in a jerky motion unlike her natural athleticism, and when I catch up with her, I see the strain in her face. Guards stand on either side of the double doors at the back of the platform, both of them in silver tunics unlike any garment I've seen in the city. They rotate smartly to open the doors, which are decorated with the same vine-like pattern from outside. Before we go in, Angelica catches my arm and leans close.

"Remember," she whispers. "No staring. Lots of *your majesty-ing*. And—"

"I know," I say. "Curtsy. Whatever that is."

She tries a smile, but it's more properly a grimace. Then she lets go of my arm and pushes me into the room ahead of her.

It's not the slightest bit dark. Dozens of torches line the walls in the metal holders I've learned to call *sconces*; hundreds of candles, many of them grouped together at the top of tall silver candle-holders, dazzle me with brilliant pinpricks of light. All the illumination shows me a chamber easily five times as big as my bedroom, with a high ceiling in which the sweet candle-smoke gathers. There's a chair at the far end, though to call it a chair is like calling an urthwyrm a worm: this chair is double the size of any I've seen, raised above floor level and wrought, so it seems, of the same metal as the candle-holders. The woman who occupies it shines so brightly it's as if she's spun a cocoon of silver threads around her.

"Get moving," Angelica whispers, and I follow her as she approaches the throne.

Queen Celestina might be young, but I can't tell from looking at her. And despite my teacher's orders, I can't stop looking at her: she's without doubt the most beautiful woman, the most beautiful person—the most beautiful creature—I've ever seen, with skin so dark as to be almost black and silvery hair that falls over her shoulders in a profusion of thick braids. The silver color, I assume, isn't natural but the effect of some art, because it matches her flowing dress, her painted nails, her glittering eyelashes and silver-lidded eyes. Amidst all the ornamentation, it's a moment before I find her actual eyes, but when I do, I discover them to be a striking shade of gray as close to silver as can be, like the sheen of moonlight on water. I also discover that they're looking straight into mine, and I quickly drop my gaze to the blood-red floor covering.

"Your Majesty," Angelica says, and performs what must be a curtsy: a quick bobbing at the knees with one foot in front of the other. I do my best to imitate her, but I'm afraid I move with all the grace of a juvenile prowler monkey.

"This is Sarah?" the Queen says, and again, I'm having a hard time hearing youthfulness in her rich, throaty voice.

Angelica pokes me in the back, and I stumble forward, performing a second awkward curtsy, hoping it doesn't cancel the first. "Yes, Your Majesty."

"I welcome you to our city," she says. "I would have greeted you sooner, but I have been engaged in matters of great importance to our people."

"Yes, Your Majesty," I say again, and though this might be rude, I look around the room for my father. "I've been busy too. Learning to read."

She smiles, showing teeth as white as her skin is black. "Have you met with success?"

"Yes, Your Majesty." If I say this one more time, I might have to kill myself. "Angelica taught me."

I turn to my companion, but the attempted

compliment is met with a frown. Maybe I'm not supposed to bring her into this.

"Gabriel has achieved his purpose, then," Queen Celestina says, jerking my attention back to her. "He proposes to teach you the ways of the healers, after his fashion."

She rises from her throne, and the light rises with her. As she steps down, I see that her dress carries the same embellishment of sinuous vines as the outer and inner doors, though the way the fabric moves makes the vines curl as if alive. With all the brightness, it's a second before I realize that the vines end in blossoms, silver flowers sprinkled over her small frame. For she is small: when she stands before me, I see what the elevated throne disguised, and it's I who look down to meet her eyes. As soon as I realize I'm doing that, I drop my gaze further, staring at her small, bare, silver-nailed feet.

"Angelica, you may go," the Queen says, and I note out of the corner of my eye the deepening of Angelica's frown before she curtsies and leaves.

Alone with Celestina, the panic I thought I had under control edges upward. She's not trying to intimidate me, not that I can tell, but her outlandish beauty and gentle manners make me feel far beneath her in ways the screaming hissy fit I'd anticipated never could have done.

"Do not fear," she says, and I startle when I realize she's detected my nervousness—picked it up, I assume, through her skin. "Your father waits outside."

She's no sooner said that than the door Angelica exited swings open, and my grateful eyes fall on my father. He's followed by two additional figures, both in the silver costume of the queen's guard. He crosses to where I stand and places a hand on my arm, letting the defensive shield fall just long enough for me to feel his attempt to steady me. I turn my attention to the guards, who are dragging someone or something into the room. Their flashing uniforms momentarily blind me, but when they succeed in coaxing their burden closer, no warning of my father's could have prepared me for the sight.

It's Gideon.

OR IT WAS Gideon. Who—or what—it is now isn't entirely clear.

The old firestarter is naked to the waist, recognizable by his long white beard and hair, his single eye, his muscled arms. Yet every inch of his flesh—his chest, his throat, his cheeks—is obscured by a network of black threads that might be veins if not for their abnormal density and color. Peering more closely, I see that the threads lie not beneath his skin but upon it, as if he's been covered by the strands of a black web. Even his beard is braided with it, while the corners of his eye are encroached on by fine filaments. Reluctant though I am to come too close, I focus on his eye and find it glassy and immobile, more like the eye of a cicatrix's molted shell than that of a living man.

"Black vines," I murmur, forgetful that it's surely the Queen's place to make the first remark. The old firestarter doesn't respond to the sound of my voice, doesn't seem aware of anything around him; he stands, if he stands at all, only thanks to the guards who grip his arms, their hands protected by thick gloves.

Celestina addresses my father, her tone much sharper than when she was speaking to me. "You have attempted to heal this man?"

"Yes, My Queen," he answers. "But, as you see, my efforts have failed."

"And you have no notion of what this manifestation might be?"

Gideon staggers despite the guards' support. When they pull his body upright, he seems to have no will or strength of his own, but hangs between them like an animal hide cured over a fire.

"We have heard reports of emergent species," my father answers the Queen's question. "In this case, however—"

"I know of the black weed," Celestina cuts him off. "I have detected it in the Ecosystem. Can you assure me it is not contagious?"

My father lowers his eyes. "We have taken great care, My Queen," he says. "But I lack the wisdom to determine all potential risks. I have brought this man here, as you commanded, to undergo further analysis."

"Indeed," Celestina says. "And I have summoned another pureskin to perform it."

"Your Majesty—" my father objects, but a single glance from her lustrous eyes silences him.

Celestina turns to me. She's barely up to my shoulder, but for the first time since entering her council room, I understand why Angelica was scared of her.

"Come, child," she says, though it's likely we're the same age, or I a bit older. "Here your lessons in true healing begin."

She holds out a silver-nailed hand; gleaming bracelets clink at her wrist, their pattern similar to the vines that decorate her dress. I'm momentarily unsure what to do, until it occurs to me that she can't be inviting me to reach for her hand. So I take a step toward Gideon instead, or the new species that has become of him. As I do, I detect a putrid scent rising from his body, more pungent than the candle-smoke. At nearer inspection, I determine that the web-like strands don't merely rest on the surface of his skin but have worked their way into living tissue as if rooted there. I reach out toward his forehead, its wrinkles darkened by black threads, only to be interrupted.

"Do not touch him," the Queen commands. "A pure-skin has no need of touch."

I halt, then place a hand on either side of the old man's face, so close I can feel the black threads rippling faintly, in a motion independent of Gideon's breathing. For he is still breathing, though in shallow gasps unlike natural breath. With trembling fingers an inch from his cheeks, I close my eyes and try to search inside him for the source of this awful plague.

Images form slowly in my mind. I see the old fire-starter alone in the forest, walking erratically as if under the influence of some intoxicating plant. I see him fall, feel his pain as something lances his side. Then it's as if a shadow passes over my inner vision, and by the time it's gone, the infestation has taken hold. I feel it everywhere on his body, know that it's spreading even as we stand here, but can neither name it nor determine how to uproot it. The man beneath the alien coating has receded from me; his mind is hidden, his very self lost behind a veil of dark-ness. I could attempt to penetrate it, sink my fingers into it and tear it down, but a warning tingle tells me that if I do so, Gideon will die. In my mind, I call his name, but he fades from me, and when I reach for his hand, there's nothing to hold on to.

"Sarah!" my father's voice breaks through my trance,

and I open my eyes to find that my hands are a mere hair's breadth from Gideon's cheeks. For a moment, it seems as if the black threads are straining toward my fingers, but when I pull away, they lapse into a random waving, like the antennae of thousands of ants.

The Queen watches me beneath half-closed lids. I feel a mixture of exposure and mortification, as if she knew all along that I would fail.

"I've...I've heard of this before," I say. "One of our Sensors detected it on the way to the city."

My father glances at me, and I feel a fresh wave of shame that I never told him.

"Can you heal it?" the Queen asks.

I bow my head, and wonder why I feel so humbled in her presence. "I'm sorry, Your Majesty. I can't."

The Queen smiles, her eyes closing fully. I feel a sudden warmth in the air around me, though when I catch my father's eye, he seems not to have noticed. Gideon goes rigid, his arms clamped to his sides; the guards struggle to hold him upright, but he falls, landing heavily on the blood-red floor. With the black threads covering him, he looks like an oversize insect caught in some monstrous arachnard's web.

Celestina opens her eyes. "I have assessed this man's sickness, and judge him a threat to our city," she says. "Place him in isolation, Gabriel, and set a guard over his chamber. Let no other come into contact with him until I command."

"Yes, My Queen," he says, bowing.

"Your daughter will remain with me," Celestina

continues. "There is power within her, but she has no skill in its use. I will train her myself, as one pureskin to another."

My father's face darkens. "With all due courtesy, My Queen, I have prepared her course of study in the manner of the healers. She has learned to read, as you know…."

The Queen's brow arches.

"And with that knowledge, she is gaining an understanding of the Ecosystem's rise that may help her to grasp the present disquiet—"

"That *may* help her," the Queen repeats, "or that *will*?"

For the second time, the confident man who is my father seems as abashed as I feel in this small girl's presence. "No one can tell the future, My Queen. And yet my daughter's training has prepared her—"

"For the lessons only a queen can bestow," Celestina interrupts him once more. "If she is truly ready, then what profit can there be in delay?"

"My Queen—"

"Go now," she says, dismissing him with a shake of her silver hair. The guards stoop to lift Gideon, but after a moment's struggle, they decide to drag him from the room instead. I can't say for sure, but it seems as if the threads that bind him seek to gain a grip on the floor-covering as the guards wrestle him from the council chamber. When the door bangs shut behind them, my father lingers a second longer, looking as if he would speak. Then, performing a bow far more elaborate than Angelica's curtsy, he follows the guards from the room.

I'm left alone with Celestina. She dazzles me with a smile, then slips a slim arm through mine. My skin burns at her touch, while the heady smell I'd taken to be candle-smoke wraps me in a dizzying mantle.

"You have only begun, child," she says. "I will show you things of which you never dreamed."

BOOK THREE
HARM

It may be difficult, but we ought to admire the savage instinctive hatred of the queen-bee, which urges her to destroy the young queens, her daughters, as soon as they are born, or to perish herself in the combat; for undoubtedly this is for the good of the community; and maternal love or maternal hatred, though the latter fortunately is most rare, is all the same to the inexorable principle of natural selection.

—Charles Darwin, *On the Origin of Species* (1859)

I AM TRANSFORMED.

The Queen leaves me in the hands of three women in silver dresses, their hair covered by silver veils, who escort me to an adjacent building. Stairs to a lower level open onto a room whose floor, ceiling, and walls are covered in mirrored tiles; at the center lies a circular pool where, the women indicate with nods of their heads, I'm to bathe.

My cheeks warm when I realize they don't plan to give me privacy, but their gazes are insistent, so I slip from my tunic and, clutching my mother's token in my fist, step as quickly as possible into the pool. Thankfully, it's deep enough for me to immerse myself to the chin. The water's pleasantly warm and scented with some aromatic herb, pleasing to the smell and relaxing to my tightly wound muscles. The art of bathing is new to me; in my village, water was so precious that occasional rinses with a wetted rag were all we could afford. I splash ineptly in the depths, using the soft pad the women give me to wipe myself down. If not for their staring eyes, it would be quite invigorating.

After a time, they signal for me to step from the pool, which I do, though with one arm concealing my chest and the other athwart my hips. They clothe me in a silver robe as soft as the bed in which I first awoke, then lead me to an antechamber where I'm laid on a table draped with a clean white spread. At this point, they remove the robe and gently force my arms to my sides until I give up on modesty and simply close my eyes while they work. The women rub my warmed flesh with fragrant oil and sprinkle a sweet-smelling powder over top of that. One of them undoes Leah's handiwork; a brush glides through my wet locks, then fingers fashion tight rows. I lose track of time while the women silently labor, the only sound being the lap of water from the room next door. At last, their hands encourage me to sit, and I open my eyes to see one of the women holding a long silver dress. With some difficulty, I pull it on, lacing the strings across my stomach and tucking the token into a convenient pouch I find over my breast.

When it's done, when they lead me to the body-length mirror that stands in a silver frame in a corner of the room, I'm astonished by the woman who appears there. Her face, neck, and hands glow from the oil, while the powder must have contained some silvery substance that sparkles in the lamplight. Her hair has been braided into parallel rows that alternate with sections of nearly bare scalp; silver beads weight the braids where they hang on the nape of her neck. Her eyelids and lashes have been silvered, a part of the procedure I have no memory of. She's nowhere near as beautiful as the Queen, and she moves clumsily in the unfamiliar dress, yet I can't take my eyes off of her. No matter how often I tell myself she's me, there's a part of me that refuses to believe it.

I find myself wishing Aaron could see me now. Or my mother. Or Isaac. Tears gather in my silver-tipped lashes, sparkling along with everything else.

After I've admired myself for an unseemly long time, the women lead me from the room and across the courtyard to yet another building in what I take to be the Queen's compound. This one is small, almost cottage-like in contrast to the towering Cathedral and the no less impressive council chamber. But it's a house built for a queen all the same, with bright chips of mica flashing from the stone walls and elaborate metal scrollwork curling across guarded front doors. Inside, clusters of candles point the way to a single door to which the women lead me before unceremoniously leaving me. I look at the last of their departing faces, and the woman lets me know with a quick scooting motion of her hands that I'm to enter.

I ease the door open, and instantly wish I hadn't. The room is nothing other than Celestina's private chamber, I know as soon as I see the massive bed that rests beneath a ceiling tiled in silver. The sheets are the same color as the tiles, and sparkling draperies on tall metal frames surround the bed. These have been pulled back and held in place by silver cords; the gray daylight falling from a window set high in the wall shows me the young queen in all her magnificence as she reclines on a silver bolster at the head of the bed.

She claps her hands and leaps from her spot when she sees me. She's dressed in a lightweight robe that reveals the outline of her girlish figure in a way her formal dress, fashioned to round her hips and boost her bosom, disguised. Her hair hangs loose on her shoulders, though for all its casual appearance, not a single strand looks tangled or out of place. I stand nearly a foot taller than her, yet in her presence I'm brought back to earth, reminded that no matter what her attendants have done to me, I'm nothing next to this vision of loveliness.

She places both hands on my shoulders to appraise me, but this time, I feel only her light touch, not the burning sensation of before. "You're a dream, my dear," she says in her surprisingly deep voice. "The very image of your mother."

"You knew my mother?" I ask, then add belatedly, "Your Majesty?"

She laughs, a light warble from that perfect mouth. "You may call me Celestina," she says. "You are of queenly lineage yourself, and if not for a quirk of fate, you might stand where I do now."

I'm not sure she sounds entirely happy about that.

"I have observed the life of your mother in a manner known only to the queens," she goes on. "I have seen her as a girl, and as a woman, too. You lie in between. And yet you have been given the opportunity to surpass her, to become what she might have been."

She slips her arm through mine and leads me to a side door made entirely of glass. We look out upon an extensive, manicured garden, with flowerbeds and walkways interspersed among sculpted hedges; though the sky remains overcast, the plots shimmer with bright greens and reds and patches of what appear to be glistening silver. At the far boundary of the grounds, a hedge at least twenty feet high stands as a bulwark against a solid line of towering trees.

"Your mother was seeking the City of the Queens when she died, you know," Celestina says. "Years ago, long before I became queen. She was traveling the Ecosystem in search of her birthright, yet what she met was her doom."

This account of my mother's final journey is a surprise to me, and I wonder why my father narrated such a different story. "I was told, Your Maj—" I begin, and try to make my lips form the name *Celestina*, but decide it's better to pronounce no name at all. "I was told that she was working for the healers of her village when she died."

The Queen smiles as if at an ignorant child. "And why would she have agreed to do the healers' bidding, if reclaiming the place of her birth played no part in her plans? How could she content herself to grub among the herbs of the forest when she knew that she might sit on a throne instead?"

"Sit on the throne?" I repeat. "But wasn't your mother queen then?"

"Indeed," she says. "And yet, there were some who wished it were otherwise, some who sought to restore Demetria's line. Among them was the man named Abraham."

"My father?" I ask in shock.

"Whom my mother, Estella, christened Gabriel," she affirms. "A new name for a new man. But he was never content to serve. He had higher aspirations, and he might have achieved them, had disaster not befallen the mother of his child."

I stare at the garden until the colors bleed, and I can no longer tell them from the backdrop of forest trees. "You mean," I say slowly, "that my father was trying to...to overthrow your mother?"

She pats my arm, gives me a regal, pitying look. "Surely you were not so easily misled by his tales as to believe—"

"I wasn't *misled*," I say, too nonplussed to avoid the incalculable rudeness of interrupting the girl who holds my arm. "If what you say is true…."

Celestina frowns, and much as she's been treating me like her confidante these past few minutes, I'm sure I've overstepped every courtesy there is. But her answer reveals no hint of the anger I feel at my father's deception. "Come, child," she says in a soft voice. "I will show you, so that you doubt no longer."

She does nothing that I can tell, but the air warms around me. Everything falls away: the Queen, the room, the garden. I stand in the midst of the desert where I encountered the urthwyrms' lair. The sky is graying to dusk, the black shapes of raveners dozing on the limbs of gash trees. Silence reigns; the grassharrowers have bedded down for the night. But something moves in the waste, something crawls forward on hands and knees. In the dimness, I can barely make it out—but I can tell that, whatever it is, it's not going to reach its destination.

The scene shifts, and I come face to face with the wounded thing. It's only then that I see it's my mother, dressed in her Sensor's outfit of close-fitting brown fur, her expression one of agony as she drags herself across the ground. How she crept this far after being struck by Nathan's arrow, how she wasn't killed by forest or swamp in the days it must have taken her to reach the desert, I don't know. She lifts her face to the moonless night, and I see the trails of dried tears on her haggard cheeks, hear her voice as it croaks out a few final words.

"I'm sorry, my love," she says. "I tried to—"

Then a monstrous shape explodes from the earth, and she's buried in darkness.

The world changes, and I'm back in Celestina's bedroom, the Queen eyeing me with her all-knowing gaze. My mouth is too dry to form words. "How...?"

"How have I seen this, when none was there to witness her end?" Celestina speaks. "The Ecosystem was there. It saw her final moments, heard her last words. I am pureskin, a queen of this realm, and little can remain hidden from me when I wish to know it. I have spoken to the earth, commanding it to yield its secrets. It has told me of your mother's death, and of your father's part in it."

I'm too stunned to respond. Watching my mother die, learning that she was called away from her home to serve my father's scheme, not comprehending how he could toy with her life that way—it's too much. If it weren't for the Queen's small but steady hand on my arm, I've no doubt I would sink to the lushly carpeted floor of her bedchamber.

"You see now why I have taken you from your father," Celestina says. "So long as he remains under strict watch, the man is a useful tool. But he is devious, and the lust for power runs deep in him, as it does in all who are descended from the original Brotherhood. He would have set your feet on a wicked path, one that could only have ended in the destruction of you both. I offer you another choice: to become, not a queen yourself, but a powerful healer, serving at the queen's side to defeat the darkness that threatens us all."

I hang my head, knowing that if she desired, the Queen could end my life—and my father's—at any moment. It was his deception that stole my mother from me and that would have stolen her mother from her, and yet Celestina is giving me a chance to atone for his crimes. How can I refuse her, when the worst of those crimes is me?

"What must I do, Your Majesty?" I ask.

Her grip tightens on my arm. A calming strength flows through me, and I'm aware that she's the one providing it. I'm also aware that my thought lies naked to her: she knows that I yield to her under duress, not loyalty. Her smile is at once an acknowledgment of that and a reminder of how defenseless I am in her hands.

"Let us begin the lessons," she says. "That you may see to the heart of things, before it is too late."

WE WALK IN the garden, arm in arm. Celestina wears nothing but her gossamer robe, but we're protected from prying eyes by the hedges that border the walkways. She leads me to a stone fountain, clear water bubbling from a statue that looks like a bearded man with killdeer legs.

"Do you mark that flower?" she says, pointing to a pale shape that floats on the surface of the water. "I look at it, and I see you: a lovely thing, but one that can only drift at the whim of the wind and water. What if there were a power able to restore it to vitality, to lend it the strength it needs to fight for its own survival?"

With a smile, she scoops the wilted flower into her palm. She holds it before me, and I feel her power stir. The pale petals quiver, then fold into the perfect shape of a silver bloom. The Queen blows it from her palm, and it floats away on a breeze I'm unable to feel, trailing a scent as sweet as her breath. I watch it whirl through the air until it finds a bush of the same silver flowers and joins the colony from which it came.

Celestina reaches for my hands, which feel cold. Maybe that's because hers glow with such warmth.

"When you sought to heal that man," she says, "you reached inside him to cure his sickness, did you not?"

"Isn't that what I'm supposed to do?"

She tips her head, smiling not unkindly. "It is a

common error, when one lacks a proper understanding of the healing arts. Illness lies within the body, so the body must be the source of recovery. Is that not right?" She wraps her hands tightly around mine, and once again I feel their singular heat. "But illness cannot heal itself, can it? So the source of healing must lie elsewhere. And where could that be?"

It's not an idle question; she wants an answer. "I don't know," I confess.

"Think," she says. "Think of the place from which healing flows."

I cast my mind back to my one successful attempt at healing, when I cured Isaac of a histeria infection. I remember reaching inside him the way I used to reach out with my Sense, finding the poison in his blood, drawing it out. But I had another medium then, something to help me: a witch hazel concoction that Rachel had instructed me how to brew. "You need...medicine." That was Isaac's word. "To aid in the healing process."

Celestina cocks her head, and I cringe when I remember her words from minutes ago: *How could she content herself to grub among the herbs of the forest?* I feel the way Leah must have felt during my bee lesson: like a dull child among demanding elders. I try again.

"My father cured Rebecca by touching her," I say. "So the power is...in the healer? In his hands?"

"I have told you that touch is needless for those of pure skin," Celestina says. Her voice is soft, but she's beginning to sound like a teacher who expects her pupil to commit every word to heart. "A lesser healer such as

Gabriel may rely on contact. A queen need only reach out and take the power that is there to be found."

She squeezes my hands as she says this, and the feeling of warmth grows stronger, to the point where I fear that she might burn me. I'm missing something obvious, something simple, or the Queen wouldn't be getting so peeved. I close my eyes and picture the silver flower blossoming in her hand. What power on earth can make a dying bloom return to life? Then I think back to the books I read, the bees spreading their gene-pollen throughout the Ecosystem, not only to plants and animals but to us as well. I don't know if the thought comes from me or her, but it's there before I know it, shining as brightly as the girl-queen who holds my hands. I open my eyes, and I know from her smile that she anticipates my words before they leave my mouth.

"The Ecosystem," I say. "Healers draw their power from the Ecosystem."

"Very good, child," she says. "Your father invoked the wyrms' power of regeneration, and the girl was healed; I called upon the power of growth that lies within all living things, and the bloom was restored. We are one with the Ecosystem: its seeds lie deep within us, and healers are nothing less than conduits for its awesome potential. You have thought to open your patient's body and peer inside. It is when you open *yourself* to the Ecosystem that true healing will begin."

A lifetime's hiding from the Ecosystem, shielding myself from its ever-roving eye, rebels against her words. "I'll try."

Her smile broadens. "You will try now." To the look

of alarm that must show in my face, she goes on: "Do not fear, child. I will assist you, this first time."

My hands tremble in hers, though I'm not sure why. "What do I need to do?"

"Only this," she says. "Reach out to the Ecosystem, as you have always done. But when you hear its answer, do not flee. Keep still, and let it find you. No harm can come to you while I remain at your side."

I have my doubts about that, but I have little choice but to obey her bidding. I close my eyes again, feel myself anchored to the earth by Celestina's small, strong hands. I calm my breathing as Aaron taught me so many years ago, lower my heart rate. In stillness, I reach out beyond my own frame, listen for an answer from the life around me. Everything is stiflingly silent, as I feared it would be. I resist the urge to strain or struggle, which I know will only interfere with whatever might be trying to communicate with me. The minutes pass by without the slightest stirring, and I'm about to tell Celestina we might as well give up.

That's when I feel it. A tingle, a pulsation that seems to come from inside me but that I know isn't of my body's making. It's been so long since I've Sensed anything, I'm not sure I'm experiencing it for real, not sure if it's my power reviving or Celestina's filling the gap in mine. Yet it grows, this Sense of the wild, and it feels dangerously familiar, the spoor of an old enemy as I approach its lair. My instinct is to shield myself, but with the Queen's hands gripping mine, I ignore that impulse, open myself fully to the power that flows from the earth. As I do, I feel something else stir inside, something I can't say I've felt before.

Or I have, but on a much smaller scale: in those rare, unguarded moments when the cicatrix, the mangraves, the wyrms saw me. When the defensive shield that keeps *me* hidden from *it* slipped and fell away.

A strangled gasp escapes my throat as the full weight of the Ecosystem presses on me. Clothed though I am in the fancy dress of a novitiate, my skin coated in glistening oil and my hair weighted with silver beads, I feel utterly naked before its prying eye. This must be what the common villagers feel, this sense of exposure, of helplessness. But it's far worse, for people like Leah are blessedly unconscious of the Ecosystem's baleful gaze, unable to detect the thing that hunts them. I'm like a child abandoned in the woods, wailing piteously while predators with gleaming teeth circle in for the kill.

Dimly, I'm conscious of the Queen's hands holding mine, but whether she's protecting me or preparing me for the slaughter, I have no notion. With what feels like my very last effort, I wrench myself away, and feel myself slipping into darkness as the wall that separates me from the wild falls into place once more.

I open my eyes to find myself cradled in Celestina's arms, my body shaking like a leaf in a squall. She strokes my newly braided hair as if I truly am her child, and in her smile I see a depth of wisdom and sadness far beyond her years. I wish I could say something, ask for her blessing or her promise of safekeeping, but I can do no more than bury my head in her chest and shiver for a warmth I may never feel again.

"Hush, child," she says, her deep voice almost a lullaby. "You have taken your first step into the world known only to the queens, and you have glimpsed the terrors that world holds. But see: knowledge hard earned yields treasures of its own."

I pull my face from her bosom. She smiles again, sadly as before, and holds something out to me.

A silver flower, new-grown, glistening as if with morning dew.

CELESTINA ORDERS A couch to be brought into her bed-chamber for the night. It seems she's concerned that I might sink into despair without her, and she's not far wrong. I worry what Leah will think when I don't return to our room, but I know I can't depart without the Queen's permission, and I'm selfish enough to long for the comfort only she can provide.

The couch is as soft as my bed, the room infused with the soothing fragrance that follows the Queen wherever she goes. Yet I'm unable to sleep, unable to rid my mind of the Ecosystem's tormenting eye. I remember my first days in my grandfather's home, a girl of three who'd newly lost her mother, lying beside his great stone bed and pulling the animal-skin blanket to my chin as if I could hide from the world. It worked no better when I was a child than it does now.

In the depths of the night, I hear the Queen's voice. "Sarah," she whispers. "Are you awake?"

"I am," I say. "Your Maj...Celestina."

"I, too," she says. "Do you wish to talk?"

I lift myself on an elbow. Moonlight floods the room, and the flower we produced glows in a vase atop her night-stand. "It was terrifying," I say. "Being exposed like that."

She breathes out a sigh. "It is a strange fate," she says. "To see to the root of things, when those around you see only the leaves and branches. To be open to all, yet belong to none."

"I don't like feeling vulnerable," I tell her.

She's silent for such a long time, I think she's fallen asleep. Her breath sweetens the room, and it occurs to me that the scent that surrounds her isn't some perfume derived from the wild. It's the Queen's essence, the attar of her being.

At last, she speaks. "I perceive that you possess the strength of a queen. Even with my aid, to produce so flawless a bloom on one's first attempt is remarkable."

She draws in another breath, lets it out.

"But the queen's vulnerability *is* her power," she says. "I cannot deny that such power comes with much suffering, but this you must embrace as well."

"I don't know if I can."

"Then you will fail, and the healing you seek will come to naught." She pauses, breathes. "Tell me. When you were brought to this city after the urthwyrms' attack, did you never wonder why your legs were not fully healed before your father's wyrm-courier returned you to your village?"

"I thought your healers lacked the power," I say. "But when I saw him heal Rebecca, I knew that couldn't be it."

"You were wise to distrust your first thought," Celestina says. "The truth is that you had offered yourself to the Ecosystem as a willing sacrifice, and even the queen is obligated to respect that bargain. The girl Rebecca was blameless. But then, she has not the blood of a queen."

I lie back on the couch, raise my eyes to the room's ceiling. Flashes of moonlight ripple across the silver tiles as if they're the scales of an enormous fish. I reach into the pocket of my gown, take out my mother's token and watch the light flicker across its scales. When she joined the village healers as a girl of sixteen, did she know the burden she'd taken on? When, as a woman and a mother, she allowed her beloved to tempt her from the village, had she prepared herself for what she would face in the city of her birth, the trials one of her blood would be called on to endure? Or did he lie to her about that, too?

"Sleep now," Celestina says. "In the morning, these things will seem more clear."

I hear her rise from bed, see her pulling her filmy robe about her. She pads to the door that leads to her garden.

"Aren't you going to sleep?"

"The queen does not sleep," she says, and I'm struck by the mixture of wistfulness and bitterness in her voice. "Goodnight, Sarah. I will return at first light of day."

My eyes close as if some power other than weariness commands them. I breathe deeply, Celestina's scent filling my lungs even in her absence. I know that I'll sleep soundly tonight, and that I will not dream.

I WAKE ALONE. Pallid light seeps through the glass door that leads to Celestina's garden, but when I raise myself to glance at her bed, I find it empty. Its covers have been cast aside, but no indentation from a body is visible on the feather mattress. It's as if the Queen is too light to leave a mark, or as if everything that's happened over the past day was a dream.

I rise and walk to the glass door, thinking I might find her outside. A scan of the garden shows me nothing but flowers and fountain, hedges and trees. The sky remains clouded, the silver flower-bushes providing the only spots of brightness in the pale dawn. I reach out to them, thinking my Sense might stir now that the Queen has reawakened it, but nothing happens; maybe I can't Sense through glass. I open the door and step onto the stone terrace, feel its chilliness beneath my feet. This time, when I cast my Sense at the flowers, I do get a response, weak and unsteady, like the voice of a child trapped in a deep firewell. I descend the stone stairs, and with each step, the voice grows louder. When I stand directly in front of the bush, I can make out its words.

The flower's name is silverbloom. It was made by Celestina, bred by drawing out the properties of other flowers. She created it to adorn her garden because it reminded her of something she loved as a child. My Sense isn't finely enough attuned to know what.

And it's sickly.

My Sense tells me this, but even if I lacked my Sense, my eyes would tell me the same. The edges of the silver blossoms have curled and browned, becoming brittle with a nameless malady. Petals fall from time to time, and only their maker's power, I know for a certainty, can restore them. Every night, when she walks in the garden, they recover their shine. Every day, when she attends to other business, the process of decay begins again.

I cast my eyes to the sky, see the forms of birds wheeling against the gray. Some are familiar by sight: bloodbirds, fire-tailed hawks. Others are unknown to me, and too far away for my recovering Sense to name. I hope that, in time, the gift Celestina revived will grow strong once more. But I think of the withering silverbloom bushes, and I wonder if, like everything else in the Queen's garden, my strength is sustained only by her power. What will happen to me, to the city, to the woods and fields beyond, if her power weakens? How can one person be tasked with healing the world?

Hesitantly, I open myself to the silverbloom bush. I feel like a novice, the way I've not felt since I was a girl of three, learning the ways of the Ecosystem under my grandfather's care. Back then, I was taught to listen without being heard, to watch without being seen; now, though it makes me feel faint to do so, I close my eyes and reach out, beseeching the health that remains in the belly of the earth to flow into me. It's there, I can feel it, but when I try to close my hand around it, it pulls away from me. It's like what happened when I tried to heal Gideon: darkness stands between us, and I can't reach through it. With an effort, I gather myself to try again. This time, my hand catches hold of something, and I draw it toward me, not sure what it is but hopeful that it might be what I need.

I've succeeded in wrapping it around my fingers and am about to send it in the direction of the failing silverbloom when it pulls tight and drags me to the ground.

My eyes fly open as my knees hit the sod. I find my hand clenched in a fist, so tightly closed my nails bite my palms. I can't tear the hand open, not even when I grip it with my other hand and try to pry the fingers apart. I see nothing around my hand, but it feels as if invisible strands bind the knuckles, constricting like an angerconda's coils. I shake the hand, pull at ropes that aren't there, but it's useless: the blood has drained from my skin as the strands tighten, and I fear the entire hand will be severed from my wrist.

"Sarah!"

The Queen's voice cuts through my anguish a moment before her hands catch hold of my shoulders. She lowers me carefully onto my back, then fills the air with a pulse of power. As it washes over me, the pain retreats, the gnarled strings of my hand loosen. Though I'm gasping for breath and the hand beats with a pulse of its own, I know that she saved me before too much damage was done.

She kneels beside me, helps me sit. She's still wearing the nightgown, her hair loose on her shoulders. Her silver-gray eyes narrow with concern, but then her face softens, and she manages a smile.

"My dear," she says, "what did you think you were

doing? You are not ready for such a test without me. See," and she holds up my hand, the wrist and knuckles striped with dark blotches like a fresh bruise.

"I was…I was trying to help," I say, struggling to catch my breath. "So you wouldn't have to do it all by yourself."

Her eyes widen, and for the first moment since I've known her, she looks like the girl she is, or was: a girl like Rachel, chary and shy. Then she wraps her arms around me, and the aura of the queen returns.

"You are brave, my dear, but also foolish," she murmurs in sweet-scented breaths. "The time for such valor may come, but not if I lose you now."

She helps me stand, and with her arm around my waist and my smarting hand tucked against my chest, we make our way up the steps to her room. I glance behind me, and find that the silverbloom bush has lost all of its blossoms, the dead petals lying in blackened crisps on the stone.

WHILE CELESTINA DRESSES for the day, an attendant arrives to wrap my hand in a soft white bandage soaked in witch hazel. I could ask the Queen why she doesn't heal the wound herself, but I know what she'd tell me: my sacrifice was willing, and she can't undo the damage without violating the bargain between her and the Ecosystem.

I sit on the couch in her bedchamber while I wait for her to return. There's a clock on the wall, and I've become expert enough at time-telling to know that many minutes pass. Recalling Celestina's elaborate hairstyle and face-painting the day before, I imagine it'll be many minutes more before she reappears. I rise from the couch, though I can't think what I'll do other than pace her room. I certainly won't make another foray into her garden.

Just then, the door to the outside hallway opens. I rush to meet the one who enters, but it's not the Queen. It's another of her attendants, dressed identically to the rest but considerably taller than the women who've waited on me thus far. She carries a silver pitcher and basin, and her apron pockets overflow with combs and canisters. I sigh, return to my seat. More grooming.

The attendant sets her supplies on the nightstand. She's about to pour water into the bowl when she pauses.

"You're wearing a dress?" It's a moment before I recognize the voice, match it to the green eyes.

"Angelica? What are you doing here?"

She pulls the veil loose, letting her hair spill down her back. "The more important question is what *you're* doing here." She tilts her head while her eyes travel over my braids, my face, my dress. "What happened to your hand?"

"It's nothing…."

She reaches for the wounded hand, lifts the bandage, probes gently. I feel some relief at her healer's touch, but the original hurt won't go away.

"Did the Queen do this?" she asks.

"Celestina? She would never—"

"So you're on a first-name basis now?"

That's one thing I've learned about fair-skinned people: their emotions show in their coloring. The more so with Angelica, whose cheeks have reddened so much they nearly match her hair. Why she should care what I call Celestina, however, is beyond me.

"She asked me to use her name," I say. "It's not like I had much choice."

Angelica puffs out her cheeks, blows loose strands from her eyes. "So how did you hurt your hand, then?"

"It was my own fault," I say. "I was trying to heal something before I knew what I was doing. The Queen was the one who stopped me before it got any worse."

"Well, thank goodness for that," she says, though she hardly sounds mollified. "What's she teaching you, anyway? You're nowhere near ready to be a healer."

"I told you, she wasn't teaching me," I say. "I did it to myself."

She lets my hand go and sits on Celestina's bed. I'm sure that's a violation of pureskin rules, but I say nothing.

"It sounds like she's teaching you plenty," Angelica says. "Her first lesson is always to make people think the worst of themselves."

"That's not true!"

"Trust me," she says. "If you'd known her as long as I have, you'd know it's as true as her eyelashes are fake."

Anger rises in me. "What do you have against the Queen, Angelica? You act like a spooked fell-cat when she's nearby, and yet you never miss a chance to insult her."

"I know her tricks," she says in a strained voice. "If she's giving you the royal treatment, that means she wants something from you. And when Her Majesty wants something bad enough, people get hurt."

She falls silent, her eyes dropping to her lap. The sadness I felt when she told me about Lavinia radiates from her, and I wonder if the Queen hurt her in some way. But I'm bristling with anger at her intrusiveness, and it suddenly occurs to me why she's here. "Did my father send you to check up on me?"

Her cheeks turn fiery, giving me my answer. "He was worried about you."

"Why? Did he think the Queen was going to hurt me, too?"

"He's just worried," she says. "He was planning to train you the way all healers are trained, first with reading and then with a structured program of skills acquisition. The Queen has swooped in out of nowhere and thrown two centuries of tradition out the window. You don't think that's a little odd?"

"What's going on in the Ecosystem is more than a little odd," I say. "Plus he doesn't know what the Queen knows."

Her eyes narrow. "What does the Queen know?"

I take a deep breath lest I blurt out anything else in anger. "That's between me and her."

"Fellow royalty?" Angelica sneers. "Don't you get it, Sarah? She's using you to get what she wants, the same way she uses everybody. Probably she thinks your father brought you here to usurp the throne. And then put you on it as his puppet."

"Like he was trying to do with my mother?" I spit back. The words have barely left my mouth when I realize my brilliant plan to keep quiet about what the Queen told me has lasted all of three ticks of the clock.

"What are you talking about?" Angelica says. "Your mother died when Celestina was a baby."

"But not when *her* mother was," I say. She's about to respond, but I cut her off. "You have no business being here. If the Queen finds you, she'll know you're spying for my father. Then you really will have something to be afraid of."

I wouldn't have thought her cheeks could get any redder, but I was wrong. She stands abruptly, readjusts the veil over her hair. The pitcher and basin clatter as she collects them, and the lotions and powders she's spread out on the nightstand remain where they are as she marches to the door.

"I thought you were a fast learner," she says. "But you're way out of your depth with Celestina. Don't come running to me when your little slumber party turns into a nightmare."

Then she leaves, slamming the door behind her.

CELESTINA RETURNS SHORTLY thereafter. She's no sooner stepped into the room, dressed in a particularly stunning gown of what looks like braided silver thread and with her hair piled in a gravity-defying topknot, than her skin picks up the hot, angry energy I'm emitting.

"My dear," she says, taking my hands in hers and providing far more of a balm than Angelica could summon, "you're positively burning up."

"I'm okay," I say. "It's just—"

She holds a finger to my lips. "There are many who envy our gift. Including some who have found a salve for their wounded pride among the lesser healers."

I breathe deeply, letting my body relax on the exhale. "Can I ask you something?" I say, and cringe at how uncouth the question sounds.

Celestina smiles. "You may ask me anything."

"Okay," I say. "I was just wondering how your mother died."

Her eyes widen fractionally beneath the lashes I can't help thinking of as fake, and I worry that, despite her invitation, this was the one question I wasn't supposed to ask. But she recovers her manner and answers.

"My mother Estella grew sickly before her time," she says. "I was with her when she died, and I swore to her that I would carry on the good works she had begun."

"I...I didn't know," I say. "I'm so sorry."

She smiles graciously. "In this, too, you and I are similar. We have both lost mothers, though mine lived to see her daughter grow, and died with the comfort of knowing that her child would become queen after her."

Her voice doesn't change from its rich, controlled tone, but I can't help wondering what it was like for her to lose her mother. I can't remember mine, yet I've felt her absence my entire life. I wish I knew Celestina's true age. Last night, in her dressing robe, I'd have guessed thirteen or fourteen. Now, in her royal gown, she seems as old as the mother she recently lost.

"This is probably a stupid question," I say, and bite my tongue when I remember Angelica's accusation. "But is it common for queens to die young? My grandmother, and now your mother...."

She takes my arm, and I feel her vitality flowing into me as always. "Queens are strong, Sarah," she says. "But not immortal. We give much of ourselves for the good of our people, and if death is the price we must pay, how can we refuse it?"

I have no answer to that, so I don't offer any.

"But come," she says. "Yesterday was a time of much learning, but I see you are eager for more." Her voice is teasing as she lays her fingertips on my bandaged hand. "I have planned an even greater lesson for today."

Arm in arm, we stroll out into her garden. I suppress a shudder at the sight of the scorched silverbloom bush; I wonder if it lies within the Queen's power to restore the blooms to life. She leads me past the ruin I created, down a long flight of stairs lined by terraced flowerbeds and herb gardens. Beneath the lowering clouds I've begun to doubt will ever disperse, ruby-throated huntingbirds provide spots of brightness as they flit from flower to flower, their needle-sharp beaks poking in and out of blossoms for the nectar they contain. The air buzzes with the vibration of their wings, and a longing for the lost bees washes over me. I wonder why, in all its mutations, the Ecosystem has never given birth to an insect resembling the humble hive-creatures of old.

We reach the end of the stairs and stand at the base of the soaring hedge that protects Celestina's garden. The Queen bids me sit on the grass, then tucks her legs beneath her and joins me, her dress flowing like a silver rain shower over her lap and onto the earth.

"You have heard that Queen Dominica never took a husband," she says. "But did you know that it has been the same for all the queens who have ruled this city?"

"Aren't queens allowed to marry?" I ask, while my thoughts go back to my mother, to Leah, and to Miriam last of all.

"Marriage would serve no purpose for a queen," she answers. "In days of old, a queen's husband—the king—shared power with her when he did not rule in her stead. Since the rise of the Ecosystem, no king could hope to stand at the queen's side, for the power you and I share is manifested in girl-children alone."

She raises a small hand, and one of the huntingbirds leaves its feast and streaks toward her outstretched palm. I'm tempted to throw myself in front of her before the bird stabs its beak into her throat, thirsting for blood as much as nectar. But it pulls up short and hovers above her hand, its wings a shiny blur. I relax, reminding myself that in this realm, much of what's wild has been tamed.

"Among huntingbirds, the males are smaller than the females," Celestina says casually. "In consequence, their bills are somewhat longer, as they require this advantage to compete with their larger mates."

As she speaks, the bird darts dizzyingly around her hand, putting me in mind of an impossibly fast child playing peekaboo. I already knew about the difference between male and female huntingbirds—my grandfather taught me in the first year of my training—but I'm mildly surprised when I realize that the one circling the Queen's hand is male, the more naturally aggressive of the two sexes. Celestina, however, seems not the slightest bit concerned.

"Among our own kind, of course, males are typically larger than females," she goes on. "This it was that convinced the Brotherhood that Sensors should, by rights, be male: to their mind, physical strength betokened strength in the Sense. Eventually, women were admitted to their ranks due to desperate need, but only grudgingly, and never in great numbers."

I know this as well. Nathan, the man who wounded my mother and tried to kill me, was only the most radical believer in the weakness of women's blood.

"Yet here, as in so many things, the Brotherhood were sadly mistaken," Celestina continues. "Had they known anything of the true life of the Ecosystem, they would have known that the most powerful creature in the hive is the queen, and that, in our descent from that line, we share the bees' preference. Queens are the rulers of the city, Sarah, because the power to rule lies within our blood."

"Do you mean," I say, "that queens carry the genes from queen bees? That that's what gives them their power?"

"It is what gives *us* our power," she says, a smile on her silvered lips. "It is a power derived from Queen Dominica herself, and transmitted to all the queens who have followed her."

"Dominica was…part of the original hive?"

"After a fashion," she says. "She was the daughter of the researchers who birthed the hybrid colony, a girl whose given name was Dominique. Newborn as her parents' experiment came to fruition, it was she who bequeathed her genes to the colony's queen. So in a sense, she *was* the queen bee, the originator of its power. And for this reason, she claimed the same power the queen bee did: the power to command the whole of the Ecosystem."

She waves her hands, and all of the huntingbirds in the garden leave their feeding and swarm around her, describing an elaborate dance so fast I can't believe the creatures don't collide with her or with each other. Through the whirling maze of wings and emerald backs and blood-colored throats, I see Celestina's ravishing eyes, her calm smile. She does no more than blink, and the birds depart, the cloud of them streaming away without upsetting a single strand of her hair.

"That's…amazing," I say. "But I can't…there's no way I can do that. You saw what happened when I tried to heal the silverbloom."

"You failed to reckon with the powers you had tapped, and you suffered the consequence," she says. "That was a fault of inexperience, not inability. In your time as a Sensor, did you not make contact with the earth?"

"Not the whole thing."

"No?" she prods. "Did you not touch the earth entire, on the day you searched for the girl Miriam?"

My protest dies on my lips. She's right: on the day Miriam went missing, I laid hands on the Ecosystem to discover where it had taken her. When I did, I had the Sensation of girdling the globe, touching every living creature on the land, in the skies and waters, beneath the planet's surface. I'd thought that was a power possessed by any Sensor who was willing to risk such deep and prolonged contact with the Ecosystem. Apparently, it was a power possessed only by a queen.

"I have witnessed your desire to heal," Celestina says to my silence. "I have heard the words you spoke at the grave of your beloved." She smiles serenely, refusing me a moment's disbelief. "What I do not know for certain is whether you have the will to carry out your vow."

She flicks a finger, and a single huntingbird separates itself from the pack and flies with a speed my eyes can't follow straight at the spot where we sit. Not at her this time. At me. I fling my hands up to protect myself from its beak—whether it's male or female I can't tell and don't care—but I know instinctively that my hands aren't enough. My body tightens as I anticipate the beak slamming into my palm with enough force to punch through flesh and bone.

But the blow never comes.

"See," Celestina says. "See what a queen of this realm may achieve."

I lower my hands. The huntingbird hovers in front of me, wings beating furiously, beak so close to my face I can see into the depths of its bright black eyes. Celestina's not holding it; I feel none of her power infusing me. *I'm* holding it. I flex my fingers, and the bird somersaults through the air, righting itself only when I instruct it to. It's not as tame as I'd supposed—I feel its rage building as it tries again and again to come at me—but it can't break through, not while I command it.

"This is the true power of the queens," Celestina says. "With this power, I defend my city; with it, I hold the living will of the Ecosystem at bay. This is the power your father thought to arrogate to himself, foolishly seeking to found a kingship where none was possible. But we have seen through his conspiracy, and we are united against it. Brandishing the power of the queens together, you and I will heal the world as only we can."

I struggle to conceive this awesome power, akin to the Ecosystem's control over its own creatures. Yet small as the huntingbird is, its presence shows me that the Queen's promise is real. I feel her hand reach out toward the bird I hold in flightless flight—not her actual hand, but the hand that wields the Ecosystem's will. The bird is drawn away from my much weaker grip and flies off to join its fellows in their swooping, wheeling dance.

"When do we begin?" I ask.

"At once," Celestina says. "And we do not end until your training is complete." Seeing the look on my face, she adds, "You will feel no fatigue while you are with me. A queen has no need of sleep."

WE DO NOT sleep.

The day passes from morning to noon, noon to dusk, while we remain in the Queen's garden. Celestina instructs me with word and look and touch, showing me where to seek the earth's hidden power, what questions to ask of it, how to receive its response. I lay myself open to the Ecosystem, and as it flows through me, I learn to catch its filaments in my fingers and pull these strands of life in whatever direction I desire. It's like Sensing, this intimate contact with the wild, the difference being that instead of merely reading the Ecosystem's mind, I command its body to heed me. It feels less like discovering a new ability than recalling a long-forgotten dream: it's in my blood, in my genes, the genes of the girl from whom all of my kind are descended. I know that what Celestina says is true: none but a daughter of queens could wield this power.

I remember, or think I remember, a time when my mother ran with two-year-old me across the village greensward, leading her chubby toddler on a chase after huntingbirds. We never caught one; she didn't know we had the power. But I know now, and while the daylight lasts, I catch bird after bird, holding them in my palm and letting them take flight in my mother's memory.

Nighttime falls. A full moon pierces the cloud cover, flooding the garden with silver. In its light, the Queen and

I are transfigured, her piled hair haloed, my hands radiant as pearl. There's no hunger or thirst, no weariness in my limbs or mind; there's only my body's response to the Ecosystem, my fingers streaming with light. By the time the moon sets, I've created my first bloom, quieted the cicatrix song, calmed the earth's hunger for a time. I long to delve deeper, to snare the wayward wyrms that devoured my village, dry up the poison of the tree-leaping frogs, discover the source of the black vines that darken my vision—the same, I'm convinced, that clutched my hand when I tried to heal the silverbloom. But the Queen forbids me to try, fearing further injury. I obey her, though by the time the gray light of day replaces the night's silver glow, I feel that I've become a queen in all but name.

The sun, the moon, the sun again: it seems to me that several days and nights elapse in the Queen's garden, but time is a dream, and we're immune to its passing. I watch as Celestina lays hands on the earth, threads fingers through the soil. The moon is out again, the garden a maze of purple shadows.

"Would you commune with your mother?" she asks.

I catch her eyes. "Can I?"

"Not with her departed spirit," she says. "But with her days upon this earth, yes."

I join my hands with hers, and we reach out into the Ecosystem, searching for the one I lost. I worry that I'll lose her again in the darkness deep below, but the earth's winding ways open before me in an instant, and finding her, I discover, is no more difficult than finding Miriam was when I searched the Ecosystem months before. Since I came to this city, I've seen my mother's life twice: once when my father showed me the beginning of her time as a Sensor, the other when the Queen showed me that time coming to an end. It's left to the Ecosystem to show me the days between.

The Queen releases my hands the moment I make contact, allowing me to relive those days by myself. The images that flow from the soil are fractured, incomplete; my mother was a Sensor, and she didn't show herself to the Ecosystem when she didn't want to. But there were times she let her guard down: times when, in her work as a healer, she gathered herbs openly before the Ecosystem's eye, or when, as a woman with child, she spoke the name she'd chosen for me to the forest glade. I watch her in those carefree moments, soak her up through my fingers, clasp her to my breast. Another nighttime passes while I savor the touch, the sound, the smell of her. Where my tears fall, the ground gives birth to tiny buds that grow and bloom before I can blink the next tear away. They're flowers of my heart's longing, and I instruct the Ecosystem to fashion them after her: orchids as slim and graceful as a reed, with soft brown petals sprinkled over with blue. I wonder if Celestina's flowers are for the mother she so newly lost, just as mine are for the mother I've so newly found.

While the Queen walks elsewhere in the garden, I search for the life of the man who was my grandfather. I find him less readily than I did my mother, for he was strict in the ways of the Sensorship, and showed himself to the Ecosystem only sparingly. I delight to see him as a boy, little older than Rebecca when he left the City of the Queens; he clutches the hand of the tall, severe woman who must have been his mother, and I think I can see my own mother's face in his. I study him when, as a much older man, he searched the Ecosystem for his missing daughter; I see him reach out toward the City of the Queens, where he must have suspected, or hoped, she'd gone. But he never found her, just as she never found her way home, and when he returned from his search, he bore only her Sensor's token in place of her body.

Another day has waned, another night standing ready to take its place. I make one final search for Isaac. I know that if I find him, learn how he died, it won't comfort me, and yet I'm unable to resist. For the first time since this dream began, though, I'm frustrated; the Ecosystem won't show him to me, not a single moment of his time on earth. That shouldn't be, for I carry in my own memory the many times the Ecosystem saw him: in the forest the night he joined me on my search for Miriam, at the swamp where we shared our one and only kiss, in the cave of the urthwyrms where I thought I'd lost him for good. It's as if he's been erased from the Ecosystem's memory, swallowed by the deeper darkness the Queen won't let me fathom. I search until exhaustion nibbles at the edges of my nerves, but at last, I'm forced to admit he's gone.

I stand and find the Queen, who seems to float toward me in her gown of moonbeams. She takes my hand, and I know this stolen time has reached an end.

"For all your days, you have hidden from the Ecosystem," she says. "Now you have awakened to your true calling, and nothing will be the same again."

"Yes, My Queen," I say.

"Come, then," she says with a smile. "You are weary,

and must rest. Tomorrow you and I will heal the great sickness that gnaws at the heart of our world."

I bid the past farewell as she leads me from the garden. The places where she sets her feet glow silver in the moonlight.

I wake in the Queen's bed. Her sweet breath bathes my face; her fingers stroke my braids. The hazy sunlight I've come to expect shines through the door to her garden, but whether it's the next morning or a week later, I can't say.

When she sees my eyes open, Celestina smiles. "Are you refreshed?"

I yawn, stretch. "How long was I asleep?"

"One night only," the Queen says. "But six days and nights have passed since we entered my garden." She smiles at my startled expression. "Time has no meaning within the Ecosystem."

She withdraws while I sit up. I look around the room, expecting everything to be different, probably because I *feel* so different. I scan the Queen's garden, where I find the silverbloom bushes flashing like beacons. I reach out to a single flower, and despite the distance and the glass between us, I'm instantly connected to the health within the bloom, as well as the sickness that keeps it from growing to its fullest. I speak words of comfort to it, feel it calm in response. The flowers sparkle in a synchronized wave, as if they're bowing to me.

I meet the Queen's eyes, and she smiles. I notice that, though she seems to have shared the bed with me, she's already dressed. Today's gown is modest to the point of plainness; her hair is caught in a single braid, her face unpainted. I slide from bed and find that my own gown smells as fresh as the day I first put it on. Even more surprising, I discover that while I slept, the Queen has slipped two of her bracelets on my wrists, one on each arm.

"Are you hungry?" she asks.

"Not really." That's another surprise; though I can't remember the last time I ate or drank, I feel as strong as I ever have.

"Come, then," she says, and takes my arm. Despite her smile, there's a solemn air about her this morning. At moments like this, she looks much older than her true age, whatever that might be.

"Are you all right?" I ask. "My Queen?"

Her smile broadens, but the sorrow settles in her eyes.

"There is one further trial to be undergone," she says. "Now that I have unlocked the power within you, it is time for you to learn the deepest source of the queen's strength."

"I'm ready," I say.

She lightly touches my cheek. "I know you are, child. I have prepared you for just this moment."

We leave her room and head for the front door, but before we reach it, she turns to the side and leads me down a short passageway I didn't notice the day I came here. There's another door at the end, with the familiar pattern of metalwork branching across its surface. The Queen reaches inside the bosom of her gown and withdraws a metal object that flashes gold against her usual silver; this she fits into a slot in the door and turns it until I hear a click. On our initial tour of the Cathedral, my father explained the foreign concept of locked doors to me, but he also explained that for reasons of both trust and expediency, Dominica did away with locks when the university became her city. This one door, however, is apparently an exception.

The heavy door opens with a groan. I expect the gray light of dawn to spill through, but instead, I see a night-time gloom, accompanied by a breath of moist, earthy air even the Queen's fragrance can't mask. Celestina takes a many-armed candle-holder from a table beside the door and shines the light inside, showing me an alcove walled in stone with a stairway at the farther end. The stone steps lead down, curving out of sight into the darkness.

"You will have to follow," the Queen says. "The way is too narrow for two to walk abreast."

She lets my arm go and starts down. Her dress drags on the stairs, which are cold against my feet. The stair-case curls tightly as it drops into the depths, the smell of earth growing stronger with each step. In the light of the candles, I see that the walls have yielded to bare dirt, and within a minute or two, I realize that the stairs we're step-ping on are no longer stone either. I shudder, not from cold but from my memory of the urthwyrms' attack on my village. This place appears to have been fashioned by human hands, but it's as close as I can think of to the bot-tomless abyss that swallowed what little was left of my former life.

Yet it's not, after all, bottomless; long after I've lost count of the stairs, they come to an end, and we step onto level soil. We must be very deep beneath the surface, in a vault tall enough for us to stand but so rife with the cloy-ing earth-smell I have trouble breathing. The candles feel the stuffiness, too; they flutter, dying to points of bluish flame that do nothing to push back the dark. The Queen herself appears leeched of radiance, her gown and hair dulling to a sepulchral gray, her almost-black skin ashy. When she speaks, her teeth show as little more than pale flickers, like sunlight fighting through leaden clouds.

"We've a distance to go," she says, her voice muffled like everything else. "The way is dark, but trust in your power to guide you aright."

She turns from me and plunges ahead. After a few steps, the candles sputter and die, and Celestina makes no effort to revive them. I close my useless eyes and discover that the Ecosystem's life-force is unusually strong here, its aura penetrating my nostrils like an animal musk. Even the Queen's presence is overwhelmed by it; I can't hear her feet padding across the ground, can't smell her sultry essence. I reach out with the power she taught me and feel the Ecosystem watching us, waiting with barely contained eagerness as if it's been expecting our arrival for years.

A measureless time passes before the darkness behind my eyelids gives way to a dim glow. I open my eyes to discover that Celestina and I have entered a cramped passage where the cavern walls are covered with crystalline shapes, six-faceted and emitting a golden light. The trail ahead of us is composed of shining, six-sided plates, whose translucence creates the illusion that I can see through to the deeper depths from which the light emerges. The plates feel smooth and slick when I follow the Queen onto the glowing trail, but what's producing the light is impossible to tell.

All at once, Celestina holds up a cautioning hand. I stop while she sets her candle-holder on the floor. Just ahead, the tunnel ends in a wall of the golden substance; a six-sided opening, barely large enough for a human body, rests at floor level. Through this aperture, golden light shines with such intensity I have to squint to look at it.

"You have walked in the queen's garden, and slept in her bedchamber," Celestina says. "But what lies ahead is the queen's true abode, the very heart of the Ecosystem."

Realization dawns on me. "Do you come here every night?"

"Every night, and every day that I can," she says. "I tend first to my garden, as you have guessed." Her teeth gleam in a golden smile. "But when I finish there, I resort to this chamber, where my mother came before me, and the queens before her all the way back to Dominica the first. It is where your grandmother would have come if her fate had been otherwise—where *you* would have come, had your grandfather not stolen your mother from the city of her birth. And, coming here, you would have given yourself to the living will of the Ecosystem, as I prepare to do now."

She kneels and wiggles through the opening, her hair catching as if the material is tacky. I'm much larger than her, and it's a struggle to crawl through, the walls clutching at me as I force my way past. The room we enter is composed entirely of the gleaming substance, the light so strong we seem to swim in a sea of gold. My eyes burn from the brightness, but when I squint, I'm able to make out angled walls and a low ceiling, and in the center of the room, marks like human feet sunk deeply into the waxen floor.

Celestina lays a hand on my arm as if in warning, then

takes her place in this spot, her diminutive feet fitting easily inside the depressions. She closes her eyes, spreads her slim arms out to her sides. The silver bracelets clink at her wrists. My eyes deceive me in the punishing light, and I think the bracelets are slithering up her arms, fastening in place like finely scaled chains. The earth groans, and the light in the room dims just enough for me to see snaky appendages emerging from ceiling and floor. Roots or vines they may be, but they're golden in color like the rest of the chamber. I watch as the ones from below climb the Queen's body, twist about her girlish waist, twine with her bracelets; the ones from above enter her hair, braiding with her silver locks until only their color tells me which strands are hers. She holds perfectly still, or perhaps she's bound too tightly to move. Her eyes flash open, and I fall back when I see that not only the irises but the whites have been replaced by solid gold.

"I touch the earth," she says, though her voice is no longer hers: it's many voices, too many to count, sibilant as serpents' tongues, harsh as the call of bloodbirds. "I know its mind, and am one with all that lives. See!"

The chamber glows unbearably bright, forcing me to shield my eyes. Blindly, I reach for the place I last saw her, but some force repels my hands. As if through a pillar of light, I see the Queen writhing in the Ecosystem's grip, her body caught in a web of golden strands like a chrysalis. A dark aperture opens in the brightness as if she's drawing breath, but no scream emerges but my own.

Then the fiery shape stumbles forward, and without thinking, I drop to my knees to catch her. My hands burn at her touch, but it's the burning of cold, not flame. With the dying of the fire, I'm able to see again, and I watch the living threads that held her retreat into the cavern's ceiling and floor. The Queen shivers, drawing several deep, racking breaths before freeing herself from my arms. Her eyes are wide and wet, but their color is her own once more.

"My dear," she says, her voice quavering. "I'm sorry to have frightened you. You see that I am well now."

"What happened?" I ask. My voice shakes as badly as hers. "What did the Ecosystem do to you?"

She strokes hair from my forehead, and though her hands tremble, I'm relieved to find that they've recovered their warmth. "It is the bargain the queen must make," she says. "The compact that holds her people and the Ecosystem in balance."

I stare at her in horror. "*This* is the bargain Dominica struck?"

"There was no other way," she says, smiling sadly. "When the scientists of old birthed their colony, they housed its queen here, where they could guard her at all times. They did not foresee that she would bridle against imprisonment, and command her brood to rise up against her captors. Yet humanity might have withstood this attack, had the scientists—Dominique's parents among them—not become fearful of the queen's power and destroyed her in this very place. Then the Ecosystem, grown wild with rage and grief, redoubled its assault against those who had spawned it, as if to teach them what it was to be bereaved."

"The book I read didn't mention anything about this," I say.

"By the time Dominica came, the record-keepers had fallen into death or despair," she replies. "The true nature of the queen's sacrifice is known only to those of her blood." She pauses, her gaze turned inward. "Dominique was but a child when she forged her compact, enchaining herself to this place so that she might serve in the original queen's stead. I think of her often, motherless and alone, and with the very weight of the world on her shoulders."

I try to picture this girl-queen, but all I can call to mind is the sad, stately woman in the many-colored window of the council house. "How old was she?" I ask.

"She was seven," Celestina answers. "But from that day forward, she was a child no longer."

She bows her head, the way I saw people bow theirs before the burial stones. When she speaks again, her voice is uncharacteristically tremulous, carrying a plaintive note I hadn't thought to hear from her lips.

"When I was no older than Dominique, my mother brought me to this place," she says. "Here, she showed me the trials the queen must endure. As a young girl, I was enchanted by the prospect of ruling the globe, even if it came with such travail."

A tear brightens in her eye, slides slowly down her cheek. Its trail is silver.

"But as the years passed, I learned the truth," she says. "I watched my mother shrivel, watched the Ecosystem sap her strength and eat her life away. I heard tales of the Brotherhood, and of the intrigues that swirl ever around the queen, your father's not least. I had been raised in comfort and in the arms of love, and I knew that I was unequal to enduring the queen's fate. I consulted the Ecosystem, and in its wisdom, it has sent me an answer." She touches my cheek with trembling fingers, and for all her magnificence, it seems as if the years have fallen from her, revealing the pampered girl of whom she speaks. "The day I have longed for has come at last."

I shake my head in confusion. "My Queen?"

"No, Sarah," she says. "I am queen no longer. The Ecosystem has chosen another." She lays a finger on my lips. "It has chosen you."

I'M SURE SHE'S joking. But her eyes are serious, her tears real. Crazy as it sounds, she means what she says.

"A queen?" I say. "Your Majesty—Celestina—I'm nowhere near ready for that."

"You are," she says fervently, and holds out one of my brown-and-blue orchids as if to prove her word. "You are strong, having grown up without mother, partner, or beloved friend. The Ecosystem has tried you, tempered you. You are the queen it wants, the queen it has sent to this city."

She sits with hands folded around the flower in her lap, looking every bit the frail girl she was and maybe still is. A new thought arises in me, a suspicion I don't want to give credence to. "I came here because I had no other place to go," I say. "That wouldn't have happened if the city's wyrms had stayed put."

She drops her eyes. Tears cling to her thick lashes, fall like specks of golden light.

"Celestina," I say, "did you command the wyrms to destroy my village?"

"No!" She shoots a look at me, half frightened, half pleading. "I sent them to retrieve you only. But once they were free of the city, some other force fell between their will and mine, and I could not control them. I am weak,

Sarah, and will never be able to assuage the world's pain, much less bear my own."

My body trembles anew. I can hardly bring out the words I have to say.

"People died in that attack," I say. "People I knew, and…and loved. There were almost two hundred people in my village. Because of you, there are only twenty-three left."

She lowers her eyes again. The flower she holds has withered, its petals forming a ring of death around her.

"You killed those people!" I say, gripping her shoulders. "You're the queen, and you killed them! All because you were too afraid to accept your responsibility."

I shake her, hard, feel her slender body quiver in my hands. She doesn't respond, only gazes at the floor of the brood chamber as if she could pierce its golden depths. I would strike her if my own strength didn't desert me, my breath turn to a wail. I wrap my arms around myself and huddle beside her.

Isaac didn't have to die. None of them did. I could have seen him again, if only from afar. And now, I never will.

Celestina has risen to her feet. I look up at her, find that the tears have dried on her face. She appraises me coldly, the very image of a queen. When she speaks, her voice is devoid of pity.

"The queen is a slave," she says. "Do not judge her until you have worn her chains."

She plants a foot on my chest and shoves with a strength I don't expect, and I'm thrown onto my back. I push myself to my feet, clench my fists to return the blow. But I'm held in place by something as strong as grabgrass, and I can't take a step toward her. I look to the floor of the chamber, discover that my feet have sunk into the waxy spot where Celestina stood minutes ago.

"I had hoped to avoid this treachery," she says. "I do not know whether the sacrifice will be acceptable if it is forced upon you. But you would never have stood in this place of your own free will, Sarah granddaughter of Seraphina."

Golden tendrils emerge from the floor, climbing my legs like vines. Their cousins drop from the ceiling and grip my wrists where Celestina's silver bracelets gleam. I'm pulled fully upright, my arms pinioned, the living threads of the Ecosystem's will working their way into my hair and holding fast to the silver beads the Queen's maids placed there. I gather the power within me and try to shake them off, but the strands only grip me the harder. Against their irresistible might, the warm wave that issues from my body dissipates into nothingness.

I find the strength to lift my eyes to Celestina. She smiles, but it's a smile of mingled grief and scorn. Much as I struggle, I'm held utterly motionless while she leans forward and kisses my forehead.

"I did not ask for this power," she says. "I did not ask for the blood that flows in my veins. And now I am free."

She shakes her bracelets loose, and they drop to the floor. I would scream, but the tendrils tighten around my throat to choke off all sound. Celestina crawls carefully through the brood chamber's sole exit, stoops in the tunnel to retrieve her candles. I hear the scratch of a flint, see the spots of flame through the waxy shield. She holds the candles against the opening for a long time, until the wax softens and drips under the heat. Within minutes, the doorway is completely sealed, and all I can see is the blur of Celestina's figure through the translucent wall. Her nails tap the wax to test its solidity; her fingers spread as if to wave goodbye. Then even that is gone, and I'm alone.

Or not alone. I feel the power building in the strands that secure me, the strands that ensnare me. Last night, in Celestina's garden, I told myself that my own power was great. Now I see that it's nothing compared to the monstrous force that holds me here.

The golden light sears my eyes, and everything fades away.

BOOK FOUR
STORM

*It is not a futile purpose to decide definitely what
we mean by the so-called species among living
bodies, and to enquire if it is true that species
are of absolute constancy, as old as nature, and
have all existed from the beginning just as we see
them to-day; or if, as a result of changes in their
environment, albeit extremely slow, they have not in
course of time changed their characters and shape.*

—Jean Baptiste Lamarck,
Philosophie zoologique (1809)

I AM CONSUMED.

The pain is knife-sharp, blade-deep. It strips my flesh, dissects my body. Its edge is so keen, it cuts me to parts too small to see, then slices those parts again, until I feel the pain in my body no longer. I try to scream, but I have no throat to scream. Try to flee, but I have no limbs to carry me. Try to fight, but can't summon the will to defend myself.

This is because I have no self. I've been broken down, transformed into coils and spirals of soil, detritus working its way through the slow entrails of the earth. I'm spread far and wide, a kernel here, a grain there, nothing so solid as flesh or bone or muscle or nails. I'm all mind, earth-mind. I no longer feel the Ecosystem's assault, because I have no body, nothing with which to feel.

I am the Ecosystem.

An immense buzzing fills me as my consciousness spreads throughout the numberless minions that make up my hive. I roil and gurgle like water, hiss and spit like fell-cats. I shake with tremors of my own making. I bud, and my buds open, and my openings close, and my closings bud again. Wyrms crawl through me, hearkening to my directions, hastening where I send them. They meet at crossroads in my belly, and if I wish to, I devour them, and if I don't wish to, I let them pass. I tend the cycle of cicatrix, grub and nymph and shell-mate. The flameflies' dance I approve, the flare of life and death no wonder to me. No pity either, for I birthed these things after eons of labor in my secret laboratories, and if I didn't get it right this millennium, there'll always be time for further experimentation. For now, for as long as now is ever, I'll breed bloodbirds and moss, scaramanders and soil-serpents, and make things to startle and humble the two-footed enigmas that cross my broad fairways.

For I made them, too. They can build their sanctuaries of stone on my stomach, but they can't evade the truth of where they came from.

I alone remember their birth. That, it may be, is what separates me from them. I remember.

And I endure.

Yet there's one thing that troubles me. Deep in my gut and bones, I feel it. It's a shriek in my root-ends, a shiver in every leaf I cultivate. It hides from me, shadowy and silent, while at the same time it seeks to tear me apart. It's not meant to be there, but much as I try to free myself, it remains.

It's what makes me always hungry. Always vigilant. So long as it lasts, so long will I be drawn to the one place that brings me comfort. So long as it's with me, I'll never, ever be able to escape into the releasing, the letting go, the falling silent and still that these curious ones call death.

Or is it sleep?

CONSCIOUSNESS RETURNS SLOWLY, painfully. I wake to find myself lying on the floor of the brood chamber, my cheek pressed against the wax, which feels slimy with sweat or tears or worse. I lift my head to discover that the golden tendrils have let me fall and vanished into ceiling and floor. Yet I know this is only the beginning. The Ecosystem has gotten what it wants from me for now: the soul-draining communion with its queen without which the hive can't exist. But it won't be satisfied with a single sip. Time and again it will return, flooding my mind until I've lost all memory of who I am and surrendered all desire to return to the world above.

I push myself from the floor, the footprints in the center of the chamber clinging to me briefly but no longer holding me in place. The sealed doorway is another matter. Wax it might appear, but it's as solid as stone, impervious to my hammering blows. I pull my mother's token from its hidden spot in my dress, try to use the serpent's tail as a blade, but it leaves nothing so much as a mark. Recalling Celestina's lessons, I reach inside for the power I gained in her garden. But though my flesh tingles and grows warm, it cools the second I lay my hands against the wax. The power that seemed so strong in my moonlit dream is useless here. In the depths of the Ecosystem, the queen of the realm truly is a slave, her body and soul existing only to serve her hungry brood.

I sink to the floor, catch my head in my hands. The beads that Celestina's attendants braided into my hair clack against each other, but when I try to claw them free, they grip all the more tightly. The same goes for the ridiculous silver dress they made me put on: I wrestle with it, try to pull it from my arms or slip it over my head, but it's bonded to me like a second skin. I suspect that the Queen's bracelets are what hold everything in place, fixing the other implements to my body—but that knowledge does me no good, as I can't tear the bracelets free either. Something tells me that even if I were to cut off my hands, tug every strand of hair from my head by the roots, the chains that bind me to this place would bind me still.

Dimly, Angelica's words return to me: *If she's giving you the royal treatment, that means she wants something from you. And when Her Majesty wants something bad enough, people get hurt.* How could I have known how right she was, and that everything Celestina did—taking me into her home, turning me against my father, training me in the ways of the queen—was meant to prepare me for this fate?

I detect a stirring in the chamber, raise my eyes to see the inquisitive strands of the Ecosystem emerging from walls and floor. I must not have supplied them with enough energy on our first melding. The strands reach my wrists, jerk me upright, drag me to the spot in the center of the chamber. My body rebels against the nauseating sensation that's about to come, the feeling of losing myself to the hive's labyrinthine mind. But there's nothing I can do. The Ecosystem has me in its hold, and I'm plunged once more into a pit so deep I can't see a trace of light.

I come out of the trance choking, shaking, blood streaming into my eyes where the fall sliced my forehead. I can't take much more of this, and in a way, I'm grateful: at least my suffering will be short, the erasure of my existence total. With the shred of self-awareness that's left to me, I wonder how previous queens survived this torment for the long years of their reign. Angelica said that my great-grandmother Leonida ruled for over sixty years. Even Estella, sickly as Celestina claimed she was, lasted for twenty. Maybe, after a lifetime of training instead of mere days, they learned techniques to defend their sanity. Or maybe the fact that they weren't imprisoned here, that they could replenish their humanity in their beds and gardens, gave them the strength to face each night's torture in the brood chamber.

Whatever they did, it won't help me now. If I'm to have any chance of survival, I have to figure out a way to fight before the Ecosystem returns.

Gasping with nausea and weakness, I push myself to hands and knees. I can't stand, so I crawl to the spot where the tendrils emerged, try to determine if there's any way to stop them from returning. The floor of the chamber is as smooth as if nothing ever troubled its surface. The ceiling is the same; it's as if the wax dripped and then solidified to form the golden strands, then melted back when they were done. Another round of bruising my fists against the doorway convinces me I'll never break through. Desperation rises in my chest as minutes I can't count tick away and the time for the agony to repeat itself approaches.

With the skills I first learned under my grandfather's instruction, I steady my breathing, settle my heart. If the brood chamber is truly connected to the entirety of the Ecosystem, can I use the tricks of the Sensor's trade to hide from it, the way I used to mask myself in the forest? Can I slip through the gaps in its consciousness, so that when it comes back, it'll be as though no one is here?

But no, there *are* no gaps in its consciousness, not in this room where the hive was born. Here, the queen is open to every impulse of its mind, every touch of its hands. Like that first day in the garden when Celestina instructed me to bare myself to the Ecosystem's eyes, there's nowhere to hide.

I think back to that day, which seems so long ago it might have been in another life. The Queen's vulnerability, Celestina told me in her bedchamber, *is* her power. Did she teach me that so she could weaken me for this final assault? Or, selfish though her motive might have been, was she telling the truth? I recall what I felt during the endless spell in her garden: surrendering myself, opening myself more fully than I've ever dreamed or dared, gave me the strength the Queen promised. The strength that Dominica, though only a child, must have found when she struck her bargain in this very place.

I do not know whether the sacrifice will be acceptable if it is forced upon you, were the next-to-last words Celestina spoke to me. Is *that* why the Ecosystem tortures me so—because, as an unwilling sacrifice, I've resisted it thus far? If I honor Dominica's bargain, will I gain her power?

The tendrils stir once more. They're hungry, and I'm convinced by now that the reason they're so persistent is that I'm not fulfilling my end of the bargain. It's a huge risk: if I accept the sacrifice, I might succumb to the Ecosystem entirely. But if I keep going as I've been, this next episode of contact will surely kill me. It's my choice. If I'm wrong, I only hope the end will be quick.

As calmly as I can manage, I place my feet in the prints at the chamber's center. The wax seals at once; the strands of the Ecosystem unfurl from ceiling and floor. I hold my arms out, close my eyes, breathe deeply as I feel the filaments curl around my arms, twine through my hair. I speak to them, in a voice that might be only in my mind.

I am the Queen, I say. *I accept this fate, and all that comes with it.*

The golden strands pull me to my feet. Do I deceive myself, or do they grip my arms more gently?

I feel a jolt as the mind of the Ecosystem courses through my frame. I see its multifarious lives, hear its infinite voices. It surrounds me, desperate to commune with its queen. But it's different this time. It's not the assault of an invading army, driven mad by the lust to consume. It's more like a child returning to its mother's arms, wounded and afraid, seeking the solace she alone can give. It needs my strength, and it offers me a bargain: guide it, help it, and it will serve me always.

I nod my head. *Yes,* I tell it. *Yes. I hear your call, and I will return.*

The golden strands release me. I step easily from the spot on the floor, find my body unharmed, my mind untouched. The bracelets gleam on my wrists, but I know I can remove them whenever I please, replace them whenever I need. The golden wall, however, I can't breach. I have little time to search the Ecosystem's vast, sprawling consciousness for the right tool, so I take the first and fastest offering that presents itself.

Come to me, I think, or say. *Your queen has need of you.*

Minutes pass in silence. I fear the distance might be too great for my plea to be heard. But at last, a loud buzzing builds in the tunnel outside the brood chamber. I have just enough time to step to the side when the sealed wall explodes inward.

A barrage of huntingbirds enters. Their beaks, propelled by the speed of their flight, have burst the wall my hands could never have torn down. They circle me, a rainbow of emerald and ruby and ivory. When I step through the shattered wall, they move with me, their invisible wingbeats fanning my face like a cleansing breath.

I see at once Celestina's mistake, and her mother's before her. They resisted, refused the sacrifice. The Ecosystem withheld the true measure of its power from them because they treated it as a foe. When the bargain is accepted with all her heart, the queen is no slave. She is freed, and her children with her.

The huntingbirds dancing about me, I race up the tunnel to the distant stairway. There's much yet to be done, immediate and far-off dangers of which the Ecosystem warned me. I've gained a powerful ally, but time is against us all.

I TAKE ONLY the time I need in Celestina's residence to fling away the ungainly dress and slip into a more comfortable tunic before I speed across the courtyard to the Cathedral, seeking my father. My legs ache from climbing the stairs from the brood chamber, but urgency lends me strength.

He's not in his laboratory, nor in his classroom. I hunt through the first few floors of the tower, but my random search is in vain. That's the problem with a city this size: whereas in my village one could hardly avoid bumping into people, here there are too many places to roam, places to hide. I consider trying Angelica's room to see if she knows where he is, but shame stops me. I summon my huntingbird guard, dispatch them to search the grounds; they're faster than I am, and they're fifteen to my one. As soon as the birds zoom off to the far corners of the city, I climb the stairs to Dinah's room.

It sits at the end of the upper-floor hallway where the members of my village were housed, right before the staircase. I have to walk past the room I shared with Leah to get there, but I don't approach the door; the last thing I'd do is involve her in this. Nothing obvious alerts me to the danger that resides within Dinah's room; if anything, an unusually deep silence broods over the place. I rest a hand on the door, then an ear; something stirs inside, for I hear a creaking, groaning sound more like the branches of an ancient tree than anything that might come from a human throat. I test the door, but it won't open. It's not locked—the handle turns like normal—but something holds it firm. I knock softly, call out in a voice as pleasant as I can.

"Dinah? It's Sarah. Can I come in?"

There's no response, unless it's the groaning sound again. I put my shoulder to the door, shove with all my strength, but it doesn't budge. I reach out to the birds, call them to my aid once more. They're so fast that within minutes, I see the majority of them streaming down the corridor, and I step aside to let them do their work.

The huntingbirds batter the wooden door, flinging themselves against it time after time. Their beaks are like knives or awls; chips of wood fly, the door dwindling until it's too weak to hold them back. The first bird to break through dies instantly, its body smashed by the thing on the other side. The others I beg for caution, and they comply, darting against the door to open holes wide enough for me to clutch and tear the wood away. I'm nearly overpowered by the rotten stench that escapes the room, but I continue to work alongside the huntingbirds until we've created a space I can squeeze through. I take a deep breath and order the birds to remain behind, but in this, they won't obey me.

I've reason to be thankful for that.

If not for their buzzing, protective shield, I'd be crushed at once by the black vines that come hurtling at me when I step into Dinah's room. The birds deflect the blows, and die defending me. The room is filled with flailing appendages, so densely woven it's impossible to see through them. They fall back for a moment after their initial assault, and I'm able to locate their source.

It's Dinah, or what Dinah has become. The woman's body is recognizable in shape as it sits heavily on the bed, but that shape is covered from head to foot with black tendrils that writhe like hundreds of extra limbs. It's the culmination of the process I saw with Gideon, a human being transformed into a monstrous hybrid of plant and living web. Some of the tendrils have worked their way into the stone walls and floor, rooting what was once Dinah to the spot; I've no doubt that if they'd been given time to grow, these strands would have forced their way into other bedrooms within the Cathedral, then farther down into my father's dissection room, and finally to the depths of the brood chamber. There, whoever stood in the queen's place—whether Celestina or me—would have been overwhelmed by them. My thought flashes to Gideon, taken more than a week ago to a cell somewhere on the city grounds; if he's become a monster comparable to this one, I don't know if I'll have the time or strength to defeat them both.

That's my last thought before the thing on the bed opens what remains of its mouth and issues countless black tongues that hiss through the air like whips.

They strike at me, seek to curl around my arms and legs and throat. I fight them off with my hands, helped by the few remaining huntingbirds, which harry the vines with their sharp beaks. But my queenly power is useless; the moment I reach out to the monstrous appendages, I know they're beyond my command. Even if Dinah weren't too far gone for me to heal, the power that controls her is much greater than my own.

I duck beneath a barrage of black vines, send my last three huntingbirds to distract the creature while I seek a retreat. When I turn, I find that the monster's limbs have snaked up the ceiling and trailed down to cover the space before the broken door, weaving a web as thick and strong as a net. If I put my hands into that black morass in an effort to escape, I'll be snared for good. Holding my breath against the fetid odor that fills the room, I spin to confront the creature once more. Despite the distance to the stone pavilion, the window is my only hope. I reach out to the bloodbirds circling nearby, call them to bear my weight when I make my leap for safety.

But I'm too slow. As if sensing my thought, the monster emits another burst of tendrils that weave a second net over the room's sole exit.

I regard the thing that's about to kill me. It has no eyes to stare back; all it has are inky sacs where its eyes once were. These burst like seed pods, spewing more of the black vines to consume me.

All at once, the strands retreat, scores of them whipping back into the body of their host. I smell something burning, turn to find my father wielding a sconce in each hand. Where the monster's roots are anchored to the wall, fires are spreading, emitting an acrid black smoke. The thing that was Dinah shudders, groans, but its roots have sunk into the stone of the building, and it can't pull itself free. In a last effort to save itself, it wraps limbs around my father and hugs him close. With a heavy blow, he drives one of the metal sconces into the thing's chest, and it shrieks in agony. I grab his hand and drag him from the monster's clutches as its body bursts into flame.

We tumble through the scorched web into the hallway. I beat at my father's clothing where flames flicker, then call on the Ecosystem's power to mend the burns he's suffered. Charred flesh returns to health so fast it startles even me.

"Are you okay?" I ask.

He doesn't answer. Instead, he holds me at arm's length, and if we hadn't almost died, I might laugh: his eyes are comically wide, while the huntingbird that retrieved him circles his head like a ruby-colored halo. He lets me go and kneels.

"My Queen," he says.

I take his hands and gently raise him from the floor. The wall between us is there no longer, and never will be again. I touch his face and let him feel the power that flows through me.

"I'm not your queen," I say. "I'm your daughter."

Arm in arm, we stand at the doorway of the room where the creature burns. There's little to fear from it in this fortress of stone, but we watch until the fire has utterly consumed its body, leaving nothing but a mountain of ash that stinks of decay. My father enters the room and douses the smoldering remains with a basin of water from the bedside table. I wonder if Dinah ever used that basin to cleanse herself, to view her face when the metamorphosis began. Silently, I reach out to the Ecosystem, beseeching it to receive her wounded spirit. Then I turn to my father, and to the challenges that lie ahead.

"Take me to Gideon," I say. "I think I can heal him now."

THE HUNTINGBIRD LEADS the way as we descend the stairs of the Cathedral. It's hard to imagine the solemn man who is my father laughing, but he comes as close as I've seen when he tells me the story of how the bird found him.

"I had traveled to the edge of the city," he says. "It circled me, and when I sought to defend myself, it poked me. Lightly, in the back. I had never heard of such behavior from these birds. It took me some time—and some further damage to my pride—before I realized it had been sent to find me, though I did not know by whom."

"Sorry," I say. "It was all I could think of."

"And you control these creatures?"

"Not exactly," I say. "The Queen taught me how to communicate with them. It's less control than cooperation. It works with pretty much anything in the Ecosystem," I add, though I know that's not entirely true. I'm not ready for that conversation, though, until we've found Gideon.

My father is quiet for a long time, digesting this. It must be strange for him, to have served as the leader of the queen's healing corps for years and only now glimpse the true extent of her power.

"The Queen is gone," he says at last.

"Celestina?"

"She has abandoned the city," he confirms. "Her attendants grew anxious when she failed to return to her bedchamber this past night, and they came to me. I was searching for her when your companion called." He pauses, then says with a heavy sigh, "Angelica has disappeared as well."

I'm saddened, but hardly surprised. "The two of them hated each other. Maybe the Queen took her hostage. In case we followed."

"We must follow," my father says. "We must learn where Celestina has gone, and why. I have grave fears for the city's safety if she has turned against us."

We've reached the first floor of the Cathedral by now. I hesitate to tell him what else I know of Celestina, but I'd rather he learn it from me than through some accident in the field. I place a hand on his shoulder, hoping my touch will soothe the hurt my words are sure to cause.

"Celestina released the city's wyrms to come and get me," I tell him. "She's the reason the village was destroyed. All because she didn't want to be queen."

A spasm of pain crosses his face as we start down the stairwell to his underground laboratory. The huntingbird hesitates before joining us, but I beckon to it, and it finds a comfortable roost on my ear.

"Estella was a girl of fourteen when she assumed the throne," my father says to me, his voice soft but his words echoing in the stairwell. "Few considered her ready, but when your great-grandmother Leonida died without an heir, there was no other choice. Estella was a mere thirty-four years of age when she died, leaving the throne to her only child, Celestina, who was but sixteen when she was crowned."

"Celestina was taught by her mother?" I ask.

"Estella would permit no other to come near her child," he says. "Normally, the healers play a part in training candidates for the throne, instructing them in the common medical arts, as well as the more subtle art of rule. But with Celestina, never."

"Father," I say, "were you trying to force Estella from the throne?"

He sighs so deeply the huntingbird rises up in anxious flight. I signal to it, and it settles down as my father continues his tale.

"It was Estella who welcomed me to the city," he says. "She gave me my name, opened the secrets of the healing arts to me. I honored her for renewing my life, and pledged myself to her service. You must believe me."

His eyes are pleading, but his expression is grim.

"When she gave birth to a daughter, a great change came over her," he says. "She grew weak in body, troubled in mind. My offers of aid she met with allegations of treachery. I watched her retreat into seclusion with her babe, and doubt grew within me. Much as I feared to introduce another schism into the city, I thought that your mother, as the sole surviving woman of Demetria's lineage, might be brought here and trained for the throne in case of desperate need." He turns to me, his face anguished. "I made a terrible mistake, my daughter. It caused your mother's death, and confirmed Estella's heart in suspicion against me."

"Her suspicion ran deeper than you knew," I say. "After she commanded the wyrms to kill my mother, she used you to breed a host of their offspring for war. Her own, or her daughter's after her."

As if reflected in his tears, I see the image Celestina showed me of my mother crawling across the desert, succumbing to the monsters from below. Though wounded by Nathan's arrow and badly off course, she might have found her way to the city if Estella hadn't sent the creatures to intercept her. That tale must have been told to Celestina, along with instructions for commanding the denizens of the deep. But when the young Queen sent her mother's legions to retrieve me, a power far greater than hers lay in wait beyond the city walls. And I've learned enough by now that I begin to suspect what that power is.

My father has stopped on the stairs, his shoulders slumped, his tears unceasing. I touch his cheek, but not to heal him. Only to let him know I understand.

"You must never lie to me again, Father," I say. "I'll have need to trust you from now on. Plus, if you do," and I try a small smile, meanwhile opening my hand to let the huntingbird hover above my palm, "I'll know."

GIDEON'S CELL SITS off the main chamber of my father's underground laboratory. The wyrm remains stretched across the floor, massive and inert, its innards exposed to view. Knowing the part its kind played in my village's death, I can barely stand to look at it as I cross the workroom and peek through the barred window of the cell.

The space is little more than a closet, rough stone unlit by any fire. My father shines a torch through the bars, and my breath is taken from me at the sight of the old firestarter's body. The black threads cover his face and naked torso, though whatever Celestina did to him seems to have halted their growth. The rotten smell I remember from the throne room is so thick it makes me gag.

"I would have deemed him dead, except decomposition has not taken place," my father breaks the silence. "Yet I cannot think how to heal him."

He produces a key like the one that opened the door to the brood chamber. With his torch giving me light, I kneel beside Gideon and survey his body more closely. He lies so still, he might be cousin to the wyrm: I can detect neither breath nor pulse beneath the black shroud. All the same, I know he lives, even if the signs of life have been stolen from him.

"Did Celestina bring this plague upon us, too?" my father asks.

"No," I say. "She was as confused and frightened as we were. She couldn't remove the parasite, so she placed its host in a dormant state."

"And can you heal him?"

"I can try," I say. "You might want to stay back, though. In case I fail."

"I will remain here," he says. "In case you fail."

I give his hand a squeeze. Then I close my eyes and reach out to the Ecosystem, calling on its power to come to my aid.

It unfolds before me, within me, a force of life beyond measure. As I finger the strands that flow through the motionless form of the old firestarter, I feel what I felt when I scanned Isaac's mind, what I felt in the queen's brood chamber: something beyond my sight, cloaked in darkness. The problem doesn't lie with my Sense as I believed on Miriam's wedding day; it's a presence, actively withholding itself from me, contesting my probing mind. It's so strong, my hands seem to wither at its touch. But I have one advantage: it seeks to snuff out many lives, while I seek to heal only one. If I'm silent and quick, it might not notice me before my work is complete.

I recall the queen's bargain, allow all fear and doubt to slip from me as I open myself to the Ecosystem's might. The life that remains within Gideon stirs at my beckoning, gasps awake. As it does, so too does the entity that slumbers with him. Carefully, my mind's fingers working with a nimbleness my actual hands will never know, I snip the black threads that bind the old firestarter, pull the clinging strands from his body one by one. Some are so small, others rooted so deeply, I worry that I'll miss them, and the entity will grow anew. But finally I manage to draw them all away, and before they have a chance to return, I bind Gideon in the healing power of the Ecosystem, wrap his body as gently as I would a sickly child. Then I stand and prepare to dispel the parasite forever.

That's when it strikes.

The black web leaps at me, eager to claim a new victim—to claim us all, for if I'm taken, the rest of the city will follow. My mind darkens, and my heart races at the thought of allowing this malign entity to gain hold of me. But I master my fear, send a surge of healing energy to meet the creature as it makes the leap. The Ecosystem's power singes the web to nothingness in midair. My legs give out, but strong hands catch me as I fall.

I open my eyes to see my father's face, just before he clasps me to his breast. I allow him the indulgence; frankly, I'm too weak to do much more.

"The darkness surrounded you," he says. "It filled the chamber, and I feared that you were lost. But then it was gone."

"I had help," I say.

I hold out my mother's charm, its pink scales shimmering in the glow of the fallen torch. My father's eyes brighten in recognition, and I wonder if he was the one who gave it to her. He clasps me even tighter, so tight I'm tempted to remind him that I'm not his baby anymore. The sound of another body moving in the cell gives me the excuse I need, and I turn my head to the place where the old firestarter lay.

He's awake, having pushed himself into a sitting position. For the first time since we met, I can believe him to be a man of seventy years: his limbs shake as if with palsy, his eye wobbles in confusion. But his flesh is cleansed of the black threads that covered him, and I can feel his strength flowing back into his body.

"Mistress Sarah," he croaks, his voice that of a man who hasn't spoken in years. "Where are we?"

I smile at him, and together, my father and I help him stand. He totters, but with my arm around his back, he finds his feet. I'm trying to figure out a way to explain everything that's happened when my father speaks.

"You are in the City of the Queens," he says. "And you have been healed by your liege." I cringe when I hear it coming, but he speaks the words anyway. "Queen Sarah, sovereign of this realm."

Gideon's eye widens, and it's all I can do to keep him from tumbling to the floor.

AFTERWARD, WE MEET in my father's private chambers, opposite Gideon's cell. It strikes me that this might have been where the experiments that bred the Ecosystem were conceived—possibly where the original queen was created using Dominique's genetic material. It might even have been the place where, if my father's dreams had been fulfilled, he would have trained his beloved in the healing arts. Now, it's been turned into a council room, and we've summoned a host to hear the dire news I bring.

Michael has come, along with Caleb and Noah, who started the training while I was with Celestina. The captain of the city guard, a woman named Aurelia, joins us at the table, as do Michael's boyfriend Luke and the two guardsmen who discovered Gideon. Gideon's there too, strong and hale as before. One of Celestina's maids attends, though I don't know her name or if she even has one. Finally, I've sent an invitation via huntingbird to Leah, and she's accepted, which gratifies me in more ways than I can say. She sits to my right and won't quite look at me, but I'll take that over the openly hostile stares of the majority, who plainly see me as a pretender to the throne.

I decide to address that right off. "As you know, Celestina has fled the city, taking the healer Angelica with her. What you don't know is that before she left, the Queen chose me as her successor. She—"

"Impossible!" Aurelia bursts out. An imposing woman with skin a shade lighter than mine and a hairstyle I've seen on no other—shaved on both sides of her skull so that only a crest of rusty hair is left—she glares at me across the table. "The Queen would never abdicate the throne to a stranger from beyond our lands."

"If by 'abdicate,' you mean offer me as a living sacrifice to the Ecosystem, that's exactly what she did," I shoot back. "Celestina didn't want to be queen, and she tried to force me to take over."

Aurelia's mouth opens to hurl back an objection, but my father silences her with a hand. "My daughter speaks truly. I have seen her heal this man"—he points to Gideon, who draws himself up to show how healed he is—"and she could not have done so were the power of the queens not within her."

That draws a shocked silence. Aurelia and the two guards continue to eye me with suspicion, but Michael and Luke's expressions soften. Caleb and Noah shake their heads as if they've been rudely awakened from a pleasant dream. Leah still won't look at me, and the maid's face I can't read.

"Anyway," I say. "The point is, Celestina is gone, and I'm here. I've gained access to the Ecosystem, and I've learned two important truths. Both of them are vital to our survival, but one is a matter of life or death."

"Not to scare anybody," Leah mumbles into her lap, half-smiling.

I wish I could half-smile back. "The first thing has to do with the events of several weeks ago," I say. "We've assumed that the forces that destroyed the village are identical to the ones producing the current disturbance in the Ecosystem. But that's not true. It was Celestina who sent the city's urthwyrms against the village, and once that was over, her part in the Ecosystem's unrest came to an end."

The members of the Queen's coterie emit sounds of outrage at this revelation, though whether their anger is directed at me or her, I can't tell. At least I've discovered that her maid has a voice. That could come in handy down the road.

"The reason we were misled is that we've misunderstood something essential about the Ecosystem," I continue. "We've believed all along that it's a single entity, a single consciousness spanning the entire planet. There's no doubt it started out that way: one hive, with one queen. But there have been times over the past two centuries that new colonies have split off from the original body. It happens when multiple queens within a hive vie for control. Then there's a swarm, and part of the hive separates to follow its own queen."

My father looks stunned. "How did you learn this, my daughter?" he asks.

I hold up one of my library books. The picture on the front shows a tree fairly covered with a squirming mass of bees. "Reading."

He smiles, fleetingly. I make a mental note to return the book when I'm done with it.

"So anyway," I say, "what this means is that the Ecosystem we've known all our lives is only the oldest and largest of the parts—the original hive, answering to this city's queen. But within the past two months, a new queen has arisen who isn't content to rule her own hive and wants to take control of ours. She's already produced new life forms to attack us, such as the poison arrow frogs. And she's colonized members of the city itself, including Gideon. If I hadn't destroyed the organism that lived in him, it would have spread to others as well."

Gideon nods gravely. Knowing the old firestarter, he's less thankful that I saved his life than that I stopped him from becoming the source of a city-wide epidemic.

"Where does the rival colony lie?" Luke asks.

"In the village," I say. "Or what's left of it. I've felt the new queen there. She's terribly strong. Celestina felt her power too, which could be one of the reasons she abandoned the city to its fate."

"And who is this new queen?" Aurelia challenges.

"I don't know," I admit. "All I know is that she isn't descended from either of the daughters whose lines have ruled this city. There was only one woman of queenly blood who left the city for the village, which means the new queen must be the heir of Divina's daughter, Delilah."

I expect another exclamation from the guards, but the only one to utter a sound is Aurelia, who curses softly. The memory of Delilah and the Brotherhood must strike fear in the residents of the city, and though I'm not about to show it, I feel pretty much the same. The darkness I sensed in the brood chamber, the malevolence that produced monsters like the poison arrow frogs and the nameless thing that conquered Dinah, is beyond any evil I've known in all my years as a Sensor. But who Delilah's heir could be, and why she's waited this long to launch an assault against the place her ancestor left eighty years ago, I can't fathom.

Michael interrupts my thoughts. "Queen Sarah," he says, and I brace myself for another bout of *It's just Sarah*. "What do you advise us to do?"

"There's really only one choice," I say. "We've got to learn what we're up against, which means we've got to return to the site of the village."

"But if this new queen is as potent as you say…" Michael begins.

"Even so," I answer. "We can't sit here waiting for her army to arrive."

"We have no force capable of confronting hers," Aurelia says in a low tone. "This city is a place of healing, not of war."

"I'm not talking about a fighting force, "I say. "More like a scouting party. A delegation. Maybe we can come to terms with her. Or discover her weaknesses. If she has any."

"You had to add that," Leah says, but this time, she raises her eyes to mine and smiles fully.

"I didn't want to lie to you," I say.

Her hand grips mine beneath the table. Through our touch, I feel the things she hides behind a smile and a wink: her fear of abandonment, her longing to be loved. How can it be that my body holds such power, and yet it's so useless when I need it the most? I could reach inside her right now, call on the Ecosystem to mend a limb, suture a wound, make her heart beat again. But not to heal what truly ails her. That part, I can't touch.

"Every queen has weaknesses," I say, and though my eyes are on the group as a whole, my words are for my friend. "Dominica was a little girl who didn't know how brave she could be when she made her bargain with the

Ecosystem, and Celestina was mourning the death of her mother while trying to figure out a way to serve her people without losing herself. You look at us like we're all-powerful, but we're just people. We need other people to be close to us, to support us. To help us heal."

The others lower their eyes, but Leah holds my gaze, smiling as if I'm some impossible child she's been hoping would finally grow up. She gives my hand a squeeze before letting go and standing.

"I'm with the Queen," she says. "Anyone else?"

Gideon and my father rise at once, followed shortly by Michael, Luke, and the twins. It's a minute before Aurelia and the guards join them, the Queen's attendant adding her vote last of all. I let out a grateful breath, while Leah crosses her arms and smirks like the carnary that's eaten the fell-cat.

WHILE THE OTHERS get ready for our journey, I return to the brood chamber. I stand in place, reach out my arms, and let the strands of the Ecosystem's will join with my own. Through the connection we share, I thank it for the strength it's given me in the past, ask it for the strength I'm going to need in the future. I try to locate the new queen who lies hidden in my ruined village, but I'm no more successful than before; it's as if she knows I'm searching for her, and she's built a wall of darkness around herself so strong I can't breach it. When it occurs to me that she might be trying to infiltrate my mind from her own brood chamber, I shut off the attempt to make contact.

Next, I search the woods for Celestina and Angelica, if only to learn whether they're safe or not. But though their feet must have passed over the Ecosystem's floor, they've evidently masked themselves the way a Sensor would have done, and the forest has been unable to register their presence. I stretch my consciousness to the breaking-point before admitting I'm not going to find them. It could be that they've died, victims of the new power that's arisen in the west. Or it could be that they've joined that power, adding their strength against the little we have.

I am like Dominique, like Celestina. I didn't ask to be queen. I take up this burden because it's in my blood—because, if my grandmother had lived, I might have grown up a little girl in this city, watched her sit on the throne, and my mother after her. I owe them this. I didn't ask to be queen, but in the end, I choose to be queen, to serve the realm that might have been theirs.

The Ecosystem, that mystery that's been more a part of me than I realized from the day I was born, tells me it approves. Its arms release me, and send me on my way.

MY FATHER WAITS for me in the courtyard of the Cathedral. It's nighttime, the moon peeking from behind clouds. Celestina was right in this respect: time has no meaning in the Ecosystem. It was barely midday when I entered the brood chamber.

Leah is next to join us. Gideon pleaded to come along, but I told him I needed him here to prepare for the defense of the city if our embassy fails. Caleb and Noah would have come as well if Leah hadn't put them in charge of Huldah. From what my friend tells me, it's going to be a long night for all three of them.

"Where are the others?" I ask my father.

"Michael will remain behind to direct the healing corps in my absence," he answers. "The captain of the guard and the queen's attendants are likewise needed in the city. Will you be able to commune with them from the field?"

"I should," I say. "With the healers especially, since they're best attuned to the Ecosystem. But don't you think we could use…."

His eyebrows lift.

"…some reinforcements?" I finish. "This might not be a friendly gathering."

He nods, but not at me. From the shadows beneath the Cathedral, two guards wearing dark-colored uniforms emerge, wrestling with something large at the end of bridles. When the reluctant creatures slide onto the pavilion, my heart misses a beat.

They're wyrms, two of them, saddled for riding behind their blunt, eyeless faces. Rings of teeth glint in the moonlight. My father places a hand on the larger beast's flank, but I can't bring myself to copy him.

"These steeds are my private couriers," he reassures me. "They were the first I trained, and their allegiance to my blood is unquestioned. They rescued you twice, from the lair of the wild wyrms and from the glade of the spitting frogs. They will answer to me, and to you, my daughter."

He holds a hand out to me, and I take a hesitant step closer to the wyrms. They buck against their halters, rear high above our heads. My father lays my hand against the flesh of the larger one, and as I touch its slimy hide, I tamp down my fear and open myself to its will. The might of this creature makes me shudder, but it's only a moment before I realize its power is restrained, held in check by the compact between itself and those of my blood. In some of the picture books I read, children played with what were called *pets*, harmless animals that shared their homes. This wyrm is no pet—if unleashed, it'll crush solid rock to powder with its jaws—but it lowers its snout and nuzzles my hand with the gentleness of a caress.

My father helps me mount, Leah behind me. He makes sure we're securely strapped in then lifts himself onto the second beast. A wyrm-guard joins him, the second guard rounding out the trio on my steed. It takes only a touch of my father's hand for his wyrm to wheel about and point toward the gate through which we first entered the city.

"We ride at top speed," he says. "We should reach the village by morning. Hold tightly."

I touch the wyrm's snout and feel its will synchronize with my own. I do no more than picture our destination before it takes off, racing across the pavilion and through the gate like a bird in flight.

THE FOREST SHIMMERS with luminescence. Not only does the moon shine through the clouds, but the flameflies are out, pirouetting around our train as if eager to show off their dance. I take some credit for that: my hands aren't needed to guide the colossus beneath me, so my mind is free to embrace the woods. Nothing approaches us with ill will; even those creatures that fail to recognize their queen out for a jaunt don't dare contest the coursers on which her company rides. Some trees suffer damage when the wyrms press their bulk through narrow spaces, but I'm quick to mend the hurt as we roll on.

The moon sets and the flameflies retire, but the leviathans need no light to show their path. Leah has stayed awake to this point, her voice exclaiming breathlessly in my ear; now that darkness closes around us, she wraps her arms about my middle and rests her cheek on my shoulder to sleep. I had some hesitancy about her joining us, powerless as she is before the Ecosystem. But I've decided that if the most she can do is hold my hand, point out some blunder of mine, make me laugh, I'll be glad she's come.

My eyes are useless, so I reach out with the thing I once called my Sense, and for the first few leagues of our journey, I feel the life of the wild carrying on very much as it would whether I could see it or not. Yet I'm not so blind that I can't detect a change in the Ecosystem as we draw closer to the village, a shift from that part of the world that acknowledges me as its queen to a part that knows me only as its enemy. The black vines are everywhere, threaded through the understory, the ground cover, the root system; though our wyrms tear through them as if they're made of paper, I can feel the darkness spreading inch by inch toward the city, and my heart quails to think of the power capable of producing it. No matter how close we come to her realm, the owner of that power refuses to reveal herself, stays masked in shadow and silence. She's waiting for me, charting our advance, preparing her reception. But she keeps me truly blind to the form that reception will take.

The sky's paling at our backs when Leah stirs against me, then lifts her head from my shoulder. "Sarah," she whispers. "Are you awake?"

"Never went to sleep."

"Are you afraid?"

I stare into the dimly lit shapes of trees. Black strands show like veins against the bark. "Yes."

"Of what?"

"Many things," I say. "That my power won't be equal to hers. That I won't be able to talk her out of whatever she's planning. That one of you might get hurt."

"Are you afraid to die?"

I look over my shoulder into her wide, dark eyes. They're glossy from sleep, but she's wearing the brave smile that first told me she was someone I could trust.

"I've never been afraid to die," I tell her. "When I was a Sensor, practically my first lessons were about life and death. It's different now. If I fail, other people might die. My family. My friends."

"Are you sure you're not being too hard on yourself?"

I laugh. "That's what I do best. When I'm not being too hard on everyone else."

She's quiet for a time, resting her cheek against mine. Birds trade rumors of daybreak in the trees, joined by the rising chorus of cicatrix song.

"We're almost there," Leah murmurs.

"I think so."

"If you have to leave me," she says. "To face the queen. I want you to know you should go ahead."

I look into her eyes. They're perfectly dry. "I could never do that."

"Just if you have to," she says. "I'll understand."

Her arms tighten around my middle. I clutch them to me, close my eyes. The wyrm, undisturbed by my inattention, plunges onward. Against my cheek, a sound less heard than felt, Leah sings the notes of the lullaby she favors to soothe Huldah to sleep.

It's a moment before I realize we've come to a stop. I open my eyes to see my father astride his wyrm-mount, one arm outstretched against the backdrop of dawn.

"The village lies ahead," he says. "My daughter, if you would treat with their queen, the time is upon us."

WE DISMOUNT AND lead the wyrms to the edge of the wood. It was only weeks ago that I last looked on this place: it's the spot where I comforted Rebecca, consulted with my lieutenants, faced off with Dinah and Levi. Now, it might as well be an entirely different world.

The ache trees of times past have disappeared. In their place stands a towering hedge of crisscrossing black vines, identical in appearance to those that grew from Dinah's infected body but much more densely woven. I reach out to the growth, try to discover its name and source, but even with so much of it right in front of me, it resists my probing. The black mass seems too solid to penetrate, but I know the strands are animate, capable of moving aside if their queen desires an audience. Or of crushing her visitors if she wants to remain alone.

She must be in the mood for company. The threadlike vines pull back when I step toward them, opening a space for us to walk.

One of the guards stays behind with his wyrm while the rest of us lead my mount into the gap. It's wide enough for all, including the wyrm, but when I glance over my shoulder, I find that the hedge has sealed all trace of the way back. Doubting even our wyrm can force its way through this morass if the path before us closes, I hurry my companions toward the light that's barely visible through the tangled web.

We exit the hedge onto what used to be the village sward. Now it's a field of blackened grabgrass choked with a palisade of uprooted trees. Ache, hexlox, sickenmore, and others have been planted at angles facing the hedge, their branches stripped and their crowns shaved to lethal points. Gray smoke hangs over the field, mirroring the gray clouds that blanket the sky. I realize that with our passage through the outer barrier, all sound of birds has ceased, and I think back to the book I read while Angelica looked on. To myself, I recite the sentences that struck me then: *No witchcraft, no enemy action had silenced the rebirth of new life in this stricken world. The people had done it themselves.*

Leah places a hand on my arm and leans close. "I can't tell where the village used to be," she says in a whisper.

"Look there," I say. "Just beyond the trees."

A mound of earth rises behind the angled trunks. The wyrms that destroyed our village must have continued their work after the buildings fell, heaping soil around the hole they created. My gut sickens at the thought that the queen has taken up residence in this crater, with the bodies of more than a hundred villagers buried around her and the monstrous wyrms prowling the catacombs. An image flashes through my mind of a dark-haired woman seated on a pile of bones, and though the vision lasts only a second, it strikes me that I've had my first true glimpse of the adversary I must face.

My father stands beside me. "What is your will, my daughter?"

"The rest of you stay here," I say. "I'll take the wyrm. If I don't come back...."

"We'll die anyway," Leah says. "Look, Sarah."

I don't need to look. I feel the ground shake. The dark queen's wyrms are on the move, and anyone who remains behind will be cast into the pit they're digging beneath our feet.

"Mount the courier," my father says. "Our path lies ahead."

The four of us scramble aboard the creature, which has plenty of room to spare. I touch its back, and it glides through the blockade of downed trees, knocking them aside when it can, suffering stab wounds when it can't. Its pain registers in my mind, but when I beg it to be careful, it answers in a wordless rumble, assuring me it's tolerated worse injuries than this. As if to prove itself, it puts on an extra burst of speed to force its way through the last line of the palisade, and I see what's become of my former home.

The blocks of stone left over from our village—from the gathering hall, the Sensorium, the pavilion, the houses we lived in—have been piled in a ring around the crater, serving as a foundation to anchor the earthen mound. Combined, the rock-and-dirt barrier rises to a height of fifty feet above ground level. Our wyrm snakes up the nearly vertical wall and pokes its head over the top, enabling us to see inside. Except there's nothing to see: the hole, several hundred feet across, is covered with swirling smoke the weak sunlight won't pierce. If we enter, we'll be at the wyrm's mercy, trusting it to find something it can cling to without pitching us, or itself with us, into the depths.

"Are you certain?" my father calls as we balance above the rim.

"There's no other way," I answer, and at a final touch from me, the wyrm dives through the smoky cloud into darkness.

For a breathless instant, I'm attached to the world only by the feel of the wyrm's body against my legs and the sound of Leah's scream in my ear. Then the creature collides with the interior wall of the crater and somehow clings there, for I can feel that our velocity has slowed, our movement a descending spiral instead of a freefall. We must be circling the inside of the crater, the wyrm gripping with I don't know what while the rest of us hang on by the straps of its saddle. Leah's still screaming, but it's less a scream of pure terror than one of mingled fear and release. I join my voice with hers, our screams echoing off the crater walls. For the second time since this journey began, I'm glad she wouldn't let me leave her behind.

There's another jolt as the wyrm strikes bottom, my scream—and nearly my tongue—being cut off by the impact. I'm no longer guiding our mount, but the creature shows no hesitation as it slithers along one of the passageways created by its kin. Ahead, the tunnel brightens just enough to show me something clinging to the earthen walls, though we're too far away to tell what it is. As we approach, the shadowy mass resolves itself into a sight so horrible I can't tell whether the gasp I hear is Leah's or my own.

Trapped against the walls of earth, held in place by snaky strands of the dark queen's power, are the bodies of the lost villagers. Some are almost certainly dead, their frames crushed by the collapse of the gathering hall or mauled by the teeth of marauding wyrms. Others might be alive, if their feeble movements aren't those of the black vines that ensnare them. I see Esther, her limbs pinned to the walls and her head twisted to the side; her dark eyes seem to follow us as we rush beneath. Two members of the Sensor corps flank her, Judah and Adam, both of them as helpless as the Chief Sensor they betrayed. Daniel is there too, his ceremonial furs matted with blood but his chest, I convince myself, drawing shallow breaths. Among the common villagers, there are some I know by name, others I recognize only by look: babies who'd be in someone's arms if the black threads didn't hold them, mothers and fathers who'd reach out for their children if they weren't chained to the prison walls. That these innocents might be alive to bear such torture appalls me far more than the thought of their death.

We're nearing the last of the colony when my eyes fall on a tall, willowy woman whose face I know I've seen before, though I can't place when. It comes to me just as we flash beneath her and she reaches out her arms to Leah.

"Beulah!" my friend sobs, and I feel her body tense as if she's about to leap from the wyrm. At the speed we're going, she'll surely die. I wrap my arms around her, knot my hands in the saddle to hold on.

"Let me go!" she screams, fighting my greater strength. "Sarah, let me go!"

"Don't look," I say. "Please, Leah."

"I thought she was dead!" she cries. "I can't leave her…." She struggles a moment longer before collapsing in my arms. "Beulah," she moans, and I think I hear a faint answering call. But when I look back, Beulah has gone limp, her head fallen on her breast and her arms dangling at her sides. That's the last I see of her before the wyrm whips around a bend in the tunnel, and the colony vanishes from sight.

The tunnel darkens again now that the queen has shown us her victims. There's just enough light to see that the black tendrils have multiplied, carpeting ceiling and walls as densely as the hedge aboveground; the strands curl and wave, and for some reason I'm reminded of hair, unruly hair blowing in a breeze. But there's no breeze in this place, only stale air filled with the tang of soil as cloying as blood. Ahead, I see a circular aperture that's too black for my eyes to penetrate, and I know our journey has reached its end.

The wyrm knows, too. It pulls up short of the dark queen's brood chamber, dirt spraying as it skids to a halt. We climb from its back, and I take a moment to pat its flank in gratitude. A pulse of light issues from the chamber, too weak to show me anything more than the strands of the web that drape the opening. I'm struggling to make contact when a voice emerges from the walls around me, soft yet tinged with menace. I feel as if I should recognize it, but it echoes belowground, and I can only make out its words.

"Enter, queen of the city," it says. "Leave your vassals."

Black tendrils lash out from the walls, grip my companions, drag them beyond reach. Leah's cry is strangled in her throat; the guard's attempt to use his blade is defeated by a vine that snaps his wrist and flings the weapon from his limp fingers. Even our wyrm is caught off guard, so many threads lassoing its body it can do no more than wriggle against its bonds. My father is snared as fully as his creature, and as the black web lifts him overhead, he looks down at me with an expression of unutterable regret.

"I should have come for you years ago," he says. "Only cowardice kept me away. And now, my child, it is too late."

I reach out to him, but our fingers can't touch. The best I can do is send a healing wave to soothe his sorrow.

"It's all right," I say. "I'll get us out of this."

He tries to smile, but his face is obscured by the black web. I turn to the portal and, ducking beneath the strands that part before me, enter the dark queen's chamber.

SHE SITS ON a throne of skulls. Her black hair streams in every direction, joining with the web that clots her chamber. In the room's ghostly light, I can't tell if these strands are extensions of her hair or a new organism that holds her in thrall as the Ecosystem once held me in Dominica's place.

I know her.

Her arms are as bony as ever, but her once beautiful eyes have turned solid black. She wears the remains of her wedding dress, torn to strips that barely conceal her not-quite-woman's form. At her throat, fastened by a cord that might be a lock of her own hair, the token I gave her— my Sensor's token—is smeared with something oily and unclean. Just beneath it, the hilt of a stone knife protrudes from her breast, and though it's been over a month since the blow was delivered, the wound weeps tears of what I realize is black blood.

"Miriam," I say.

She makes no sign that she hears me. Something scuttles along her web, and I flinch as a red-haired creature drops to the floor. It hunches beside the throne, its head jutting to show me the sharp nose and sparse beard of Levi. Its mouth opens, and a bright stream issues from its throat: frogs, all colors of them, their tongues flicking in and out, coated with poison. The dark queen's web pricks what's left of Levi's body, and it collapses like an emptied water-bladder, the frogs leaping about the brood chamber until other strands of the web descend to smother them.

"Miriam," I say again. "What's become of you?"

Her eyes turn to me, fixed, unseeing. Their color is that of a two-day-old bruise, while the unnatural way her hair curls around her face reminds me of the times she used to beseech the Ecosystem to deliver its dead. Her lips move, and the voice that emerges from them is Miriam's, but it's as cold and hollow as wind rattling cicatrix shells.

"You took it from me," she says. "Now I will take it back."

I try to think of what she could mean, but I'm at a loss. "Took what? Miriam, took what?"

"You will see," she says.

Another figure emerges from behind her throne. Unlike the thing that was Levi, this new servant of the queen walks upright, though with a limping gait, one leg dragging behind the next. Strands of the black web bind the broken leg, but my healer's power tells me instantly that it's been set wrong and causes incredible pain with every step. The flowing mass of Miriam's hair blocks the newcomer's face from view, and nothing can prepare me when he steps clear and his eyes meet mine.

"Isaac," I say. "Oh, my Sense, Isaac."

It's him. His face is covered in gashes, his hair caked with dried blood. He's stripped to the waist, one arm palsied against his side. A loop of Miriam's web cinches his neck, so tightly his throat labors for breath. His brown eyes are alive as hers are not, but there's no softness to them, no remnant of the boy he was. I worry that his madness has worsened, but the quickest of scans convinces me that the dark queen, having taken control of his mind to draw him to this place, has released her hold on him, no doubt to relish his grief and fear. His mouth opens, but not to spit vermin as Levi's did. Instead, it spits words more venomous by far.

"You were a fool to come here, Sarah," he says. "She'll kill you, and then she'll destroy everyone you love."

"But why?" I ask him, while tears flavor my words. "What did I do to her?"

He stares at me in disbelief. "You know exactly what you did. You lied to her, and spurned her, and when you had a chance to save her, you left her here to die—"

"Enough!" Miriam screeches, the sound shivering every line of her web. The noose circling Isaac's throat tightens, and his eyes bulge. He tries to raise his good hand to claw free, but other strands snake around his shoulders, pulling him toward the roof of the chamber with one leg kicking and the other hanging crooked and immobile. By the time I wipe my tears away, he's vanished amid the blackness that hangs above the dark queen's throne.

"I didn't know," I plead, and hear the lie in my own voice. "I'm sorry, Miriam. You must believe me."

For the first time since I entered her chamber, the queen's face stirs, forming a cruel smile that makes a mockery of her girlish features.

"You have said that you did not intend to start a war," she speaks. I gasp, remembering my words to Isaac on the day he told me of his wedding. "But war is upon you. Your city must arm itself as it can, in the absence of its queen."

Web-like strands descend from the ceiling. They

surround me on all sides, blocking escape from the chamber. I try to reach out to the Ecosystem, to open myself to its power and call it to my aid, but in this place, there's nothing to heed my call. Whether it's Miriam who controls this monstrous colony or some malign force that works through her, the Ecosystem here answers to her alone. To her, the last heir of Delilah, lost queen of the city.

"I'm sorry, Miriam," I say. "For everything. But I can't let Isaac die."

I hold out my hand, and the last of my huntingbirds takes wing.

It flies directly for the queen, who commands her web to bat it away. But the bird's too fast even for her, and it drives straight through the flailing strands, aiming for her throat. I expect some reaction from Miriam, but there's none: maybe there's no blood left in her veins to defend. At the last instant, the bird shears away from its target and slices through the web that holds Isaac captive. He tumbles toward the ground, neither his arm nor his leg prepared to break his fall.

But I'm there to catch him, and as the dark queen rises from her throne, a curse forming on her bloodless lips, my sole other ally emerges from without.

THE WYRM'S HEAD bursts through the door of the brood chamber, tearing the dark queen's web from the earthen walls. Teeth sharp enough to chew through mountains make short work of the few remaining strands that block our exit, and before she's able to fling more at the beast, I've mounted its back with Isaac in my arms. The wyrm's tail lashes out as it turns, scattering the pile of skulls and knocking Miriam from her feet. She falls to hands and knees, and if I directed it to, my courier would wrap its coils around her and squeeze what life remains from her body. I feel its eagerness as it awaits my command.

No, I tell it. *I can't let things end this way.*

Though it doubts my wisdom, it refuses to challenge my word. It rears and, with its cargo of two human beings and one very excited huntingbird, charges from the brood chamber.

The outer tunnel shakes with the approach of Miriam's wyrm army. Her web tries to slow us by constricting around my trapped companions, but our wyrm wolfs huge mouthfuls of the black stuff, and the strands recoil in agony, dropping their prisoners to the floor. I help the shaky survivors onto the beast's back, and we're off again, careening down the tunnel with all the speed a determined urthwyrm can muster. In no time, we've reached the near edge of the nest where the members of my village are held.

I rein in the wyrm, cast my eyes on the figures who hang from the tunnel walls.

If I leave them here, they'll die—die, or become slaves of the dark queen, strengthening the force she plans to send against the city. But our single mount can't carry them all, and in the time it takes to free them, Miriam's wyrms will have reached us. Much as I've planned this assault and escape, I never counted on having to make such a choice.

I'm no closer to a decision when I feel Leah's lips press against my cheek. Before I can think what she means to do, she slides off the wyrm to throw herself at the limp form that hangs above us.

"Leah!" I call, but the strands that hold Beulah have found my friend, and they pull the two into an embrace. Leah claws at the black threads to no avail. I leap from the saddle to help her, but before I can lay hands on the web, it retreats suddenly, dropping the two to the floor.

The following instant, the tunnel wall explodes and a wyrm even larger than ours thrusts its head above Leah and her beloved. Our mount reacts instinctively, wheeling to lock its mouth onto the enemy wyrm. The two leviathans tussle in the cramped space, my father and the guard leaping free. Isaac utters a weak moan as he rolls from the saddle. I try to protect his body while at the same time reaching for Leah, who's struggling to raise Beulah from the ground. But the taller woman's legs keep collapsing under her, and the wyrms block me from coming any closer.

Just then, my father vaults over the tangle of coils and stoops by Leah's side. He's about to lift Beulah into his arms when our wyrm smashes the other's head into the low ceiling, causing tons of earth to pour from above. I'm knocked to the ground, but not by the cave-in; instead, my wyrm has shoved me out of the way, forming an arch with its body to shield me. When the shower stops and I rise to my feet, choking on the dust-filled air, I find that of our wyrm's passengers, only Isaac and I have been spared. The others—my father, the guard, Leah, and Beulah—lie buried with the enemy wyrm.

"Father!" I scream, pounding my fists against the wall of soil. I scratch and claw, but there's no chance of my breaking through. The wyrm hears my silent entreaty and begins chewing into the debris, then pauses as if listening. The walls of the tunnel vibrate with a guttural booming, and I know that the dark queen's legions can't be far away. But that's not what the wyrm's responding to; there's another vibration, too faint for me to feel but strong enough to attract the notice of this dweller in the ground. I place my hand against the wyrm's flank, and then I hear it too.

It's a voice, small and weak. With the wyrm's senses communicating the sound to my ears, I can just make out its words.

"Sarah?" There's a cough, and a long pause. Then the voice again: "It's Leah. Are you there?"

"Leah!" I know she can't hear me through the barrier, but I shout as loudly as I can. "Are you all right? Are the others alive?"

There's nothing but silence. I strain to hear, reach out with my healer's touch. At last, with the wyrm to assist me, I learn what lies beyond the wall.

My father rests in the ground like my mother before him, his body crushed by falling rock. The guard is dead too, having been torn to pieces by the enemy wyrm in its death agonies. Leah and Beulah were thrown clear of the cave-in, and they're alive—alive, but beyond my reach. Even now, strands of the dark queen's web enfold them, preparing to drag them back to the brood chamber.

A sharp jab behind my ear makes me turn, where I expect to find the teeth of another wyrm at my throat. But it's no wyrm. It's my faithful huntingbird, pecking anxiously at my ear. In the tunnel beside me, our own wyrm waits, its head bowed to the ground to ease my mounting. I wish it could ease the grief in my chest, but it has only one desire.

Numbly, I lift Isaac into my arms and climb onto the creature's back. The bird finds shelter where my healer's token rests. I have no need to direct my courier before it wheels and arcs like lightning down the tunnel.

We ascend through darkness. Other wyrms nip at our heels, but none can match our beast's desperate speed. It explodes from the crater with such force that I'm nearly thrown from the saddle when it lands. The sky's too dark for me to see the trees of the queen's palisade or the surrounding hedge. Somehow, the wyrm forges a way through. The guard who remained above, however, is nowhere to be found, nor is his wyrm.

I raise my head, draw air deeply into my lungs to clear away the stink of death. I can't understand why it's so dark, when we arrived just this morning. Can the Ecosystem have cheated my sense of time again? I shiver atop the wyrm, and I realize what's amiss.

It's not only dark but cold. Something falls on my cheek, a brief sting that turns to water when I touch it. The clouds have opened up at last, releasing frigid hail that pelts my flesh. The wind howls around me, and it's only thanks to the wyrm's saddle that I'm able to keep myself and my companion from being hurled from our perch.

I pull Isaac close to preserve our warmth. I feel the bird beating against my breast, a second heart to make up for the one I've lost. And I speed on through the dark, an orphan on the way to the city of her mothers, to prepare for war.

THE END

ACKNOWLEDGMENTS

What fun would a book be without acknowledgments? Here's to all who helped me with *The Devouring Land*:

My agent, Liza Fleissig, who's been first on all of my acknowledgments pages (and deservedly so).

Caroline Gessner, who suggested a major innovation that played a decisive role in the development of the City of the Queens, and who read the manuscript to make sure I got things right. Whatever I got wrong, though, is on me.

Jennifer Bardsley, who's my unofficial cheerleader/pep-talker/marketing guru. Now if only I'd listen to her!

Kat Ross and Stephanie Keyes, without whose expertise and enthusiasm this journey would not have been possible.

Christa Yelich-Koth, who edited the book with her typical eye for detail (not to mention for stupid mistakes).

The writers and bloggers who participated in the tour for *Ecosystem*: Katie L. Carroll, Christina Farley, Kristi Helvig, Larry Ivkovich, Darlene Beck Jacobson, Margo Kelly, Matthew Phillion, Erin Rhew, Kai Strand, Jean Vallesteros, and Yvonne Ventresca. It's really inspiring to be part of such a selfless and supportive community.

Classic Lines Bookstore, The Penguin Bookshop,